Short story writer and novelist Owen Marshall has written, or edited,
eighteen books to date. Awards for his fiction include the PEN Lillian Ida
Smith Award twice, the Evening Standard Short Story Prize, the American
Express Short Story Award, the New Zealand Literary Fund Scholarship in
Letters, Fellowships at the universities of Canterbury and Otago, and the
Katherine Mansfield Memorial Fellowship in Menton, France. He received
the ONZM for services to Literature in the Queen's New Year Honours,
2000, and his novel Harlequin Rex won the Montana New Zealand Book
Awards Deutz Medal for Fiction in the same year. In 2002 the University
of Canterbury awarded him the honorary degree of Doctor of Letters.

Owen Marshall was born in 1941, has spent almost all his life in South
Island towns, and has an affinity with provincial New Zealand.

GW00690043

When Gravity Snaps

short stories by

OWEN MARSHALL

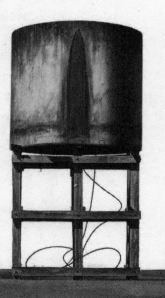

V
VINTAGE

National Library of New Zealand Cataloguing-in-Publication Data

Marshall, Owen, 1941-
When gravity snaps / Owen Marshall.
ISBN: 1-86941-528-0
1. Short stories, New Zealand. 2. New Zealand fiction—21st century.
I. Title.
NZ823.2—dc 21

A VINTAGE BOOK
published by
Random House New Zealand
18 Poland Road, Glenfield, Auckland, New Zealand
www.randomhouse.co.nz

First published 2002

ISBN 1 86941 528 0

Text design: Elin Termannsen
Cover painting: Grahame Sydney's "Drought, North Otago" 1989. (detail)
    Oil on linen. 580mm x 780mm. Private Collection, Christchurch,
    New Zealand.
Cover design: Janet Hunt
Author photo: Rosslyn Hood
Printed in Australia by Griffin Press

CONTENTS

WHEN GRAVITY SNAPS

We were waiting in the Pathways bus a block from Cologne Cathedral, which was the reason for the tour's morning stop. The stained glass was fiery in the dark church and, if I closed my eyes, the narrow windows rose in my mind like brilliant, illuminated candles. Other tours in other buses waited beside us in the morning sun, and the busy city swirled past. The couple from Gibraltar were holding us up of course. At scenic or heritage stops the Gibraltar couple were always late; after shopping stops the Wisconsin Foursome were inevitably to blame. Our tour guide, Malcolm, bounced in and out of the bus as his impatience grew. 'Anyone seen the Gambaegges?' But no one replied. Malcolm began a tuneless whistle, and shot his wrist abruptly from his jacket to make a watch check. The departure of our Rhine tour boat was a deadline beyond any negotiation.

All bus groups have their Gambaegges and Wisconsin Foursomes, and they become the scapegoats for everything malign and disappointing that happens. Maybe they weren't directly responsible for the snatching of Irene Hamble's bag in Marseilles, or the bruising fall suffered by amiable old Chester at the Lourdes Grotto, but if they hadn't got the whole party behind schedule and hassled, those things wouldn't have happened. Irene Hamble said she only took her bag because there wasn't time to go back and lock it in the bus.

The Wisconsin Foursome were not vicious or immoral people, just two brothers who had married two sisters and, through excessive and humdrum wealth, come to the view that the world exists for their personal satisfaction. The times so clearly enunciated by Malcolm meant nothing to them: shopping finished when the Wisconsin Foursome had made all the considerable purchases they considered necessary, dinner would no longer be served in hotels sometime after the Foursome deigned to arrive for theirs, the bus would not leave until they occupied the seats for which they'd paid. The Wisconsin Foursome were not competitive in their late arrival, and at those stops they termed 'heritage' — galleries, churches, ruins, monuments — would demand the refuge of the bus after a brief territorial examination of the lavatory arrangements. They would sleep in the seats, each face hidden by a baseball cap, each body attired in soft, pastel, unisex clothes, so that gender could be gauged only by size: the six-foot ones were women, the six-foot-four, men. The Gambaegges could be relied on to be late at heritage stops, so the Wisconsin Foursome didn't freak out.

The Foursome were preoccupied with their plumbing, which was the term they used for the whole range of bodily functions. I thought maybe their wealth had been founded on plumbing in a more mechanical sense, but no, brother Delmar told me the family business was in remote-controlled security doors and shutters. 'Sliding, rolling, folding, tilting, pop-up, just the whole thing really, I guess,' said Delmar. 'And dressy: clients want their security to look dressy these days, now that's for sure.'

At breakfast the Wisconsin Foursome would check out their night's plumbing history in voices that rattled the pots in hotel kitchens in Brugge and Berlin. 'You got rid of yesterday's gas, Sissy-Anne?' Roy might holler. 'This continental food is something else, isn't it?'

'I haven't had a satisfactory movement for a week, no word of a lie,' Delmar would boom. I had this idea that Wisconsin must be a very under-populated place with passing acquaintances shouting to each other over great distances. In all the time we spent on tour, my wife never could work out which sister was married to which brother, they were in and out of one another's rooms and lives so readily. Delmar, Roy, Sissy-Anne and Blanche appeared interchangeable to us, but each must have had an individual shining core of being locked away in that substantial body.

In Vienna our hotel was in the suburbs, close to a wooded park, and although the shoppers of the party complained, I was happy there. After two days, and a visit to the Summer Palace, I was convinced Austria was a calm, courteous and well-appointed place, and have continued to promulgate that view. How assuredly trenchant we become about brief impressions. What powerful shorthand for state of the nation a brief visit may be.

The only downer was that Trevor started to seek out my company in Vienna. He was a single guy, my countryman, and his ambitions for the European tour were all of sexual gratification. I hoped it was common citizenship and not libidinous interest he thought we shared. Trevor's fantasies were depressingly predictable: he told me at the bar in our Vienna hotel that on his flight to Britain the blonde hostess leant over him with a light ale and murmured, 'Follow me to the starboard aft toilet and you can fuck me over Turkey.'

Trevor did manage to lay one of the Pathways tour: a skinny Dutch girl with better English than he possessed. They copulated behind one of the abutments of the Mount Pilatus lookout, but at lower altitudes thereafter she treated him with disdain.

At my age I should be immune from apprehension about the opinion others have of me, but I found it unsettling to be long in Trevor's company, for the assumption of unseemly topics hung over every conversation, and laughter, or confidences, drew the disapproving glances from the women in the bus. My wife told me not to encourage him, and I never accepted his invitations to alternative evening activities, but stuck to those things sanctioned by the brochure: folk-dancing, yodelling and weaving fests.

More vexing to me than Trevor's gonad philosophy was his dangerous combination of logic and ignorance. He considered mountain tops should be the hottest places because they were closest to the sun, and argued that people were progressively taller the further from the equator because in winter they were stretching, plant like, for the light. Almost everything Trevor said cried out for denial, but he was set in all his views, and I learnt it was best to let things pass. I didn't want his prejudices and anomalies to take root in my own mind. My wife said it was too early to say for sure about that.

Greece is a wonderful place, but unbearably hot. I stood in awe at Thermopylae, and was seized with the sense of occasion on the Acropolis despite the relentless sun, and the vigilant whistling custodians there to keep us from touching the marble. The heat drove me down to the bus park, where the Wisconsin Foursome lay across double seats with baseball caps for faces, and allowed their plumbing a rumbling ease. Old Chester sat beside me with his wrinkled, sunburnt arms, and answered the questions the official guide had glossed over. Chester had been Reader in Classics at London University and was full of esoteric and loving information if you took the trouble to ask. Equally, he was happy to watch all in silence and, no doubt, annotate his observations within his capacious mind.

A few days later, when we were sailing back to Piraeus from our Greek Island tour, the setting sun caught the Parthenon in a pink, luminous glow. For a moment I was transported nearly two and a half thousand years, for I saw just what weary Athenians had seen from their homecoming triremes, and the wonder of it overcame the crowded gossip of my fellows at the deck supper tables, and the pounding of a modern engine. The thin Dutch girl complained of the shipboard wine, and Chester's mouth dropped open as he stood in the slump of old age and marvelled at history recaptured in the setting sun. I wanted to join him and share the moment, but Nick Guillermo began talking to me about the exchange rates arranged by our tour guide, Malcolm.

Nick was an Australian Italian: his parents had emigrated in the late fifties and made a new life in Melbourne. Nick was born in Australia, or was very young when they went there, and he was on the tour with his widowed mother mainly so she could return to her home town close to Turin and see if she was remembered. If his mother was well received she might not want to go on with the tour, and he was worried they wouldn't get any refund. He wasn't going to say anything about it to Malcolm, though, in case it all came to nothing. There was some ambivalence about the family's status in the village: from the little Nick said about it I thought maybe his grandfather had been a Fascist.

'The assistant engineer told me all the tour guides work a swiftie with currency transactions,' said Nick. 'Malcolm's ripping us off for sure.' Nick had a lugubrious conviction that all the world was corrupt, while Mrs Guillermo was cheerful, trusting and a favourite on the bus. Nick at various times told me that the Greek waiters were pickpockets, the wine was watered on the Cote d'Azur, the Swiss had a spy in each hotel, and Russian women trapped you into marriage by sexual provocation. From my own experience I could comment on only one of these accusations: the wine was indeed watered in the seaside cafés of Nice and Menton. It was a weak rosé, chilled to hide its faults. 'Oh, maybe it's better that way,' cried Mrs Guillermo, who was practising, perhaps, to placate her Italian relations.

The greatest test of friendship is the good fortune of one of those involved. Gillian Heading and Naomi Browne were mid-career friends in the short-term contract world of regional television. There was a thunderstorm on the night we stayed in Brindisi and the lightning showed the ancient port at its worst, all choppy water and debris. In the morning, as we waited for the ferry, squeezed between the damp land and the falling cloud, Naomi had a cellphone call saying she had been appointed presenter for a twenty-six-episode series on Scottish cuisine, and Gillian heard she was out on her ear. No one says the world is fair, but the obvious can be a form of injustice too. Naomi was younger, better looking, had a more outgoing nature and long, pale hands that suited Scottish cooking.

Both Naomi and Gillian had to carry on the tour, though at a stroke all was changed. Naomi could see everything in the rosy tints of success and anticipation; Gillian must have felt the chill of descent. But how wonderfully she persisted in her friendship and in her openness to new experience. I wanted to congratulate her on her character, but knew no way of doing so that wouldn't seem like commiseration.

In Barcelona, after the tour to see the Gaudi architecture and some underground Roman ruins partly exposed, like fat women's thighs, I wandered in a broad avenue that went down to the sea. The centre was crowded with market stalls along its length, and the mass of people in the warm dusk pushed past each other with accustomed indifference. By a trestle table of original and execrable miniature art was a bench occupied by two men and a woman, but there was half a rump of seat exposed and I squeezed on, smiling and nodding to excuse myself. The three Spaniards showed no annoyance. They each gave up a little of their own space, because they were accustomed to living in a crowded city. They didn't seem to know each other, and the four of us sat tightly packed amid the noise and surge of all the walking people. I could feel the body warmth of the elderly man next to me, and he had a slight smell of dry vegetables, or sacking. He held a stick upright between his legs and rested both hands on its top. He looked at the faces flowing past with a slight smile, as if acknowledging their energy, their urgency, but savvy to the outcome just the same.

Among all those people it was Trevor whom I had to recognise, propositioning a small, deep-chested woman behind a counter of bags and wallets. Trevor had a quiff of hair, like a quail's crest, and a habit of baring his teeth in a false yawn. Even at a distance it seemed to me she didn't find him attractive as a client in any form of transaction. A whole clutch of bumbags hung from her stall and the zips swung loosely as if their necks were broken. The woman had a blue scarf of very light material, and it fluttered slightly in a breeze I couldn't feel as she rebuffed Trevor, speaking without looking at him and continuing to arrange her stock.

The man beside me stood up with a sigh. He checked the seat to see if he'd left anything of value, then raised his stick slightly to the three of us left on the bench, and was carried off by the flow. He left just the faintest scent of vegetables and sacking, and a less obscured view of the tourist miniatures of the art stall which were, however, gradually being expunged by the night.

In the hotel, much later, I was woken by the Gambaegges arguing in the next room. They began in English and I caught enough to know he was in a fury at her extravagance, and she enduringly bitter concerning his treatment of their only son, whom she thought driven from the family by her husband's jealousy and rigidity. Disparate themes to an outsider, but for the Gambaegges a perfectly connected dialogue as such things are in the web of marriage. The volume declined with the intensity of their anger until English itself was abandoned, and they were hissing at each other in Spanish, or Italian. Finally there was just the sobbing of Mrs Gambaegge, insistent and with a terrible sadness through the wall, and I fell asleep thinking that wherever we are in our life we find happiness to be elsewhere. In all the public face of the tour the Gambaegges were never apart, but after Barcelona I could never find any irritation in myself when they inconvenienced the rest of us.

The broken-necked bumbags swaying to Trevor's false seduction, the courteous smell of sacking in a warm crowded evening, Gaudi and the midnight weeping of Gibraltar's Mrs Gambaegge, are what I have of Barcelona: a pot-pourri quite exclusive and true to me.

Malcolm, our tour guide, was a young man from Worcester with slightly bulging blue eyes and impatience just below the surface of his pleasant nature. Both impatience and goodwill were essential and not assumed, so that sometimes he was a little at war with himself. He wanted the best for us all and was convinced he knew what that was. Malcolm was knowledgeable and not blasé about the places to which he took us, though most he had visited several times before. He told me he had been saving to attend the University of East Anglia and take a degree in languages and history. He could speak

French and Italian well, and had some German. When his arrangements were under pressure from the Wisconsin Foursome, the Gambaegges, or Irene Hamble who constantly wished to use the on-board toilet despite the comfort stops, Malcolm began his tuneless whistle — the sign he was at odds with himself.

The day we visited the Rhine Falls was a particularly long one, and followed a beer fest during which poor Chester was struck on the head by a porcelain stein with bas reliefs of pigs and grapes. Malcolm stood at the front of the bus with his microphone, telling us about the significant Second World War events that happened thereabouts, but almost all of the tour lolled in their seats — Chester with a little blood showing through his medical turban. I could see that Malcolm was mortified by the indifference to his commentary, and in between battle sites his amplified whistle whined down the aisle, a sort of falsetto counterpoint to the rumblings of plumbing and snoring from the Wisconsin Foursome and others. Biological imperatives are stronger than manners, or the desire for educational instruction: Pierre continued to drive through the pleasant countryside we had all paid to see; Malcolm continued to provide his commentary; the majority of the passengers slept with eyes closed and mouths open; Irene Hamble sidled towards the on-board lavatory.

The British conquered the world because they realised the benefit of a substantial breakfast. In our Madrid hotel I ate only a small sugar bun on three successive mornings. Nothing else was on offer. On that third morning we began the long trip to Lourdes, and I sat beside Glenda Waley who was barely fifty and recently widowed when her architect husband fell down the cellar steps in a client's partly finished Bristol home and struck the chassis of a 1927 Buick waiting there to be restored. Central Spain is very dry, with a lot of red earth, and for long distances nothing seemed to grow except olive trees. I didn't enjoy the views much, but the lack of eggs and toast may have been part of the reason. Glenda needed to tell me personal things about her dead husband: he had a benign enlargement of the prostate, she said, but was convinced he was dying, and he used to imitate his father in his sleep, talking dogmatically of Harold Wilson and the decline of English cricket. I felt sorry for Glenda, but even more so for her husband: he was dead, unable to keep up pretences any more, and his wife told strangers intimate things about his body and his inability to get free of his father.

'He'd hate it here,' said Glenda, as we drummed through the red heartland. 'He'd hate being pressed together on a tour bus like a school picnic. I couldn't consider coming until he'd passed on. He loved to be alone in a very large room, and said there was research about crowding rats together. That was one of his problems as an architect: he kept suggesting rooms larger than his clients could afford.' Glenda Waley was a serene, well-groomed woman who got on with us all, except Trevor. She always had an apple, or orange for morning tea, and peeled it adroitly with a special instrument, the skein of skin looping unbroken into her lap. I was only one of many who watched surreptitiously in car parks and scenic stops all over Europe for the tragedy of a discontinuity, but it never came. Glenda had some fine rings from the architectural earnings of her dead husband, and my wife particularly admired a large sapphire in a raised setting surrounded by diamonds.

As we neared Bilbao the country was greener and more productive. Malcolm told us of the ethnic and linguistic uniqueness of the Basques who lived in the area, and widow Waley laid a hand of glittering gems on my knee to reinforce the candidness with which she betrayed her husband's privacy. 'Graham had an abhorrence of body hair,' she said. 'On himself, on anyone, but especially women. He wouldn't let me shave because of stubble, and insisted on both of us using a clinically prescribed depilatory cream at least once a week. Esau is what he called hairy people. He was once physically ill after sitting beside a Hungarian professor of architectural history who had a full face black beard that ran into his nostrils and ears.' Malcolm's voice was a background to our conversation, carrying a carefully balanced explanation of local terrorism.

'Maybe his father was a hairy man,' I ventured. There is something of the amateur psychologist in us all. 'An Esau perhaps.'

'Not at all,' said Glenda Waley, 'but he used to beat Graham with a dog collar that hung behind the scullery door.'

Whenever I read about the Basques now, they are in my mind's eye extremely hirsute people, flinging bombs and deeply hating their fathers. 'But I've been talking just about myself,' said Glenda. 'Very rude of me. You must tell me what you and your wife thought of the hotel in Madrid.'

On the island of Capri, Irene Hamble and the Dutch girl went missing. No one was sure if they had remained in Anacapri or taken the chair-lift to the very top of the island as Malcolm suggested. How wonderful the chair-lift was: quiet and private, flitting close over the garden terraces, rough grasses and small trees. At that height there was a cool breeze such as I hadn't felt for weeks, and in a vineyard that passed beneath, I saw quite distinctly the dismembered pieces of several pink dolls lying among the green rows. Some juvenile Latin fury had been assuaged, I imagined, as had that of emperors with greater bloodshed so many years ago.

Malcolm asked us all to be on the lookout for Irene Hamble and the spindly girl, but I put them out of my mind and went to Axel Munthe's magnificent villa of San Michele at the foot of Mount Barbarossa. Irene Hamble was a born survivor with a formidable nature apparent to any nationality: the Dutch girl would come to no harm with her, apart from obligatory sexual blandishments from local men because she was blonde.

I had read Munthe's great book as a student, and found it stirring and exotic. The content of his writing had long since leached from my mind, but I felt an odd frisson from the emotional associations of the villa. All sorts of antiquities were incorporated in the construction in eccentric ways, and I was lucky to come across Chester resting on the cool marble floor of a room that looked on to the shaded garden. Chester of course knew all the history of Capri, and most of that concerning the writer. He told me about Munthe being physician to the Swedish royal family, financing sanctuaries for migrating birds, living in Keats's house in Rome, visiting mad Maupassant, and having his sight restored by surgery after going blind. Such people seem to live heroic lives, while you and I have superannuation and ingrown toenails as topics of conversation.

While waiting for the Gambaegges at the top of the funicular, our party was rejoined by Irene Hamble and the Dutch girl, who claimed that Trevor had relayed garbled times concerning the day's activities. Only their tempers had suffered by their misadventure, but old Chester was inadvertently crushed by the Wisconsin Foursome while boarding the return ferry to Sorrento. He wasn't at dinner in the hotel that night, and my wife thought I should check up on him. I found him resting on his bed in shirt and sagging underpants, so his trousers wouldn't crease, in just the way I remember my father had done in his old age. Chester's legs were thin and white, and the knees were bulbous and wrinkled. His large nose seemed roughly modelled in clay and his mouth sagged open. The very appearance that age gives us is a form of indignity, but Chester's mind had suffered no atrophy and retained reach and power.

We had just poured a Chianti, when Gillian Heading came to see how he was. I opened the door to her, and gave Chester enough time to pull a sheet across his lower half. 'No, no,' he said, 'I'm fine. It was just some bruising from the gangway, and after such a long, hot and wonderful day I thought I'd rest a little.'

'Those people are like elephants,' Gillian said.

'I'm sure Delmar and Blanche would have noticed me if they hadn't been talking.'

'Absolutely like elephants,' said Gillian. She was disappointed she'd chosen to go to the Blue Grotto rather than San Michele, and the more Chester told her of Axel Munthe the more certain was her conviction of loss. I could see that Chester was a little embarrassed at repeating the store of information he'd already shared with me earlier in the day, and though I would willingly have listened all over again, I made an excuse, went down to the bar. Trevor and Nick Guillermo had a table by the door, and Trevor began telling us about the maid on his floor who had excellent arse and tits, and who was coming to his room after her shift.

The street between the hotel and the sea fell away steeply, and although I couldn't see Capri, above the blue neons of a pizza café was the dark, shifting shadow of the sea, and the warm air was fragrant with history. Chester was perhaps telling Gillian of Axel Munthe's visit to Guy de Maupassant in the asylum at Passy. Maupassant was planting pebbles in the flower garden and told the creator of San Michele that the stones would grow into a host of little Maupassants when it rained. How Gillian would enjoy the story. While she talked with Chester, his legs palely naked beneath the sheet of modesty, she could forget she was redundant in the world of television.

There is a gold-roofed room in Innsbruck from which medieval ladies used to look down on the uncouth market throng in the town centre below, and not far from that is a small, secluded courtyard at the back of the old clock-tower with Hapsburg crests on its faces. I sat alone in the courtyard for more than an hour, and then a young gardener in a blue shirt came to weed the tiny plot around the fountain in the centre. He looked up and smiled a good deal, and I could see that, rather than concentrating on his work, he was curious as to my nationality. After a few minutes he gave up the pretence of work and spoke to me in English. He was studying economics at the university in Innsbruck, he said, and had a cousin working on an outback station in Queensland, but before we had talked long the sky darkened suddenly and there was a violent thunderstorm. Thunder, lightning, squalls of hailstones, played about the old clock-tower. The gardener began to shout, but what I took at first for exhilaration was fear, and he dropped the hoe, held his arms aloft to ward off a strike and ran from the courtyard. His shirt had turned a much deeper blue in the rain, and he jumped the biggest puddles as he ran in an exaggerated, comic way. I took shelter in the clock-tower entrance, surprised that a young guy studying such a pragmatic subject as economics was afraid of lightning. Maybe if there had been no storm in Innsbruck that day, the student and I would have discovered a good deal in common, exchanged addresses, met since on other trips in his country, or mine.

On the island of Burano, in the Venice lagoon, is a leaning spire, and Mrs Guillermo came inside the church and translated some of the inscriptions and plaques for my wife and me, and Gillian Heading and Naomi Browne. The figurines were crudely made, but had a sort of glaring confidence. When back in the sun, Mrs Guillermo steered me aside and asked if I would spend more time with Nick, because she feared he was being unduly influenced by Trevor. How could I tell her that at Nick's age, and Trevor's, a preoccupation with sexual satisfaction is both natural and incorrigible.

Burano is famous for lace, and the beauty of it incited a shopping spree. At the café where we settled for lunch, the purchases were compared and praised. The Wisconsin wives had the most, but Glenda Waley had some of the most attractive lace, and she draped it on her smooth, hairless legs and arms for display. The rings from her dead husband glittered on the delicate material, and I thought how thankful he would be that she hadn't brought the shame of Esau on them, though the crowded tables would have been less agreeable for him. Those of the tour who could speak Italian — Mrs Guillermo, the Gibraltar Gambaegges, Malcolm, Chester and, to a lesser extent, Nick and Gillian — made harmless fun with the waiters at the expense of the rest of us, and we tried to laugh off our ignorance.

After Fettuccine Piccanti, and other courses of which only the flavours remain, my wife and I went outside with Chester, and sat by the bobbing small boats moored close to the café. They were painted with the colours of a merry-go-round: bright green, red, yellow and blue. We hoped for a breeze, which Chester said sometimes came in the evenings. He had been to the island twice before, and my wife asked him what differences he noticed when returning to places as he often had over the years. 'I began to think that my fellow travellers were more oafish each time,' he said, 'but now I realise I'm the one changing: gripped with the intolerance of old age.'

Chester had the habit of stroking the healing stein wound on his head, and the grey bristles above his ear rustled as he did so. It was a pleasant part of life to sit with an espresso and Barbera wine outside the café on Burano, and watch the twilight settling in. The

Wisconsin Foursome could be heard discussing plumbing, and Trevor seemed to have offended a local woman, but it was all at a comforting remove inside the café. 'We'll send cards to each other for the first Christmas or two,' said Chester, 'and then exist only as increasingly uncertain images in the tour albums.'

'You must come and visit us,' said my wife emphatically.

'I will. I will,' agreed Chester.

A week or so before, as we discussed euthanasia in the foyer of a diamond workshop in Amsterdam, Chester told me that although he hadn't got quite the role he preferred in life, he would act out the whole play. In youth we mount the Pegasus of our ambition, and awake in old age astride a Shetland pony with our feet resting on the ground.

Chester was right as always: the night brought a breeze that whispered through the coloured boats of Burano, perhaps exhalations from the Bridge of Sighs itself, and Mrs Gambaegges began singing in Italian in the café behind us. Her husband joined in, and their unaccustomed harmony excused all the times they had kept us waiting, and gave hope for their marriage. An elderly woman stopped to listen, hunched in her doorway like a ruffled thrush. Chester raised the empty wine bottle to a waiter as a signal for a full replacement, and made my wife laugh softly with a whispered opinion of Trevor. It was one of those rare, serene and self-sufficient moments in our passage to the grave when there seemed a complete integration of spirit and external things. So let it be.

THE DEVIL AT BRUCKNERS' POND

No matter how things prosper, a woman can always imagine better times. For Haydon Collins, though, it was heaven gained to be with Alice under the buffalo horns of a new moon. A cool drift of air from Bruckners' Pond, and Alice's gasp from between himself and the coarse weave of the car rug.

Only at such times, rare times, did he feel all of himself alive and free from the lethargies that otherwise laid hold on some part of body, or spirit. The moon's wry smile glittered weakly on the small, dark ruffles of Bruckners' Pond; the willow ends trailed back, whispering of autumn.

Alice's husband never listened to her, and she was entitled to a sympathetic listener. Haydon was an eager confidant, even to the verbatim account of a meter maid, for Alice had no skill of paraphrase, no awareness, in fact, of any such mode of discourse, so all the episodes she cropped from each fortnight of her life were delivered blow by blow. He'd suggested they meet once a week, but she considered it too physical, too taxing, and she was the coach of a under-fifteen softball team that had prospects in its grade and needed to practise twice a week.

'I ticketed the harbourmaster's Landcruiser,' said Alice, 'and his secretary rang me up and said I couldn't do it, not to the harbour-master in his own precincts. I said to her I could do it in any precincts in the city that has meters: that I could do it to the mayor himself, and I'd ticketed the Civil Defence officer three times in one week, and because no emergency had been declared he had to pay up like anybody else. That's different, she tried to tell me. The Civil Defence officer's different to the harbourmaster in his own precincts. No difference at all, not at all, I says. All's equal under the local regulations and I know it off by heart. She didn't have an answer to that.'

If Haydon raised himself on his elbows he could see the moon fragments dancing on the surface of Bruckners' Pond, and the whips of willow shaking slightly in the night breeze. Miniature waves slapped the mass of root filaments that made the small bank of the pond. There was a morepork calling from the gully upstream, and Haydon was almost overcome by his good fortune to be lying on Alice in such a night, instead of watching television alone, or playing snooker in Paul Barrett's garage.

'You've got guts, Alice. I don't reckon the other meter maids would have the nerve to apply the law so evenly.'

'There's blokes too do the meters,' she said. 'How many of them do you think would ticket the harbourmaster in his own precincts?'

'None of them,' said Haydon. 'You're a bloody marvel. I reckon I should write anonymously to the council and say it too. Someone should do it.'

'I actually should go and see the harbourmaster's secretary again now that I think about it.'

Haydon gave her thigh a light slap, which sounded barely louder than the ripples on the bank, and blew hair back from her face. 'What would you say to her? Tell me exactly what you'd say to her.' In such circumstances he could listen for ever.

'Well,' she said, 'I've come for a bit of word with you, I'd say, something of a chat about your harbourmaster in his own precincts. I'm not a person who looks to be awkward, you understand —'

Haydon wished she would divorce her husband so that he could move in with her and make love after the evening meals, while she talked about her day wearing the civic badge, and upholding municipal traffic regulations. Alice was a very warm person: he could feel the fresh heat of her body as she became animated in her hypothetical conversation with the harbourmaster's secretary. 'I'd tell her straight out. Rules is rules I'd tell her, straight out — just stop a minute, there's something hard under the rug: a stone or some damn thing. That's it — No, I'd tell her, in my way of things everybody's equal, whether you're the harbourmaster, or just ordinary Joe Bloggs — .'

A noise was coming from the lupins and broom further back from the pond. Haydon could hear it, even though absorbed with pleasure, through the sound of breeze in the weeping willows, and Alice's monologue. It demanded attention not because of volume, but because of eccentricity — it was a noise quite unknown to him. A sound that had something of whirling in it, something of disturbance to natural order, yet also a constituent of powerful personality.

Haydon raised himself from Alice enough to glance behind, and saw the Devil stroll down beside them, nod in a passing sort of way, and then stand on the lip of Bruckners' Pond. He had the goodness to face away for a time, and the moonlight caught his small horns, and the thatch of vigorous, but grey, hair at their base. Haydon and Alice scrambled to uncouple, and then arrange themselves separately on the rug. Alice was very rarely at a loss: she had fronted up to harbourmasters, mayors, media celebrities and Mongrel Mob members in the course of duty. She drew in a full breath to start in on the intruder, but then he turned, could be seen so clearly for who he was, that she let it all out in one long sigh.

'Overall it's a wretchedly poor creation,' said the Devil, 'but I must say that a summer's night at Bruckners' Pond, a warm half wind, a little routine copulation: there are worse places.' He had a voice of blandishment, rich with cynical toleration and forgiveness.

'I beg your pardon!' said Alice, affronted.

'Not at all,' said the Devil. 'Think nothing of it.'

The Devil didn't appear to have any trousers, but he wore a long frock coat of fustian green, mid-calf boots, and there wasn't much gap between. He had side whiskers and a dusky red complexion as if embers glowed within. Despite the night he was quite clearly seen; again the light that made that possible was subtly from within rather than the effect of the moon. He was like one of those unregenerate eighteenth-century squires; bluff, hearty and entirely self-serving in the most natural of ways. The Devil's tail was dark, and heavy on the ground when he moved, and with flukes at its substantial end. Haydon had the odd thought that it would make a great quantity of strong soup.

'I knew the first Bruckner here,' said the Devil, after he had breathed the lake air deeply. 'Old Anton, who bought the place in the 1860s with his wife's money, and had a vision of it as a resort in the European way, all chalets and profit. But of course the family lost it one generation before it became really valuable.' The Devil's humour seemed of an ironic turn, and his smile of reminiscence was dusky and emberish. 'The family were religious, but had a redeeming streak of profligacy,' he said.

'The Reverend David Bruckner's the vicar here, you know,' said Alice, more assured now that she had got her legs together. She wondered whether to introduce Haydon and herself to the Devil, but it was that sort of awkward situation in which you get too far into conversation with a stranger for introductions to be comfortable.

'Quite,' said the Devil, 'and I believe the vestry are at this moment taking a particular interest in the church accounts.'

Haydon feared that he was to be excluded from the conversation with the Devil, and that afterwards his silence would be taken by Alice as a weakness. Remember the time we met the Devil, she might say, and I talked to him, but you had nothing at all to say for yourself did you, nothing at all.

'Bruckners' Pond belongs to the ratepayers now,' he said.

'So it does,' replied the Devil equably, but his smile continued to be for Alice.

'We don't come here often,' she said.

'More's the pity,' said the Devil. 'It's not what you do, but who knows about it, isn't it?'

The three of them considered that, and watched the moon and the willows of Bruckners' Pond for a time, then the Devil wished them well and said that he had to be going. He gave the faintest of bows, but with the assurance of the landed gentry, and his coat was a rich, verdigris green for a moment in the moonlight and his face dusky and glowing, and he walked past them and into the bushes.

As Haydon saw the Devil walking on two legs and with a tail, he realised how fitting and natural it was, and that ordinary people on two legs seemed ungainly and incomplete, while the Devil walked with the grace of a tiger, and his tail made a firm and steadying contact with the ground behind him.

The Devil's departure prompted that of Haydon and Alice. You couldn't just carry on regardless after talking to the Devil. The two of them gathered up the rug and pillows and climbed into the off-roader. 'I'm damned if I know,' said Haydon. 'What can you say that makes sense of that?'

'I wish I'd thought of more to say,' said Alice. It was a feeling foreign to her. 'Anyway, I won't be seeing you again — not like this anyway,' she said clearly. 'The Devil's quite right you know.'

Haydon was so angry that he couldn't get the key into the ignition, but he kept his voice down because he wasn't sure how far the Devil had gone. 'What do you mean, the Devil's right?' he said bitterly, but he knew in his heart the absolute authority of the Devil. The Devil had done for him, no doubt about that, had scotched the greatest of his pleasures. 'What if it had been God, eh?' said Haydon. 'What then?'

'Just the same,' said Alice serenely.

A BUM STEER

I wear a pair of thigh waders when I clean the car. My wife laughs at me because, she says, I look a fool. My sons snigger too, as they slouch past with adolescent élan. The waders are old, and the rubber has frayed away in the crease lines, but they do the trick for me when I'm using the hose on the car. It's annoying to get your feet wet at such a chore.

For years the waders have been used only at home, but there was a time when I did a good deal of trout fishing — not salmon fishing, because I always found that too competitive, too crowded. I fished as much to be alone in the countryside as anything else, and jostling almost shoulder to shoulder with others after salmon at a river mouth didn't do much for me.

I bought the waders in the year that I shifted to Oamaru to be information officer at the council. 'You'll have to get decent waders of course,' said Ted. Ted Mumsome was my immediate boss there, and a very keen fisherman. In the season most of each Monday's morning tea break was filled with Ted's monologue of his fishing exploits over the weekend: the relative merits of Grey Ghost, or Yellow Dorothy, until his colleagues were driven back to their desks. In retrospect at least, these excursions showed Ted to be a sort of

Bwana of the waterways, replete with knowledge and expertise to outwit the most wily of trout and fellow anglers.

Once he knew that I fished a bit, Ted decided to take my education in hand, and given his seniority and possible effect on my career, I went along with it. One of Ted's rather irritating habits was that he was a contradictory conversationalist: one of those people constitutionally inclined to propose the opposite of anything you suggest. If you said the day looked promising, he was full of dire prognostication. If you praised someone for affability, or talent, Ted gave a rueful laugh and said you didn't know the half of it. Any suggestion concerning timing, or venue, of any activity whatsoever, was met by Ted's determined alternative. To express any view at all was the preamble of inevitable debate. It got rather wearying, and was probably the reason that Ted didn't have many friends among the council staff. Anyway, he realised that as I was a new chum of no great status, he could be the chief to my Indian, and I found it politic to go along, at least at first.

The Waitaki is a big river, but I never found it as good for trout as I expected. The main channels were a great deal swifter than I was used to. Ted took me out four or five times that first year, and I tried to escape his persistent instruction and criticism by going off down a bank by myself as much as I could. Then, late in the season, on a long, warm, still North Otago evening, we drove up from Oamaru on what was to be our last fishing trip together. There was a sign at the Glenavy camping ground which said 'Fish In River Now', and most of them would stay there it seemed to me.

'So what spot do you reckon would be best on a day like this?' asked Ted.

'Maybe the old crossing?' I said.

'Hopeless. Absolutely hopeless. The stone wall is the place to go today. There's more trees and we want shadow on the water.'

'Right,' I agreed.

We drove up the north side of the valley and pulled off to park by the stone wall. As we stood by the car boot, putting on our waders and getting our gear sorted, Ted gave me a lecture on where the fish lie when there's broken water. He had expensive, green, one-piece waist-high waders, and a flap cap on which he carried most of his flies. He looked a bit of a pillock actually, but I wasn't going to tell him so to his face. Job security was an important part of my philosophy in those days.

'Should we go upstream, do you think?' I asked him.

'No. There's better water below.'

'Maybe I'll just mosey up there a bit and then come on back towards you,' I said. I put up a carefully calculated resistance from time to time so that I didn't lose my self-respect entirely.

'You'll learn the hard way, but suit yourself,' said Ted. 'Don't come crunching into the top of any water I'm fishing.'

We walked together across the greywacke stones, the scattered bleached grasses and docks, through the patches of lupins and broom and gorse. The sun burnt fiercely as if to deny that it must fall down soon. Ted and I parted at one of the channels, and I tried not to seem eager as I turned away from him and went upstream. 'Good luck,' I said. 'See you later.'

'Luck's got nothing to do with it,' said Ted. 'You remember what I told you last time about not moving about too much in the water.' He clumped off downstream. The waist-high waders accentuated his almost womanly hips, and his shoulders were stooped from desk work. He had a high, arched nose and the bone and cartilage whitened the skin as if to split it at any moment. I wondered what he thought about when he was fishing alone.

Autumn is almost always drought time in North Otago, and the side channels of the Waitaki in particular showed on the stones algae lines of successively lower levels. They weren't letting a lot out of the dams. I headed for a turn of still water, with a small cascade at the top end, hoping there'd be a fish or two there waiting just below the broken water.

I was only a threadline fisherman and never aspired to the almost holy realm of the dry fly. I had one strike at the top of the pool below the rapids, but the medium-sized fish flipped into the air free of the lure, and after that I never even saw a rise. I worked down the reach quietly, looking and casting unhurriedly. Much of the time I just stood there, enjoying the cool of the back channel through my waders, and watching the sun go slowly down. A long arrow of Canada geese went up the valley and their honking echoed in the evening air. I saw the momentary, syrup strip of a weasel over a pale clay bank; gone before its recognition. Magpies were quarrelling somewhere beyond my sight, and the air was a rich mixture of country fragrances.

Then I heard Ted coming from downstream, marching with slow deliberation among the vegetation. 'You said you were going to work your way down to me,' he said, as if I'd left him stranded at a city bus-stop.

'I was just about to.'

'Well, you're the loser.' Ted held up a resigned-looking rainbow of two and a half pounds or so. 'I could've given you a few tips if you'd been with me. There's no substitute for experience, you know.'

'I guess you're right,' I said.

Ted made himself comfortable on a small bank and investigated the guts of his fish for my benefit, asking me to identify the various items of the fish's recent diet, and contradicting each of my answers. Ted did a post mortem on every fish he caught, and recorded the results in a notebook along with the details of the weather and water conditions at the time of the catch. 'Knowledge is power, you see,' he said. 'That's the same in business as it is in fishing. What's the use of anything if you don't learn from your experience? Eh?' He was right no doubt, but I've always been perverse in not wishing to analyse my recreations.

'Anyway,' said Ted, 'let's take a last half hour or so downstream. I saw a likely place with a bit of depth.' He washed out his fish, wrapped it in newspaper and put it in his bag. 'Move yourself then,' he said, although I was standing waiting for him.

We scrambled up the small bank and made our way through the long grass and longer shadows of gorse and broom of the island flat. A commotion began in the bushes towards the main river. We just had time to see a thrashing line of broom and lupin tops heading our way, before a large Hereford steer burst out a few metres from us and stood glaring, with snot and saliva gleaming in the last of the setting sun. I'm not easy with big animals, and that Hereford was an impressive brute with horns. Anything with horns, from the devil down, deserved respect as far as I was concerned. I backed up and stumbled, to end ignominiously on my back amid the gorse and bleached grasses.

Ted lifted his head and gave a piercing laugh. 'Come on, come on,' he said. 'It's only a steer for Christ's sake, not a friggin bull.' The Hereford waited just long enough for Ted to finish, then charged him. Maybe it was gripped by a fury at the fates that had decreed its emasculation long ago. Ted was caught high on his waders and driven into the gorse behind. The horn tore through the rubber and the steer continued on, trampling over Ted and bursting away through the undergrowth. It was over in a few seconds, and I hurried over to Ted, expecting to find him seriously injured. Luckily the horn had caught the waders only, and the worst Ted got was a nasty abrasion on his shoulder from the steer's hoof and a face full of gorse which drew blood.

I did my best to be supportive on the way back to the car, but shock, and wounded pride perhaps, made Ted angry. 'I don't want to talk about it. I will not talk about it. Do you understand?' he exclaimed vehemently.

We never did talk about it, not driving back to Oamaru, not at morning tea at the council offices, despite the comments on his marked face which gave me an opportunity, not ever. Ted never again invited me to go fishing with him, and that was no great loss. Afterwards, though, he seemed to have a better attitude towards me, even agreeing with me once or twice at staff meetings, which surprised our colleagues. Knowledge is power indeed, as Ted had often told me.

THE LANGUAGE PICNIC

Prof Carver Glower was there, Assoc Prof Teems, Dr Podanovich, Dr Johns, Dr Fell and Eileen the department secretary. Only Dr Allis-Montgomery refused to come, because of a vendetta going back seventeen years.

The English department had just that week completed the fourth and final volume of *Antipodean English: Growth of a Variant*, and Eileen had suggested a picnic. Prof Glower had appropriated the idea, as was his wont and prerogative, and put it to the faculty. 'What do you reckon?'

'Cracker,' said Assoc Prof Teems.

'Bonzer,' said Dr Podanovich.

'Yeah, why the fuck not,' said Dr Fell. 'Out in the boohai, eh. As long as us sheilas aren't expected to bring all the grub.' She preferred not to socialise with her academic colleagues, but knew what was politic in establishing a career. Also she found something generically plaintive in picnics: they reminded her of the desperate efforts her mother had made to placate family disharmony by such occasions. 'We should have Eileen along.'

'Bingo, already come up with that,' replied Prof Glower.

From the carpark amid pine trees the track led down to the

beach of black sand. Because the sand was easily kicked out, the track was almost a ditch, and Assoc Prof Teems stumbled. She couldn't recover her balance because of the open basket she carried, and after wild oscillation she tumbled into the heart of a small gorse bush. Her apricot muffins were shaken into the marram grass, and the blue gingham cover she'd had over them caught in the gorse and became a taut pennant in the ripe sea breeze and beneath an effulgent sun. 'Bugger,' she said.

Solicitous as ever, and rendered clumsy by his concern, Dr Podanovich scrambled down to assist her. 'You did a real header,' he said. 'Arse over tip.' He began to pluck the gorse prickles from her pale arm and cheek, his fingers long and nimble from subtle play on the computer keyboard.

'Crapped out badly there,' said Dr Johns, who couldn't disguise that elementary human relief which is a response to the misfortunes of another. He was a small, neat, waxy man, rather like a Belgian detective. 'Come a real greaser all right,' he said, and gave his quick-fire, harsh laugh. Dr Johns was not essentially a malicious man, but he was suffering from an uneasy conscience, and attempting to assuage it by some acerbity towards his colleagues. Within the department he was normally a somewhat devious, and not fully disclosed, ally of Dr Allis-Montgomery, but he'd not had the courage to join him in boycotting the picnic. It was too unequivocal an alignment for him to commit to, but he half despised himself because of his decision.

Prof Glower picked up several of the muffins in a lordly, offhand manner, and shook them free of sand. 'No probs, she'll be jake,' he said. 'Nifty kai, I reckon.' In his heart, though, he was a disappointed man. He led the way down to the beach, and with his fingers combed the remaining long strands of grey hair across the pale luminosity of his head. Already he could feel sand grating there from his hand. Most of his staff were amiable enough, but he had academic respect for none of them, except perhaps Dr Fell, and all the time he felt his leadership under insidious siege by Dr Allis-Montgomery. Prof Glower told himself he should be satisfied with a chair in a New

Zealand university, but he yearned for a vice-chancellorship, even more for a professorship at a name overseas institution. *Antipodean English* was his final play for scholastic distinction, and the first three volumes had received only qualified critical reception. 'Let's find a pearler possie out of the wind,' he said in his falsely jocular tone, and looked over the empty, black beach.

The group set up with their car rugs, baskets and chilly bins in the lee of the last dune before the beach. Assoc Prof Teems was immediately absorbed in removing the remaining gorse prickles; Dr Fell and Eileen caught each other's eye and had a long, exclusive smile at the mismatched socks revealed as Dr Podanovich awkwardly sat down and crossed his lanky legs. 'Just as well we're not wearing our best mocker,' he said. 'Old dungers for the beach I say.' Prof Glower talked to all, and nobody in particular, about the need to leave their offices occasionally, and Dr Johns rather pointedly yawned and lay back with his hands behind his head.

Assoc Prof Teems was an intelligent, gentle woman increasingly buffeted by the winds of change through tertiary education. Her passion was the poetry of Robert Herrick, but that was treated with boisterous derision by first-year students, so she proffered it only to the occasional postgraduate, and even more occasional Herrick conference. She was English, and her interest in the New Zealand vernacular was entirely a reflection of the department's focus. She disliked gorse, lupins and the coastal smell, which made her think some great kipper was rotting out beyond the swell. But she was loyal by nature, and had a strict sense of duty, and so although seventeenth-century English poetry was her spiritual home, she tried to find a place to stand in a new country. No chance of a place of subtlety, of nuanced reflective comment, or classical allusion, she thought wryly, and ran her hand over her skin to check for more thorns and found none. 'Well, here's one pommie who's ready to take a gecko at the friggin' beach,' she said.

'Yeah, let's give it a burl,' said Eileen. 'Maybe there's a bronzed life-saver there.'

'More like a cockie with pig-dogs who hates loopies,' said Dr

Johns, but he went with them rather than listen to Prof Glower.

Dr Podanovich untangled his legs and stood up too, but not to go down to the beach. Already he sensed the familiar rifts and indifferences within the group becoming apparent: at least that sardonic Lucifer, Allis-Montgomery, wasn't with them, yet the taint of his eternal bitterness seemed impregnated in their congregation, as the fish-splitter carries always some olfactory reminder of his trade. Dr Podanovich retained a idealistic wish for a professional life of mutual support, respect and effervescent enjoyment. 'I'm going to get a bit of a fire going,' he said. 'I reckon you can't have a dinkum feed without a snarler or two.' Maybe a fire, that ageless symbol of communal gathering, would bring them together happily. Dr Podanovich went off, stooped even more than usual, as he fossicked in the marram grass for driftwood.

'Good on you, mate,' announced Prof Glower, and then in a lower voice to Dr Fell, 'The tight-arse didn't want to cough up for more than supermarket bangers, and now he thinks he deserves a bloody medal.'

Dr Fell permitted herself a knowing smile, but said nothing. She considered Dr Podanovich a sweet simpleton who carried far more than his share of the academic load, and he always topped the students' assessments of their lecturers. On the other hand, she knew she was the professor's favourite, and although she refused to play on that, neither would she deliberately jeopardise the career advantages that might flow from it. She alone was in his confidence regarding his increasing sense of disillusion, and that knowledge mitigated for her his public and empty pomposity. Dr Fell herself was young, had long legs, and professional prospects of even greater extent.

'I was knocked back by East Anglia for visiting prof again,' said Prof Glower. 'No hoper pricks didn't even bother to tell me until I sent an email giving them a rark-up.'

'That's bloody crook,' said Dr Fell. 'It's not on.' The black sand was warm through her fingers, and her bright red toenails glittered in the sunlight. Through a cleavage in the dunes she saw her three colleagues walking the surf line, breaking into a scamper up the beach sometimes to escape the seventh wave. Assoc Prof Teems and Eileen were close together, their heads inclined towards each other. Dr Johns attempted to relax, giving his metallic laugh from time to time, but at a distance his essential self-consciousness and uncertainty were obvious in everything he did. It occurred to Dr Fell that maybe when Allis-Montgomery was present, Dr Johns felt more at ease, because he knew he was then not the most unpopular and isolated person of any group.

'You can bet your arse it was a jack-up anyway,' said Prof Glower. 'Some Nigerian Hausa woman wearing curtain material will have been appointed, and rabbit on to packed bloody halls about the poetry of political dissent.'

'You're not shook on African poetry?'

'Poetry my arse. Everyone's got too bloody windy to say what they really think about post-colonial literature, that's for sure.'

'The new dean of humanities — ,' began Dr Fell.

'Effing commel,' said Prof Glower. He realised he had struck a sour note, and promised himself not to allow his inner melancholy to be so obvious, even to Dr Fell. 'Need a bit of old man manuka, eh,' he shouted to Dr Podanovich, who was encouraging the first flames from beneath arabesques of driftwood.

'Nah, she'll be a bottler,' said Dr Podanovich. He took a black and greasy skillet from a supermarket bag and began to lay pink sausages in it.

Walking back towards the picnic spot with Assoc Prof Teems and Dr Johns, Eileen saw a thin wisp wafting from the fire, barely smoke from such dry wood, more a heat distortion like the thermals in boiling water. She knew that Dr Podanovich would be doing all the work, while the other two watched and talked. Eileen had no degree, but often she felt exasperated with the academics she served: their tetchy self-regard and social naïvety coupled with powerful intellects and obsessive interests. During the years most important for learning to relate to others in a diverse society, they had spent their time in libraries, isolated cubicles and, less often, with small intense cabals of people like themselves. Often she felt like an ordinary mother with gifted, but difficult children.

'What's it like down there?' asked Dr Podanovich.

'Pretty nippy round the pippy,' said Eileen, 'but we're getting fit.'

Assoc Prof Teems let herself fall back on the warm slope of the dune. 'I'm knackered,' she said.

Dr Johns came last of the three. He was carrying his black shoes, had rolled his trousers up, and the dark sand clung to his wet legs. He wondered if Dr Allis-Montgomery was working alone at the university, and felt a twinge of guilt. He wished he had brought his own car so that he could have thought of some excuse to go home immediately after the picnic lunch, but then doubted his resolve to carry out something so temerarious. 'Time for tucker, eh,' he said. 'I reckon Paddy's a real gun with them sausies — you can put a ring round that.'

'Yeah, bog in, mate,' said Dr Podanovich. He experienced a sudden, poignant moment of déjà vu. The smell of sausages and burning driftwood, and the astringent fragrance of the sea, occasioned a memory that rose like an ache in his heart: his last fishing trip with his father before the latter's death. Maybe it was an omen that even his father's fishing skills had been unavailing that day, and he'd cooked sausages on the very same skillet. His father had been emaciated by radiation treatment, and although he laughed with his son, he had tragic, imploring eyes.

'Who's for plonk?' said Dr Fell. She took two bottles of Marlborough Sauvignon Blanc from her chilly bin. She had forgone an afternoon of flagrant hedonism with her personal trainer to be with the department, and thought she deserved at least a single pleasure at the picnic.

'Could I effing ever knock back a gargle of that,' exclaimed Prof Glowers. Alcohol was increasingly a solace for him, though he found double malt whisky a more rapid release than wine.

So the English department, minus just the physical presence of Allis-Montgomery, settled with somewhat self-conscious bonhomie to their lunch: al fresco academics ill at ease in a shifting landscape without books, or a dais on which to stand. The contribution of each was a significant reflection of character. Dr Fell's medal-winning white wine and cheese twists; Assoc Prof Teems's apricot muffins and Earl Grey tea; the fresh and sensible club sandwiches brought by Eileen; sherbet trumpets fashioned by Dr Johns in his modern and lonely flat; Prof Glower's salmon and broccoli quiche made by a wife complaisant as to his absence; Dr Podanovich's supermarket sausages and a six pack of Lion Brown.

'Is this good chow or what,' said Prof Glower.

'Monty,' said Assoc Prof Teems. She felt a brief frisson of despair at the thought her life provided no better option than this, and recalled her poet Herrick, driven by lack of congenial company to train a pig to drink wine with him in his vicarage garden.

'Things are cracking up big time,' said Dr Fell. The weather was in sudden change: scudding clouds driven by a building southerly, and the sea, cut off from the sun, turning leaden. The temperature fell quickly; the driven sand scurried in the lupins and grass; the wind made sad orisons along the arc of black beach; the first large drops splattered on sand and foliage, and the spread picnic of the English department.

'Turning real pear-shaped,' said Dr Podanovich. 'I think we'll have to flag it.'

All of them hastened to gather possessions as the southerly storm came upon them. They looked to their own welfare, except benign Dr Podanovich, who offered to carry Assoc Prof Teems's basket and Eileen's thermos. They straggled back up the entrenched path that wound steeply to the carpark through marram grass, gorse, lupins and the soft flanks of black dunes that flinched beneath the heavy rain. Dr Fell, immediately behind Prof Glower, heard several rain pellets strike his balding head with the sound of a kettle drum. Dr John's experienced a perverse euphoria, for the picnic was ending in disarray, and he'd be home by early afternoon. 'Send her down, Hughie,' he cried, and gave his barking laugh, not noticing one of his shoes fall from his bundle and roll to lie hidden in the lupins. How Dr Allis-Montgomery would enjoy the day recounted with the sardonic delivery of Dr Johns.

'Get your arse into gear up front,' shouted Eileen, impatient at the academics lack of athleticism. 'What drongo's holding us up?'

Prof Glower at the front refused to be hurried. 'Shut your trap,' he said sternly. Eileen was an indispensable secretary, but still a secretary after all. 'You're a bunch of sodding sooks. Wankers, the lot of you.' He strode on, refusing to hunch into the gale, professorial to the last, yet in his heart he felt an irrefutable regret that he had ever abandoned his love of Proust, and taken on the New Zealand vernacular.

DISEASES OF THE STRONG

'There's a big Easter party at the Roscoes',' Ellen told her husband. Chris's reply was mild, noncommittal, but he felt the welling exasperation at the comment. Slight, incidental information, but implied surely was his social failure: the absence of any invitation from the Roscoes. 'They say Avignon are doing all the catering, and it's seventy people,' Ellen said. So sixty-eight people definitely above themselves in the Roscoe hierarchy, and who knows how many besides. Chris wondered if perhaps the Roscoes should produce another list of those considered, but not quite there, as a consolation. But then what heartbreak for those who didn't figure even as also-rans.

'That'll set them back a bit,' was all he said.

'It's such a lovely house for entertaining: such a complete home.' Ellen had been there once to a committee meeting of the University Women's Association, and returned determined to knock out the lounge wall and create french doors to a patio. They had done so: they sat on the patio as they talked, but the expensive renovations had not achieved an invitation from the Roscoes.

The Roscoes were somebody. Bud Roscoe was senior partner in Roscoe, Roscoe and Trumpeter, and Gwen was a lecturer at the design school, despite, some said, having no formal qualifications.

Perhaps her lifestyle was sufficient and visible recommendation.

It's odd, isn't it, how much negative comment circulates concerning the privileged. Bud and Gwen weren't the richest, or most influential, people in the city, but as a couple they had attained enviable standing in the group to which Ellen and Chris loosely belonged. Bud had an easy manner and a slouching physical attraction: Gwen was all slim intensity and flair. They had a certain gloss, which attracted more humdrum people. They wielded power of association, all the more persuasive because it seemed quite unconscious.

'I suppose it'll be an arty crowd,' said Ellen, 'and legal eagles who like sport and boating.'

'Bound to be,' said Chris.

Two weeks later he played Bud Roscoe in the semi-final of the seniors squash competition. Seniors was something of a euphemism for over forty-fives, and it was a teams event. They had a long, even game and Chris won, which was the clincher for his team, Business Blue, to go through to the final. Chris and Bud had a drink at the club bar, looking out over a collection of university bike stands and a pillar box custom-made for local drama and pop band advertisements. They were well enough acquainted to talk easily of the Parkside developments, and the convolutions of the city building regulations. In the past they'd had one-drink conversations, but this time Bud asked if he had time for another.

'Funny thing,' Bud said, 'but we've a new partner at work, and almost the first thing he asked me was about you. Does it ring a bell?' Bud had very hairy arms, but a pale, smooth place on the underside of his wrists.

'No.'

'A shit-hot barrister back from London?'

'Michael Guard,' said Chris.

'Bingo.'

'Jesus. Michael Guard,' said Chris.

'He said the two of you were great mates.'

And so they were. The best of mates through school and

university, and keeping in touch for several years although in different cities, until Michael went overseas and their correspondence dropped away because of busy lives. Michael Guard: all urgent individuality, but the very best friend he had, and Chris felt something close to joy that he was back, and yet an elusive, ambiguous fear, that to meet again would be some disappointment when set against the understanding of earlier years.

'Look, I'll tell you what I thought,' said Bud Roscoe. 'Gwen and I are having a party Easter weekend, and we'd like you and your wife to come. We've been meaning to have you over several times. Michael will be there, and he'd be chuffed to see you. It's not always easy coming back after ages, and knowing hardly anyone. Gwen will send an invitation over, but get on to me if it doesn't turn up. I'm a bugger for forgetting the niceties.'

Chris said nothing to his wife until the invitation came. 'We must be replacements to get invited this late,' she said, but there was no real criticism meant; rather she reproved herself for the satisfaction she felt in being asked. Chris didn't mention his talk with Bud, or Michael Guard's return after so many years overseas. Why should he want to diminish his wife's pleasure in being invited to the Roscoes' Easter party? What was a little innocent social snobbery against all the virtues for which he loved her. And Ellen barely knew Michael, had met him only briefly before he left.

Chris was not confessional. It wasn't in his character, or background, to spill his guts in the appalling American way. Business experience had confirmed his fortitude. Yet with Michael there had been something of brotherhood stronger than he found in his own family; some wry affinity in the response to experience of which both were aware. They seemed essentially of the same humour in the medieval sense of the word.

In his honours year, Chris had a fit of despair following the sudden death of his mother: a five-month clinical depression with no warning, and never repeated. Professional counselling and medication did little, but each evening in the flat Michael would come into Chris's room to work at his studies. He said little, just worked on as he would if alone in his own room, yet his presence was the tangible support that Chris found more comforting than he could explain. And when they were together, Michael put up with long silences, for often in his illness Chris could utter not a word.

The Roscoes had great weather for their party, despite the time of the year. It's always the way for such people, isn't it, and no doubt the Roscoes never expected anything else. Their broad patio was well lit, and warmed with free-standing braziers which encouraged guests out through the double french doors. Ellen was right: it was a great place in which to entertain. The university age Roscoe kids were very much part of the night. Lots of their friends provided a free-fall informality, and a noisy band at the patio far end with drums and saxophones. Combining generations at anyone else's party would have been a failure, but at the Roscoes' of course it was a stroke of genius. Some of the adults gave way to exhibitionism long suppressed, and capered with the youngsters like missionaries at a cannibal dance.

Michael came quite late, when the braziers had begun to glow in the dusk, and the blue pool cover was indistinct. Bud waved Chris over from a group talking about safety regulations for boaties, set both up with a new drink and left them to it. 'You two catch up a bit,' he said, 'and then bring Michael over and I'll introduce him to some other folk. They're not all lawyers, thank God, eh Chris.'

Some friends of your youth never change much, the essentials of form and movement always the same. Michael had changed physically a good deal. He was a lot bigger: not fatter, but taller it seemed, broader, and with his dark, lank hair streaked with grey like that of a symphony conductor. His hand was capacious, with the thumb firm when he greeted Chris. 'It's good to see you again, you old bastard,' he said, and the voice did have an English overlay, but more noticeably a courtroom resonance.

He still had bad skin. No pimples, but a red unevenness that hadn't subsided with age. His skin was a frontier, and there was a war going on there between himself and the outside world. More than just acne, it was a rawness, the inability to co-exist, which was his personality made tangible. 'So what have we here,' he said. 'A whipped cream of the professional Kiwi middle class. Until I came back I'd forgotten just how inept, how outright fucking boring, New Zealanders are when it comes to making conversation. At least Bud Roscoe has got some half decent wine. Our stuff's going down well in Europe now.'

As they talked, Chris realised that Michael had become an impatient man; more than that, an angry man, with that sort of non-specific anger which wells up eventually whatever the topic of conversation. He was dismissive of his new colleagues at Roscoe, Roscoe and Trumpeter, scathing about the service in local restaurants, flagrant in criticism of the British judicial system that had made him Queen's Counsel, and he broke off from critical reminiscence of his university lecturers, to mock mild, bearded Colin Thurgood whom he'd never met. 'Christ, look at that arsehole over there with the full beard and a moustache like a cat's bum. I hate these losers who can gain attention only by being hairy, or wearing a bloody corduroy suit.' Chris knew Colin: there was an element of truth in what Michael said but, as well as being mildly eccentric, Colin was friendly and generous.

'He's actually a pleasant enough guy,' said Chris.

'I'll take your word for it, but please don't bring the prick over here.'

Chris did introduce Ellen, and in the conversation Michael made it clear he'd come back to the country alone after a failed ten-year marriage and a son. Bud Roscoe brought other people to meet Michael, and Chris and Ellen went inside to have something at the buffet. Ellen was intrigued to see that Avignon Caterers had a seafood theme for the Roscoes with a centrepiece of scarlet crayfish and pink crabs raising pincers around a totem of scallop shells. 'You can bet it's Gwen Roscoe's idea,' said Ellen. 'You have to say she's got flair. Look how those profiteroles are arranged.'

'What did you think of Michael?'

'Both charming and disillusioned,' Ellen said. 'I wouldn't have thought of him as a close friend for you.'

'Thanks,' said Chris.

'You know what I mean.'

He did. He knew that after twenty-five years of professional life in Britain, Michael was bound to be a different person, but there was a sense of loss nevertheless. When did a splendid sense of urgency become anger? Later Chris looked at him from across the patio. Michael's bad skin was hidden by the semi-darkness, and the confidence of his large figure, his resonant voice, made him handsome. Even at a distance he could clearly be heard in offhand, sarcastic denigration of one topic after another, one person after another.

Late at night, when the young people had left for the city clubs, and the Roscoes' guests had settled in the large rooms, Michael Guard had an argument with the manager of the ANZ Bank. Their dispute had nothing to do with the law, or banking, but arose from their opposed views on professional golf. At a party less successful than the Roscoes', it might have caused embarrassment, yet Bud and Gwen took one man each, and smoothly guided them away before an incident was born.

Bud sought Chris out soon after. 'Michael's had a fair bit,' he said. 'Would you mind giving him a lift home when you go? I've left him in the study, second right down the main hall. He's feeling seedy. He's a bit of a goer, isn't he?' Bud went off happily to enjoy time with his other guests, and Chris had to admire the deft assurance with which he'd passed on responsibility.

Michael had switched off the light in the study, and sat by the window, which gathered some illumination from the patio. He had a cigarette, and the twisting smoke drifted like hung skeletons into the darker recesses of the room. 'I'm a bit pissed,' he said.

'We'll drop you home.'

'I think I've offended one or two local stalwarts.'

'Nothing we hate more than a successful know-all from overseas. You know that.'

'You're absolutely bloody right,' said Michael. His resonant voice had no indication at all of drunkenness. The long, greying hair, normally swept back, hung over the side of his face. He smoked with grave deliberation. A male guest came across the patio and, being out of sight of the living rooms, urinated complacently in the shrubs on the far side of the swimming pool.

'Do you think Ellen would invite me to dinner sometime soon?'

'Yes.'

'I'd like that,' said Michael.

He came a week later, bringing both flowers and wine. Towards Ellen he displayed a courtly demeanour, with just a touch of self-observed affectation. When talking to them both, he felt free to let loose his insightful and cynical ridicule. His clients, his colleagues — especially Bud Roscoe — people met socially, or strangers in brief communication, were all under-cut and dismissed. Yet Chris noted that at no time during the evening, even when their student days were subject to dissection, did he mention the depression bout Chris had suffered then.

At eleven thirty Ellen said she was off to bed, and would leave them to talk, but Michael knew his manners even if he didn't always follow them. He wouldn't stay, and left with compliments, pausing at his car to stretch his arms up in the clean night air, and sigh. 'Would you like to come round to my flat some time?' he asked Chris.

'Sure.'

'I'm surprised how lonely I am here,' said Michael. 'Lots of people want to see professionally, and I get plenty of social invitations. I still feel lonely most of the time.'

'You haven't been back long.'

'Loneliness is inside,' said Michael. 'It's got nothing to do with how many people are around you.' He smiled, to show he wasn't feeling sorry for himself, and got into his large car, wound the window down. 'You're very lucky in your marriage,' he said. 'Lucky to have someone like Ellen. Not all that many women grow more endearing on acquaintance.' He lifted his hand in farewell, and his pock-marked face became slack and neutral, as he shifted his attention to the minor task of driving in the night. As Chris went back indoors, he heard the McFees' Alsatian keeping pace with him on the other side of the hedge. It was impossible to tell if the motivation was companionship, or malice.

'So what do you make of him?' asked Chris, as he waited in bed for Ellen to join him. She was hanging her clothes in the wardrobe, and he noticed how thin her arms were.

'He's very clever, very sad, and very unscrupulous,' she said.

'I think you're absolutely right,' Chris said. Then he remembered that Michael had made no mention of his depressive episode, yet it would have been such an easy hit. He didn't want to go into all that with Ellen. 'He was a really good friend to me though,' was all he said.

'Maybe he needs someone now,' said Ellen.

Chris remembered that. He no longer found Michael easy company, but for old times sake he was reluctant to let go. Almost certainly it was a time for some support. Bud Roscoe told Chris that Michael was good at his job, but a supercilious bastard all the same, and getting offside with lots of people. The two friends met several times for lunch, and Michael did most of the talking. His conversation was self-referential, but had a savage candour that cut through banality, and left odd, provocative views and phrases Chris found it hard to forget. On one occasion he talked of the sexual lustre of young women, and his middle-aged willingness to pay for access to it. Another time he mimicked perfectly Bud Roscoe's method of disengagement from conversation — the animation and colour in the voice giving way to professional distance in the farewell. He said he was increasingly captured by dreams of dread and loathing, wherein people he despised exercised power at his expense. Enervating dreams, he said, which floated at the periphery of his waking life as phantasmagoria.

He never said much about his time in England, his failed marriage and son there, any reasons for returning to New Zealand. He drank a good deal, with an almost absent-minded eagerness. He seemed impatient of the present, but had no anticipation of better times.

He rang Chris quite late on a night when a strong southerly was blowing up. His voice was particularly mellifluous, which Chris knew was a sign he'd been drinking. 'Would you mind coming over?' he said.

'It's after eleven already.'

'I know. I know.' He waited then for a concession.

'Okay, then,' said Chris. 'say in half an hour.' He put away his agenda papers, took his jacket and went upstairs to tell Ellen.

'Don't start boozing with him though,' she said.

Despite earlier invitations, Chris hadn't been to Michael's flat before. An apartment, one of ten resulting from the inner-city development of a former office block. Chris stood, buffeted by the wind, in a shallow vestibule while he spoke into a grille and asked Michael to open the main door. The apartment was on the third floor, and had large windows that looked down to shops, traffic and the strangely plastic colours of city lights.

'I've just had a call from London to tell me I'm denied access to my son,' Michael said. He sat on the large sofa close to the windows. He wore a red jersey and no tie, and looked, for once, more like the old friend Chris remembered. Chris didn't reply, because he knew nothing about Michael's relationship with his ex-wife and son, legal or otherwise. 'I appealed against the earlier decision which prevented me seeing Anthony, and now I know that's failed.'

'How old is he?'

'He's nine. We haven't seen each other for a year.'

'It's unusual isn't it, to stop a parent completely from seeing the child?'

'I was a wife beater, but Michelle didn't press charges,' said Michael.

He didn't look at his friend as he said it; he gave it no special emphasis; he watched the lights and traffic of the city. The bad skin of his face was uneven and mottled, yet his features were distinctive, almost handsome, as ever. Chris was unsure how to respond in friendship without condoning the behaviour, and he felt it unfair of Michael to come out with such a thing when he'd kept quiet about his personal life since coming back from England.

'Jesus, Michael, why would you do that?'

'Because she was a good-looking, silly woman, and I got used to her looks, but not the silliness. There's something the matter with my temperament — almost everything pisses me off these days. I've had the anger management stuff, the marriage counselling: all I could think of during the sessions was how second-rate the people were; what crap platitudes they gave as advice. There's something the matter with me. Maybe I'm one chemical short in the brain. Isn't that the answer these days? Nothing gets put down to character any more.' Michael continued to sit easily on the sofa, to drink red wine. Only his voice was different, having lost rhetorical timbre, and become softer, lower, no longer calculated for the courtroom.

'Taking it out on your wife though, that stinks,' said Chris.

'We get sick of ourselves, let alone another person always there. I hated everything except my son, and even what I felt for Anthony wasn't entirely love,' said Michael. 'It wasn't entirely love, but it was the closest I've been able to get to it over recent years, and now I'm not allowed to see him. I'd hoped he could spend each Christmas school holidays with me, well away from his mother.'

Chris couldn't come up immediately with any comfort. It was that difficult situation in which you feel you owe a friend support, but you despise what's been done. Why was it so easy to imagine a violent Michael — a man physically intimidating, and with an over-bearing intellect and fluency as well. It leapt to mind — a view of Michael at his most contemptuous, and then a blow from that large hand. That was the sort of man who had returned from England, but not the friend who had earlier left to go there.

So the two old friends sat, isolated by more recent events, and they watched the city traffic and drank wine. Chris endeavoured to think of something positive in the situation, but there was just Michael's admitted violence towards his wife, and the justifiable consequence of being unable to see his son. Maybe Michael had felt a somewhat similar bewilderment all those years ago when Chris himself had been in the pit of depression. Things go wrong inside sometimes, and no simple error message comes up.

'I don't believe it's your real nature to beat up a woman,' he said.

'I don't remember you being like that. You're so angry now, so cut off or whatever from other people. Nothing's good enough, is it.'

'The thing is, I don't give a stuff any more, and it's brought both freedom and despair.'

'You should see a first-rate psychiatrist,' said Chris.

'Oh, fuck me.'

'I mean it. Something serious has happened and you can't throw it off by yourself.'

'I've just given up all the bullshit we use to get by, and tell the truth instead. It's amazing how much resentment the truth causes.'

'If I get hold of someone who's really good, you'll see them, won't you?' said Chris.

'What's the point? I'm pissed off and disappointed, that's all. Everyone should be angry and disillusioned in this bloody world.'

'That's all bullshit,' said Chris.

Michael complained about his ex-wife, his colleagues and almost everyone else he met day by day, and Chris wanted to say he should look at himself for faults, but he knew Michael must have been doing plenty of that. So he just let his friend talk himself out while the traffic decreased in the street below, and rain brought by the southerly swirled like a whitebait shoal against the lights of the city. And when Michael was relaxed enough to sleep, had stopped drinking, Chris went home.

The next morning he didn't go to work. He talked with his family doctor, and with a friend who was a paediatrician. He talked with Ellen because, like most women, she knew a lot about the professional abilities of the city's doctors. After assessing these recommendations, particularly that of his wife, Chris rang Brendon Poole, a psychiatrist also quite well known as a marathon runner, and they talked of Michael Guard — a shit-hot lawyer, a wife beater, and an old friend.

'I've arranged an appointment with a top psychiatrist for three o'clock this Wednesday,' Chris told Michael, after finally getting through the telephone protocols at Roscoe, Roscoe and Trumpeter.

'You probably need it,' said Michael.

'His name's Brendon Poole, and he's better thought of in his profession than you are in yours.'

'Not a sufficient recommendation,' said Michael.

'I'll pick you up at your office at two forty.'

'I'm too busy for this bullshit,' said Michael.

'Two forty.'

Chris had decided to take Michael to the appointment because that was the best way of making sure he turned up, but there was another reason. After twenty-five years Chris could still remember the abject isolation of waiting alone for his own psychiatric appointments: the mind a prison of utter threat.

Wednesday was a day of full sun, and the announcement of the All Black team to play the Aussies. Chris pulled in close behind Michael's BMW in the private park behind Roscoe, Roscoe and Trumpeter. The foyer was richly carpeted and the walls hung with English sporting prints that reminded Chris of old *Punch* magazines. The receptionist had a round, good-humoured face, and a round, good-humoured bust. 'I'm here to pick up Michael Guard,' Chris told her, and she smiled, said she'd check straight away and invited him to sit in one of the upholstered, green chairs beneath the sporting prints. Michael came out immediately. He looked tired, and the left side of his face was flamed with acne. Chris and Michael went straight down to the car, with hardly a word spoken. On the way to Brendon Poole's rooms, Michael let his head loll on the headrest, and slipped a finger under the top of his tie to set his top button free. He wore a grey suit with a bottle green silk lining: the sort of tailored suit that English barristers lived in, Chris supposed.

'Why not just keep driving out to the Harbour pub,' Michael said.

'Afterwards,' said Chris. 'Yeah, why don't we go for a drink afterwards.'

'Or maybe I will just fucking shoot myself,' said Michael.

Opulence was not a feature of Brendon Poole's rooms, or his clothes. The waiting room was cream, with chrome and vinyl chairs: the psychiatrist wore loose slacks and a loose Harris tweed sports coat. He had an air of imminent athletic activity, as if he were about to cast off his casual clothes, emerge in running gear and lope off through the kindergarten playground that adjoined his office. His hand was spare and brown as he greeted them, and the fair hair right at the crown of his head stood up in a small spray. 'I think you're lucky to have such a good friend,' he told Michael, and Michael pulled a face at Chris, which meant that the compliment was justified and he wished he'd been able to make it naturally himself. Brendon Poole ushered Michael into the office, and they both looked back in acknowledgement just before Brendon closed the door. Michael put his thumb up in an exaggerated she'll be jake way, then combed his long, heavy hair back with the same hand.

Chris sat alone in the waiting room, for although there was a small office desk and chair, no receptionist had appeared. He looked out on to the play area of the kindergarten: the elephant slide, the swings, the train and the plastic tunnel were all painted in toy-town colours of red, blue and yellow. There were lots of things he should have been seeing to, some of them he'd have to catch up on later that night, but he felt that he was in the right place and doing the right thing, whatever the outcome.

When he was young he'd thought that eventually you reached some plateau of internal comfort in your life, with apprehension and confusion quite resolved, but he'd come to understand that all was a dancing flux of delight and agony, boredom and transformation, and that you needed to hold hands with those close to you, or be quite swept away.

COCK-A-DOODLE-DOO IS DEAD

Dreams came rarely to him: perhaps, more accurately, it was that he dreamt often, but seldom recalled them on waking. The dream Felix had in the night of September the twenty-eighth was a spring dream, and that was not surprising. Yet it was a dream startling for its visual intensity — not threat, or irrationality, as is so often the way.

He and his brother were sitting on the steps of the sleep-out they had shared. Their sisters had the indoor bedrooms. Felix couldn't see himself in the dream, but he knew from his brother's appearance that they were young men together. He knew it, too, from the spirit of youth he was aware of in the dream, and which he hadn't experienced for a long time. In youth there is a unity of physical prowess and imaginative reach which is at times almost euphoria, and never recaptured by the lesser intoxications which are later pursued in its stead.

Felix realised that his brother had been handsome as a young man, with black hair, thin nose, and skin pale, healthy and tight. The only lines were those briefly at the outer corner of his eyes when he laughed, or told his preposterous stories of girls. The two of them were sitting on the second wooden step of the sleep-out, with their forearms on their knees and their hands drooping.

Their view was down the long garden to the pipe gate that opened into the yards, and they could see the corner of the tractor shed and the windbreak pines behind it. All of that and more was ordinary enough, but the special thing in Felix's spring dream was that a wind was up from the south, and it shook the blossom from their mother's fruit trees and spun it like snow in the evening sun, cast it like bridal confetti on the green spring lawn. 'Anyway,' his brother said, 'we can't all stay here working for the old man, can we.'

Felix had no recollection of just those words in just that way and just that time, but he had no doubt it had been so, for the dream carried complete emotional and visual conviction. His brother left the farm at twenty-three to go and work on outback properties in Queensland. The wooden steps of the sleep-out were grey and smooth with age, and the fruit trees kept small by their mother's yearly pruning. The blossom blew and trembled just as it had each year, his brother's face was handsome and eager.

His wife was interested in the dream, for it was rare for Felix to talk about such things. She told him some of her own, which were more heightened, bizarre. 'Talking about them fixes them in your mind,' she said. 'How long is it since you've seen David? Must be nine or ten years.'

'I've been thinking about that. He's got that big op coming up quite soon.'

'Well, you should just go. Why not? You should be able to do it now, just up and go.'

'Would you come?' asked Felix. He never saw any advantage in being parted from his wife.

'Look, I can't in the next couple of months. Not with the new clinic being opened and everything, but I think you should go. David would get a real kick out of it and so would you. Ring him soon and see what he says.' She was quickly enthusiastic: she liked a project, especially for the benefit of others. She believed in snap decisions to capture happiness.

David hadn't stuck to farming. After the Queensland outback and some years at Mount Isa contracting, he had set up a firm making and erecting pre-fabricated garages. It was a considerable success, and when his wife died shortly after their retirement, he moved to Auckland and bought a house in the Waitakeres with a west view across native bush to the estuary. For all sorts of reasons it was a long way from an Otago farm.

David met Felix at Auckland airport. Still slim, but the dark gloss quite gone from his hair, his pale skin weathered to a clay colour and folded at his neck and elbows. When they shook hands, David put his free hand on Felix's upper arm and gave a slight squeeze. 'I've been looking forward to seeing you,' he said.

'Remember that guests are like fish,' said Felix. 'They go off in a few days.'

'Really, though, we haven't had a decent yarn in years.'

Felix was surprised to find his brother hadn't brought his car: he'd come by taxi, and it was waiting to take them all the way back to the Waitakeres. 'I haven't been driving much lately,' David said. 'Not in the city anyway.'

'Hell,' said Felix, 'why didn't you just tell me to get a taxi out to your place?'

'Because I wanted to be here when you arrived.'

David's house was one of the oldest places on that part of the coast, but had been often renovated by successively more wealthy owners, and because of primogeniture it had one of the best sites. It was an all wooden house, and the gables were decorated with small, carved uprights that David said were a feature of the architectural period in which it had been built, and probably replaced several times since. The house was recently painted and white in the sun, though the sloping garden had been allowed a life of its own: branches hung unrebuked over the fences, and the lemon and hibiscus shrubs of the lawn had high collars of rough grass. In the gully beyond his brother's property, Felix could see sizable kauri, and the inlet estuary was lined with mangroves. Both topography and vegetation were strangely exotic to Felix; tropical and foreign to his personal template of the New Zealand landscape. David told him there were strict rules about the trees, and that some home owners were angry that kauri were blocking their views, but they couldn't do anything about it. 'Letting in the jungle is fashionable here now, and after Aussie I'm a bit of a tree hugger myself.'

'Live and let live,' said Felix. He was relaxed in a cane chair on David's verandah, sipping a German beer.

'Mostly it's bloody laziness to tell the truth. You chop stuff and it just grows back.'

Both brothers smiled and remembered the obstinacy with which they refused to share their mother's enthusiasm for gardening. After a day hay-making, or shearing, they had no love left for hobby plants. Yet they were content to be beneficiaries: the jugs of Peace roses in the living room, the heavy, massed blooms of rhododendron and camellia on the drive.

The brothers began to talk about their families, allowing parental affection to be more obvious than if they spoke with people of no blood relation, and then they worked back through recollection till the Otago days were reached. That's where their lives had run most closely together, almost all experiences shared, with just the subtle, piquant distinctions caused by a two-year gap in age and, more importantly, their differences of personality. David had always been the more questing, the more impatient. As they talked, the bush darkened with the coming of evening, and the water of the estuary inlet turned a pale, leaden colour. Yet the heat remained, and that was another experience Felix found strange.

A black Labrador with a grizzled muzzle came quietly up the verandah steps and rested its head on David's knee. 'It pays me visits,' he said, 'and I've no idea who it belongs to. It's an old-timer and likes a bit of attention.' He fondled its soft ears, and the dog closed its eyes at the indulgence. 'Like all Labs it's a real guts, and I give it a chop or something occasionally.'

'Dad was good with dogs,' said Felix.

'He was too. I had some decent dogs when I worked in Queensland years ago, but nothing on Dad.'

'Some of the old farm's been sold for grapes — did I tell you that? The slopes along the gully side. Who the hell would have come up with grapes on that country thirty or forty years ago.'

'If you'd held on you might have come out with a packet,' said David.

'You're right there,' said Felix.

The old Labrador wandered off into the darkness under the trees without a chop, or a sausage, because David had made a reservation at a restaurant in Titirangi. They took a taxi in, and were the only men there without family, or women friends. They were the oldest as well. They both had fish, and agreed that the heavier restaurant meats and sauces imposed a penalty in the small hours. Quite a few young people were about in the warm night, drawing attention to themselves with loud voices and slightly exaggerated actions in the way young people do. Most of them seemed good-looking, confident and lucky.

'Remember the dances we went to,' said Felix.

'Those Saturday hall dances, eh.'

'You always did all right,' said Felix, 'and I'd end up with some cock teaser, go home feeling like a stick of dynamite.'

'Because you always had to have a try at the very best looking ones, didn't you,' said David, 'instead of sussing something likely.'

'Remember Tolly Mathews and the Nicholls twins,' said Felix, and David put down his glass to join in a laugh. Others in the restaurant glanced over, saw two older guys, conservatively dressed, one even with a tie. There was nothing to suggest it was a farewell. 'Cock-a-doodle-doo,' said Felix quietly, and David stopped eating for a moment to give his brother a half smile of acknowledgement. For a while that had been David's nickname at the country dance halls, because late at night, when he'd had a few, he'd give a fierce rooster's cry in the carpark before he left.

After their meal, David suggested they walk the last bit home, and the taxi dropped them at the entrance to the dead-end lane sloping to the west. The bush was coming back vigorously and many of the houses were quite hidden from the road. The street lights were widely spaced and threw shadows behind them as they neared, then stretched them grotesquely ahead. And halfway between the lights the brothers had indistinct shadows both before them and behind, as if for just a moment past and future were in equilibrium. There was still fragrance in the air from the blooms of early summer, and a morepork called from the gully. There was the yellow gleam of windows well back from the street where each family played out its theme.

The brothers had coffee sitting together at David's kitchen table, with a linen throw to protect the polished wood. Such thoughtfulness on David's part was surely a residual habit from the sensible precautions of his dead wife. Felix had only met her twice, and so felt unqualified to mention her; to ask how David had managed to live without her. Instead he said, 'What do you do most of the time?'

'Bowling. I spend a lot of time on the greens. It seems to be the thing here, and provides company.' David seemed slightly apologetic, and as if aware of his own tone, went on with a greater outward show of enthusiasm. 'No, it's a great game, and you get fresh air and exercise as well as the company of good mates.'

'I've thought of taking it up myself,' said Felix. It was a white lie and so went unchallenged.

The night was hotter than Felix was used to, and he wished he'd brought lighter pyjamas. He threw off the duvet and lay in bed with just a sheet and one thin blanket over him. He was stirred up by talking with David again: all sorts of memories trolled through his mind as he lay in a half sleep. At least twice he heard David walking through the house, and after three in the morning he went to the lavatory himself. Going back he looked from the hall into his brother's bedroom and saw David sitting on his bed facing away to the window. A small bedside light was on, but Felix didn't recognise the back view of his brother: it was the indeterminate back view of a thin, ageing man, and David was smoking a cigarette, or perhaps one of those cigarillos. The smoke twisted and spread above his head. As far as Felix knew, his brother hadn't smoked for over thirty years, and he imagined it as something taken up again as a prop during long nights.

Both of them slept in. The bright, direct sunlight lit up the house as they made breakfast after ten o'clock. Always they had been able to work together well, and in the simple employment of preparing

breakfast, harmony was evident again. David poached four eggs and
Felix made toast; together they set the table. They had the familiar
argument as to which of them was the taller, and both admitted they
had slumped just a bit from their prime. They still had a day and a
night together, and worked out how best to spend the time. David
was keen to go north, perhaps stop at Warkworth where he owned
a small citrus orchard. He wondered if Felix would mind driving,
and said that the Commodore could do with a run.

So Felix was at the wheel and David was navigator when they set
out shortly before midday: to Helensville first of all, where they had
lunch in a beer garden, served by a springy-haired Australian
woman in her fifties who was so delighted by David's familiarity with
her country that she gave them both a Queensland beer on the
house. 'Aussies and Kiwis,' she said, 'you don't get better people I
reckon, and I've been pretty much around the world. And we're so
lucky, aren't we?' She was no great looker, probably never had been,
but her energy and goodwill were attractive. Felix and David agreed
with her judgement, thanked her for her generosity and left her five
dollars in return.

'A real Aussie battler,' said David in admiration. They could hear
her husky, smoker's laugh from another conversation as they left.

Felix was surprised by the amount of bush at Warkworth, for
he'd heard that Aucklanders were moving there in increasing
numbers. 'People are coming to see bush as an asset,' said David.
'They buy land with it on even though they know they'll probably
never be allowed to mill it.' David's own land was four hectares of
grapefruit and mandarin trees. He said he'd bought it originally
thinking he might build there, but hadn't the energy for that any
more. Most years it wasn't even worthwhile gathering the crop. By the
time he paid pickers, and for boxes and freight, the Auckland market
prices weren't enough. He and Felix walked among the small trees
and then sat by the road gate for a time. On the mild wind Felix could
smell the sea which David said was only minutes away. He hoped one
of his children might come back and live on the place one day.

Felix wondered how he and his brother would seem from a third person's point of view: two men in their late sixties with some physical similarity, though not markedly so. Two older guys taking a break at the frontage of a rather run-down citrus orchard, with patches of bush at a distance behind them and the smell of the sea on the wind. Felix looked at his brother as they rested: David's forehead had deep creases like the folded seams of a rugby ball, and there were blemishes on his face caused by years working outside. On his wrist was a superb gold watch that glowed in the sun. 'When there's a crop,' said David, 'I'll send a couple of boxes of grapefruit down to you. Some of these beggars grow big as your head.'

David fell asleep on the drive back, but Felix didn't take it as any reflection on his own lack of charisma as a companion. Instead he was pleased that his brother had the trust and ease to act so naturally. Felix drove as smoothly as he could, wanting David to sleep in the comfort and warmth of the moving car as long as possible. David slept with his mouth partly open, and a slight, whispering snore. His teeth were even and white: capped, Felix supposed, because he knew they weren't false. His hair, though almost white, still had a bristling energy and close growth.

For their second tea together they stayed home, and they did have chops. The brothers sat on the verandah of David's house with their legs in the sun and their faces in the shade. They were pleased and relieved to find, after so many years, that they were still easy together, and could share personal things. Money was a personal thing: they were by generation and background unaccustomed to talk about it, but as brothers they felt able to discuss both failed and successful investments, and their shared caution regarding future possibilities. More of the talk, however, was of things a long time ago. They had reached an age at which a scrutiny of the past was more important than contemplation of the future.

The neighbourhood Labrador came at dusk again, stepping quietly from the tree shadows, and putting its head up to each of them for greeting. It accepted two uneaten chops, and the remains of those on the plates, with equal and sober satisfaction. When Felix stroked the Lab's dark coat, he felt the whole hide slide on the dog's body, and the ears were like soft suede. 'It's got a collar, you know,' he said, 'so you could find out where it lives.'

'But I don't want to find out. I don't care where the old fellow belongs when he's not with me. We're friends in our own right.'

Felix was aware of a great deal of beauty around him. Visitors had sometimes remarked to him of the dark uniformity of the New Zealand bush, but that was one of the things he loved it for: the subtle variety of greens and browns in ancient plants superseded almost everywhere else in the world. There was birdsong still from the gully running down to the inlet estuary, and the moulded sweeps of low tide mudflats gleamed in the last of the light. There was no cloud in the sky and it had an aching, darkening depth to it. David had taken over the pleasure of stroking the dog, and his forearm lay on its shoulder, the golden watch clear against the Lab's black coat.

'Before I came up, I had this dream of us sitting outside the old sleep-out,' Felix said.

'Oh, yes.'

'Absolutely clear and detailed. And there was a wind blowing the blossom from Mum's fruit trees the way it did, remember?'

'Yes,' said David. He ran his hand from front to back along the dog's head.

'The air was filled with it, and all over the lawn too. And you said you were leaving. It must have been when you decided to try Queensland.'

'We were sitting on the steps, weren't we?' asked David.

'We were, yes. In the summer we'd often sit there and yarn.'

'We did too.'

'So when do you go in for this op then?' asked Felix.

The evening had the fresh smell of early summer, the birds calls had dwindled, the mangroves far below were indistinct. Almost it seemed the world had stopped spinning in one direction, and was about to start turning the other way. Felix thought that sometime he might dream of the two of them there on the verandah, encompassed by such calm, silence and beauty.

END OF TERM

Even before the final bell kids were drifting away from the classrooms, some with special dispensation because they had buses to catch, others just up and off from teachers whose discipline was weak. Paul Broussard could have named those teachers without bothering to check the rooms, but who wanted to make an issue of it on the last day of term. All through the school there was an unclenching, a slackening, a sense that, ah, things were near enough to over. Among the teachers only the zealots took a grim pride in grinding out a last exercise before the chairs went up. And when the bell rang the students burst from the buildings, swirled briefly at the locker rooms and bikesheds, then as a human tide ebbed away, leaving debris, and within the buildings a scent of packed, reluctant congregation.

Pressure lifted away from the whole institution in a way almost palpable even within Paul's office. Sure, there would be a final flush of administrative tasks for him as teachers completed end-of-term procedures, but he would come back to the school over several quiet days and deal with those without the constant interruptions of school time. Crisis management was his habitual occupation during term, but frequency made it no easier. The

stunted glue sniffer brought to his door for the third time in a fortnight, the fifth form Chinese boy lying behind the fives courts
with teeth knocked down his throat, the choral singer who had an
epileptic seizure, the skinheads from the street refusing to leave
the senior girls' common room, the male teacher reduced to tears
by the brutal insolence of a fourth form class, the boy who had
created a large audience by shitting on the bonnet of the counsellor's car, the shoplifting calls from the supermarket manager,
the torching of the twelve, blue outdoor cafeteria tables purchased
from school gala funds, the balaclava woman on drugs screaming
to see her daughter even though Child, Youth and Family had said
it wasn't allowed, the quiet girl found at the back of keyboard
skills cutting her legs with broken glass. Such things took prece-
dence over the routine administration of exam timetables,
maintenance returns and sports day, which then had to be done
late at night, or over his weekends.

Paul intended to go through to the staffroom for a while, have a
coffee and wish colleagues a good break. Most would be as eager as
the kids to get away, but cheerful as they tidied up final paperwork
and told each other of their plans.

It was his custom to have a last walk around the buildings and
grounds before leaving the school. Often he found something that
needed action before the weekend. He walked down the corridor
lined with photographs of laudatory achievement, and the glassed
cases of trophies. He passed the open door of Gareth's office and saw
the principal stretched back on his chair with the phone to his ear.
Gareth lifted the palm of his free hand towards Paul in acknowledgement, and rolled his eyes up to show his exasperation at a call
he wished would end. That was another reason Paul liked to take his
tour of duty — it took him beyond his office, even if the cellphone
accompanied him.

Mary-ann Beale had similar intentions perhaps, because she joined
him at the large swing doors to the main entrance. Mary-ann was senior
mistress and would have had the deputy principal's job if merit always
received its just reward, but she bore Paul no grudge for the male

prejudice the majority of the board had exercised in his favour three years before.

'Thank God for the bell,' Mary-ann said.

'Why is it that with four terms now, they still don't seem any shorter?'

'We're getting older,' she said, as they moved out into the main quad which had a showpiece rose garden at its centre. As always she carried her big-format, blue diary with her to record her tasks as they arose. She was a stickler for efficiency, and famous for it. Kids knew that whatever went into Beale's book would in due time have consequence. Her dark hair was always in a page-boy cut, and her lipstick smudged on her soft, shifting face. It was the face of a fat woman, but by discipline she had kept her body from achieving its predilection. 'I've had a cow of a day,' she said. 'One thing after another.'

Paul admired Mary-ann although he never thought to tell her so directly. She fronted up to tough decisions day after day and was slagged off a good deal because of it, but more ex-pupils came back to see her than returned for any other teacher. 'Oh, everybody's twitchy by end of term,' he told her. 'Docky came to me again this morning and said he's resigning. He does it once or twice a year.'

'Accept it, for God's sake. Wouldn't it be a mercy for the kids as well as us.'

'I did, but he never puts it in writing, and withdraws it later anyway. He just wants the satisfaction of telling Gareth and me where we can stick the job. It's a therapy for him, but it winds us up, of course.'

'Docky knows he's not up to it any more, but won't admit it,' said Mary-ann. She felt better for hearing that Paul had been put through Docky's rant. There's more humour to be had in the predicament of others than in your own. She and Paul knew that within the next year they'd have to find some way of easing Docky out.

As Paul and Mary-ann walked past the manual block he thought that she was right, that getting older was as much a reason for their disillusion as anything else. What had amused him about the kids when he was in his twenties and thirties brought only impatience now he was fifty. Year after year they came on with unbounded energy and a sense of their own novelty, constantly renewed, while his finite resources were sapped just that much more by each intake. He could still remember most of the individuals of his first classes, but of later ones just the very best and worst, the majority scarcely registering at all. And from that grey majority a pleasant adult might return and expect to be remembered. Someone for whom there had ever been only one 6B Geography, and who never considered it as one of a long series for Paul.

'I think I'll check the girls' common rooms,' said Mary-ann. 'I had some classes detailed for clean up, but who knows.'

'I'll look in on the boys' ones,' said Paul.

'If you find a mess you might be able to get some of the kids from the final detention. There's a few hard core still with an hour today, I think.' And that wouldn't be the easiest of jobs — detention supervision on the last day of term. All sorts of possibilities for things to go wrong. Paul tried to remember which staff member had drawn that short straw. And there'd be those kids who didn't show up, obeying that juvenile consciousness of time which considered two weeks an eternity between them and retribution. And when eternity ended, Mary-ann, or Paul, would be waiting.

The senior common room wasn't too bad: attempts had been made, although there were still plenty of textbooks that should have been away in lockers. A least the litter had been taken to the rubbish drums by the cafeteria, leaving just the heavy smell of socks and pastry and hooliganism. The ceiling bore a dark, hachured pattern from the impact of a thousand muddy rugby balls, and the old furniture had been gutted as if in a desperate search for treasure. Everything had been worn back to a fundamental communal minimalism.

Paul walked on through the corridors until he reached the fifth form boys' common room, but even as he went in he heard someone running behind him, and a junior girl with frizzy, pale hair and the tartan school skirt almost to her ankles skidded in the doorway. 'Mrs Beale wants you to come to the main gym, Mr Broussard.' As she

spoke she looked not at him, but at the common room, which was
foreign ground to her.

'Okay,' said Paul. He went out into the north quad and cut across
the grass, under the wet-weather walkway to the school office and
on towards D block. The frizzy girl half walked, half ran beside him.
'Thanks for telling me, ahh — . Thanks for telling me. What's your
name?'

'Nadine Troy,' she said, giving little skip at the disclosure.

'Anyway, thanks Nadine. You can get away home now.'

'Mrs Beale told me to come back.'

'Okay then.'

Maybe Mary-ann had found a stash of shoplifted stuff, or copped
some kids for vandalism. Last year there'd been the discovery of
marijuana plants in the ceiling of one of the computer labs, with
bulbs rigged up for light and all. How few people outside the system
realised the truth of schools — that they weren't cosy and manage-
able but, like society at large, were places of ambivalence, jostling
contradictions, and with a small but powerful criminal fraternity.
Many of the druggies, car thieves, intruders and vandals who
contested with the police in the weekends donned uniform themselves on Monday and went off to their classes with their intentions
quite unchanged.

'So what's Mrs Beale on about then, Nadine?'

'I dunno.' Nadine trotted up beside him, encouraged by being
spoken to. 'I was just going past the gym and she came out and told
me to get you from the common rooms.' Nadine's frizzy hair shook
like metal filings and he half expected her to jangle. He guessed she
was a fourth former, but had no recollection of ever having seen her
before, though that was common enough in a large school. He liked
her openness and willingness to help. Some kids would be already
whining that they had to go, and couldn't someone else do whatever
it was that was asked of them.

Paul and Nadine went in the main door of the gym, the shadow
there a sudden reduction of light and temperature. The gym was a
cool, clean space: the high ceiling, polished wooden floor with court

markings in white and blue. No equipment visible at all except the heavy ropes drawn from the centre and secured to the wall bars.

'Mary-ann,' called Paul.

'In here.' Her voice came from one of the storage rooms by the phys ed office. Paul went to the open door and looked in to see the shelves of balls with checker-board markings, the clumped skipping ropes, and Mary-ann kneeling on the floor beside a girl whose head rested on a grey gym mat and whose legs were dark with blood.

'Oh, Jesus,' he said.

Mary-ann looked up at him, the straight hair at the sides of her face finishing at her jaw line. 'I wanted to ring from the office here, but it's locked. Could you use your cellphone for the ambulance?' Paul turned away to dial so that he wouldn't be looking at the girl as he spoke: her heavy, pale legs with the knickers half down, her heavy, pale face with an expression both questioning and oddly resigned.

He had forgotten Nadine, but facing back into the gym he found her close beside him, and as he spoke to the emergency service he tried to position himself between her and the tableau in the equip-ment room. He held up his hand though she wasn't making any attempt to push through. He felt more immediate pity for Nadine than for the girl on the floor, an irrational feeling but powerful nevertheless. When he'd finished on the phone he moved out, ushering Nadine back a bit. 'Look, Nadine,' he said, 'Mr Quintock needs to know about this. Would you go to the office and ask him to come over, and then could you please go up to the top gate and guide the ambulance down here? Don't take any notice of the no vehicle signs — come over the lawns by the swimming pool as a short cut.' Nadine whirled about without speaking, with a final jangle of hair ran noisily through the shadowed body of the gym, was outlined for a moment in the bright rectangle of the door, then was gone.

Paul crouched beside Mary-ann, and his knee popped loudly in protest. 'Have you got a clean handkerchief?' she asked him, and when he gave her the handkerchief, compactly folded, she shook it out with a flourish almost as a conjurer might. Paul took the girl's listless hand in his and could feel the slight sweat on it. Her face was forlorn, as if floating a long way below him.

'It'll be okay,' he said. 'The ambulance will be here in a jiffy. Don't you worry. Everything's fine.'

He thought that he recognised her: not by name, but as the unexceptional sixth former who always had a small, clumsily acted part in the school plays. 'She hasn't been attacked, has she?' he asked Mary-ann, though knowing he shouldn't talk in front of the girl as if she wasn't there.

'She's been pregnant,' said Mary-ann. How well she managed a minimum of specific information.

With relief Paul heard Gareth's loud, enquiring voice in the gym, with relief he went out and motioned him towards the equipment room, where the two of them stood talking in the doorway, Gareth's voice becoming more subdued as he looked past Paul to see Mary-ann and the girl on the floor. 'Right, right,' Gareth said. 'Poor kid.' He hesitated to go closer for it seemed very much the sort of thing women coped with. 'Ambulance?' he said, taking responsibility for lesser matters.

'On its way. I must go out and help Nadine guide them in.'

'Parents?' said Gareth.

'We haven't done anything about that yet,' said Paul.

'I'll see to that now.' Gareth's upper body swayed away, but before his feet moved he remembered he didn't know the girl's name. He swayed back and stepped in to be beside Mary-ann. He leant low and put a hand on her shoulder, gently, as if she were the injured party. 'And this is?' he said softly.

'This is Susan Bates,' said Mary-ann. Susan's face still floated against the grey shadows of the thick mat. Mary-ann was stroking a cheek with the back of her forefinger.

Paul and Gareth walked quickly together across the gym and into the bright sunlight. They saw the ambulance coming across the lawn. 'Jesus, what next, eh?' said Gareth. He lifted his eyebrows very high and puffed out some air through puckered lips. 'I'd better find which hospital they'll go to,' he said. Paul watched him stride off, halt the ambulance briefly with a gesture, send a trio of gawping boys packing, then hurry on to his office.

It was bread and butter stuff for the two ambulance guys. They had Susan Bates in the back, Mary-ann Beale as well at her insistence, and were on their way in just a few minutes. Paul was left in the full, quiet sun outside the gym almost as if nothing had happened at all. But he wasn't alone. There was a seat along the outside wall of the gym, and Nadine had been sitting there since guiding the ambulance in. Her hands were spread each side of her on the warm wood of the bench. She was lifting the heels of her shoes up till her feet rested on the toes and then dropping them again. She did it quickly over and over again.

Paul sat beside her. 'Thanks for helping,' he said. Her heels went up and down, up and down. The sun was warm on their faces. 'She'll be okay now I'm sure.'

'Did she have a miscarriage? My aunt had a miscarriage, but she had children again later.'

'I don't really know,' he said.

It could have been awkward because of who they were in the school, because they didn't know each other, because of what they were talking about, but events had pushed them past all that. 'Look, I'll run you home,' he said. 'I have to go up to the hospital to get Mrs Beale anyway. All this has made you late, hasn't it.'

'I don't live far,' she said. 'Maxwell Street by the park.'

'Mrs Norman lives somewhere there, doesn't she?'

'Sometimes I babysit for her.'

'Good on you anyway,' he said. 'I'm going to have a word to your form teacher.'

'I didn't do much. I'd better go now.' She stood up and he noticed how small her hands were, and that the cuffs of her jersey had been folded back twice because it had been bought for her to grow into. 'What was that girl's name, Mr Broussard?'

'Her name's Susan Bates.' He knew he shouldn't be telling her, but she deserved such a confidence. 'Remember she had a part in the last play. She was the fat witch, but it wasn't a big role.' Nadine nodded and went off down the path with her noisy shoes, and her fair, metallic hair frizzed in the sun. Paul sat and watched until she turned the corner of the science block. He lifted his heels and let them drop again, over and over. He found it oddly relaxing.

HOW IT GOES

Picture this if you will — a silky, summer's night and the grass grub moths in pale, whiskery candlewick are a clumsy mass intoxication in the warm air. There's the fragrance of the trees gathered in the still night: macrocarpa, pinus radiata and walnut around the yards, more subtle essences from the last of the native bush in the gullies higher up. The boy stands very still, the better to look and listen. He holds the .22 loosely in his right hand, and the long metal torch and a school backpack in his left. The backpack hangs with the weight of three dead possums. Far down the valley lights are winking, glowing and then cutting out, glowing again, as the car, or truck, goes from bend to bend.

The boy stands and listens, watches: at ease in the night. His face is round and smooth, his hair thick and fair and soft, but his body has begun a growth spurt for adolescence so that his arms and legs have a slight clumsiness, although outdoor athleticism is always on the point of catching up.

The lights come closer, pass the turn-off to Heyworths' and Annans'. For the first time he can hear the engine; the sound doesn't carry as well as in the frosty air of winter. He recognises the sound of the ute: his father must be coming home.

The boy begins walking back through the trees and across the yard before the farmhouse. He goes from the shadows through soft moonlight and into pine shadows again. One of the dogs slinks out of its kennel, the chain clinking like coins, but it doesn't bark, perhaps because he has the rifle in his hand. The yard is almost bare of grass, just stones and earth because of the mobs of sheep that have passed, and the movement of machinery, and the scratching of the chooks that now roost hidden in the implement shed, or the lower branches of the pines, maybe even on the perches built for them in their own house.

He throws the possums onto the jutting timber of the tank stand to be skinned tomorrow. He washes blood from his hands in the laundry and goes inside. He puts a small handful of ammunition into the box in the kitchen drawer, and after checking the chamber of the .22 he leans it at the back of the hot water cupboard. He stands in the open back door for a time looking down towards the garage, but the summer night is thick with the flight of moths and the light attracts them so that they come tumbling towards the doorway, like lobbed paper pellets. So he closes the door and stays outside with all around him in the shadows of the night, or the soft, indistinct light of the moon. Picture it. And so he waits for his father with the confidence of one who has rarely been disappointed in affection.

The ute comes up the steep, uneven drive, and its lights flare and glance on the dark mass of the macrocarpas, then break out across the open space of the yards. The ute noses into the open sheds next to the tractor, and when the boy's father turns the engine off, the noise takes time to dissipate, and the small natural sounds take time to resume: the fluffle of a chook in the lower branches, the distant dry cough of a sheep, morepork echo from the far bush. Listen and you will know them.

The father comes carrying supermarket bags, and the boy opens the door for him and follows him inside. 'You okay then?' the father asks, and the son nods. The man puts the bags on the bench without interest in them, and goes through to the lounge with its worn vinyl suite and large television. He sits well down in a chair so that his knees are almost level with his head. He is a tallish man, but most of his height is in his legs, and his bare forearms are burnt to the colour of copper. 'We'll have something to eat soon, eh,' he says.

'Okay.'

'We'll rustle up something from the can tonight.'

'I don't mind,' says the boy. The father has a habit of rubbing his hands on the tops of his thighs, and the sound on the twill fabric is like soft rain on the roof.

'Your mum sends her love.'

'When can she come back?'

'Not for a while yet, I'm afraid,' says the man. He lets his head rest back on the chair, gives a small yawn of discomfort, then sits up ready to say more. The boy is leaning on the back of the sofa, and his father flaps a hand to get him to sit down.

'She's okay, though?' The boy sits and smooths his hair down at the same time. He feels no great apprehension, as his mother talked it all through with him before she went: about the lumps in her breast and the need to get rid of them in case they became a nuisance.

'Look,' says his father, 'it's a matter of things being more serious than the doc first thought, that's all.' He doesn't hesitate much; he's obviously spent some time while driving home getting sorted what he wants to say. 'There's some more tests to be done and that, but he reckons there's no sign of anything really bad. You know that sometimes women get cancer there?' The boy shook his head. 'Well, they do, and that's the worst thing they could find, and it's not that thank God, but the doc still wants some tests to find out why your mum's tired all the time. A night or two at most. It's not worth her coming all the way home and then back again for tests.'

The father waits then, looking at his son, giving time for the boy to ask any thing else, but there are no questions. The father gets up purposefully from the chair; he claps his hands together. 'Right,' he says. 'Time for something to eat, or we'll be here all night.'

It is as they leave the room that the man turns the television on. Neither considers it unusual that they should half watch it through the open kitchen door as they make a meal. Neither of them is accustomed to continual conversation, and the lack isn't a source of awkwardness. They have Watties baked beans on toast with two poached eggs each as well. The boy has a Coke, which is something of a treat, and his father a beer, which is routine. They take their meal back to the lounge to eat, and watch a movie about gangsters which is set in a country on the other side of the world. They don't bother to draw the curtains: they live three miles from their neighbours, on a country road that is little used. Picture the simple weatherboard house with a red, tin roof set on the river terrace close to the sheds and yards. In the moonlight, of course, the red roof is another colour altogether, and the yellow spill from the lounge window shows the rough lawn, the struggling azaleas and the netting fence that keeps the stock from the garden. And yes, it's a grass grub night and the heavy moths labour through the warm air, attracted to the light. A summer blizzard of insects whirls there in the waning window light, but to the father and his son it's just life, and the soft pattering on the glass is unremarked.

When the gangster movie is over, the man tells the boy that he'd better shoot away to bed. 'Maybe tomorrow you can come in with me to see your mum,' he says. 'If I can get a good run at things tomorrow morning, we'll go in after lunch. I'd like you to help me in the yards.'

'I'll get up when you do,' the boy says. He knows his father will be outside by seven.

'No, that's okay. Just come on over when you're ready. I've got crutching to do.'

The boy is in his room when his father talks to him from the lounge; it's not far away, and with the television off there's no need for the man even to raise his voice. 'I haven't forgotten about us going pig hunting,' he says. 'It's just this thing with your mum is what's important right now.'

'That's okay.'

'We'll go soon and knock a few over. We'll get Geordie and his dogs.'

'I got three possums tonight,' says the boy.

'Good riddance to the buggers,' says his father. 'Goodnight.'

'Night, Dad.'

The boy lies in his bed with a strip of moonlight across his legs and angling across the room. It's so quiet he can hear his father in the lounge rubbing his hands on his knees, and he knows he'll be sitting well down in the soft chair, with his long legs like trestles before him. The boy thinks he'll get up really early in the morning, and be there to help when his father goes outside. He's made such resolutions before and not managed them, but he tells himself this time will be different.

Even with his father so close, there's a sense of absence in the house. The boy is old enough to realise that there are reasons his father might not be telling him all the truth about his mother, and he hopes that's not so. He's briefly shaken by an aching desolation quite new to him, and then feels better again. His father is only a wall away: tomorrow he'll see his mother and she'll maybe come home with them. Things will be okay. He has experienced nothing so awful in his life that he would think otherwise.

Picture him asleep in the small, plain bedroom of the farmhouse, with the moonlight through the window forming a pale, blank screen on the wall, as if some film is about to start and tell us more about his life.

AT BOXIT

Penners was a small, despicable man with semi-transparent ears and a hunger to witness the misfortunes of others. He was a perver as well. He would stand behind me when I worked on the wax line, and try to look down my smock. It wasn't even a personally focused reaction: he did it with all of us. If we'd dressed a female dummy and seated it there, his interest would have been equally intense. Mind you, all the guys at Boxit Ltd were unlimited in their hope of sexual possibility, and that didn't stop some from being likeable. Sexual harassment wasn't really the issue between us women and Penners. What it came down to was him being petty and vindictive, and being able to get away with it because he was the supervisor.

On an average Boxit shift there'd be about twenty women and half a dozen men, but apart from Penners the men weren't seen much. They were mainly in handling, delivery and machine maintenance, while we staffed the lines. Waxed box flats for food products was the big thing, though we also did pottles and stuff: any waxed cardboard container that took your fancy in fact. Almost every time I went to a Hoyts complex, or a fast food outlet, I recognised something from my work.

The Boxit factory was quite new, with metal girders high into the ceiling and large windows which at times allowed in more sun than was comfortable. And as factory jobs go it was clean enough: waxed products are easy on the hands and have only a faint, almost lanolin smell. I had a job in a fisheries plant once that paid great money, but no matter how much I washed, I still stank like a giant orange roughy in the bed at night. Rob reckoned the Boxit job knocked spots off the seafood one. At Boxit they provided company smocks with Velcro fasteners, but they hardly became dirty at all. About the only thing that got on our nerves, apart from Penners, was the din. It was an open-plan factory and although the noise level wasn't all that high, the template stampers were at a wearying pitch hour after hour. You could have ear muffs, but younger women found they messed up their hair, and anyway all of us wanted to talk and so make the time go. Because we had to speak loudly in the factory it became a habit, and I found myself outside work booming at people, and then feeling embarrassed.

Our topics at work weren't just about Boxit, kids, partners and visits to the doctor. You're not stupid just because you work with your hands. Some of those women had experience you wouldn't have guessed at: Nerli had been a physio in Singapore, or Hong Kong, but her qualifications weren't recognised here, Essie had an honour from the Queen for years of work with the Alzheimers Society and reading recovery, Mary Sumpter belonged to a poetry reading group and did extra-mural classes from Massey. She had a computer and knew all about the Internet. I've done polytech courses myself to keep my brain active, and I worked in the council offices before the kids came along.

I read an article about poor whites in the southern United States being savagely opposed to Black equality because they knew when that happened they'd no longer have anyone they could look down on. In a way I saw a parallel with Bernard Penners. He tried to reassure himself about his place at the bottom of administrative staff, by chivvying the workers. He was pale and ageing, with a slick of hair across his bald patch like willow roots. Rob reckoned he was a runt. When he stood at the large windows the sun behind him lit up the thin membrane of his ears so that they had a reddish glow like indicators. 'The edge trim hasn't taken, has it, Arlene,' he might tell me. 'If you'd concentrate more, maybe you'd notice these defects and save me some time.'

He always wore a white shirt and tie. The shirts were short-sleeved and polyester; the ties were old fashioned, one-colour jobs — lime green, orange, blue. On cold days he kept his double-breasted suit coat on. 'How many times,' he might say to a new girl, 'do I have to remind you to fasten the bundles buckle up, so as not to blemish the surface.' His nose took up most of the space on his narrow face, and on each side a deep crease ran down to his mouth like those on a ventriloquist's dummy. 'Toilet yet again, Susan,' he might say. 'I swear you women were at the end of the queue when the bladders were handed out.'

He was fifty-seven years old, had been in the cardboard and laminate business most of his working life and was floor supervisor at Boxit. What he enjoyed above all else were the so-called management meetings every second Thursday at eleven. Management was a sacred word for him. I've watched him going into the office for the meeting, the oldest there, deferring to the others in order of entry, yet at the same time absurdly proud to be given, and to give, that proof of executive status. Like his suit, the meetings were evidence of a position essential to his self-respect. 'When you've had my experience, Donna,' he might say, 'you'd have some basis to make judgements like that, but you haven't and you've a long way to go.'

I said the Boxit factory was quite new and clean, not bad working conditions, but the view from those large windows wasn't inspiring. Just the loading bay, the dirt and shingle yard with twitch and docks in the parts the trucks didn't use, and the high tin fence that separated Boxit Ltd from Classic Septic Tanks. Donna and one or two of the others would take their break there on some hot days rather than go to the small tearoom. They'd sit with their backs to the factory wall, their heads visible at the windows and their legs stretched into the yard. One of the younger drivers might make a swerve at them as he brought a truck in, and then stroll over and ask them to show what they've got. 'You first,' Donna would say, leaving her smock high on her legs to catch the sun. All of them would laugh, feel better about passing the time that way, and the driver would reluctantly go — looking back, smiling — to help with loading.

Penners didn't like it, of course. Work was work and he didn't like to hear laughter. And if there were sexual references made to the women then he should be making them, not the drivers who weren't managerial. He told Donna and the others that their yakking was distracting the drivers and could affect safety, and that the union had made a great fuss about tearooms for members during their breaks and here they were not even using the damn place.

There are lots of unpopular bosses in the world: it's a majority decision probably. You go into staffrooms and canteens all over and you find people grizzling. It's like politics in a way: when your life's not great, it must be the fault of people further up the ladder. Someone had to do Penners' job otherwise things would get pretty slack. If he'd just had a sense of humour, or greater toleration; if he'd been younger and better-looking even, he might have got away with it. But he and Donna took a set against each other, and that was enough.

Donna was twenty-four, nearly beautiful and engaged to a surgical registrar at the hospital. She was intelligent, lazy and only at Boxit to get some extra money together before her marriage. She and her partner even then knew people, and went to places, quite beyond Penners' reach. She called him Mr Pennies, sometimes Mr Penis, to his face, without being quite distinct enough for him to take issue. She called him The Creep behind his back. She enjoyed pronouncing the company name in his hearing as 'Boxshit', with the most innocent of expressions. She knew that life was set to carry her far above her existing circumstances, and that nothing Penners could do was a threat to her. She despised his great nose and transparent ears; she despised his desperate hold on a position of petty manage- ment; most of all she despised his lack of sympathy and goodwill. Perhaps it never occurred to her that the first characteristics explained the last.

Penners was a believer in what he called a Tight Ship, and that was something else Donna mispronounced for effect. He timed the breaks, he insisted on a doctor's chit if you were away for more than two days on the trot, he picked on the young women, he kept a log of rebukes he'd given to us in case he had to take further action, he loved pointing out your mistakes in front of everybody. He cleaned his ears with a matchstick while standing with a faraway look in his eyes, and folded his handkerchief again after each use. He had Rachel Mulveney fired for stealing tea-bags. Rachel was a solo mum with a split upper palate, but Penners set a trap three days running and stopped her at the main door on the third day. She had seven Tiger Tea bags in her coat pocket, and all of them had a biro dot in the corner put there by Penners.

At the end of the shift Penners would do a tour of the machines before leaving. If it was cold he'd put on his gabardine coat and a Norman Wisdom cloth cap under which his nose stuck out like a muzzle. He had a red and white step-through scooter which took a lot of kicking to start. Inside the factory he was always staring, but if you met him on the street he avoided your eye. They said he had a chronically ill wife and two sons who had become far more successful than him. Mary Sumpter, who'd worked at Boxit for ages, even in the old plant, said he'd been with the firm for yonks. He'd left briefly to set up a courier business that failed, and had to come cloth cap in hand to ask Boxit for a job again.

Mary was the queen of common sense among us. She was one of the quieter ones, but when she voiced an opinion it usually hit the mark. Someone told me one of her sons had been killed in an avalanche overseas. I do know she was finding all the standing in the factory more and more tiring. We wouldn't have minded if she'd spent most her time on the stools, but she was determined to do what everyone else did. She wore flesh-coloured support stockings, and had an extra holiday week because she'd been so long with the firm.

Donna wanted to have a shout for us before she left to get married. She didn't bother to say anything to Penners about it, but he got to hear. He said she needed permission to have alcohol on the premises, and if that was given it would be with the proviso that there was no drinking in work time, or on the factory floor. 'I'm prepared to consider use of the tearoom after the shift finishes,' he said. Donna gave a curtsy, pulling the two sides of her smock out with thumbs and forefingers, and that was all the application she made. What did she care for Penners and his Boxit regulations, when she was about to get married to a doctor, honeymoon in Bali, and return to a new home with a view.

Donna could have got through the last day without a blow-up if she'd wanted, and so could Penners. Good looks and popularity made Donna used to getting her own way, and Penners was equally stubborn because his authority was his only form of self-respect. Donna brought eight bottles of bubbly to work and glasses as well. She opened three at afternoon break, firing the corks through the open door of the tearoom into the factory, and laughing as the bubbles ran over her fingers. Penners wasn't about then, but it was almost as if Donna wanted to have a go at him on her last day, and she brought the bottles and glasses on to one of the packing benches late in the afternoon, saying that not all her friends could stay after work to farewell her, and she wanted to toast them all. Penners noticed that all right.

Why didn't he just stay out of sight for the last hour or so of Donna's employment? It's what most supervisors would have done. The cleverest of them might well have joined in, gaining popularity by ignoring the rules for such a special occasion, yet still keeping an eye on what went on. Penners was too insecure to do either. Rules and demarcations outside himself were all he had to rely on.

He came down the long factory, brisk and brittle with decisiveness. His long nose quivered and there was a sheen of anxious sweat at his receding hairline. Donna was relaxed on one of the high swivel stools, and she didn't get up. She filled a glass and held it up to him. 'Have a farewell drink, Mr Penis,' she said, and caught the smiles of other women with a quick glance.

'I told you, absolutely no alcohol on the factory floor,' he said.

'But it's not on the floor.'

'You know exactly what I mean.'

'Will you fire me if I don't stop, Mr Penis?' said Donna, and she whirled on the stool with her feet out, the way kids do on the fairground octopus before the rides begin.

Even Penners could realise he was on a hiding to nothing. What retribution could he use as a threat when it was Donna's last day? He was likely to get a bottle of bubbly poured over his almost bald head, if not greater humiliation, and most of the women looked forward to the drama. He couldn't think of a profitable next move, yet neither could he back down: he stood with a sort of twitching smile on his face and nothing came to him. His authority was so clearly just a husk, and his indecision such an agony, that it was oddly painful to look at him.

Mary Sumpter was the one of us with presence of mind to defuse the situation. She came over from the logo machine, and her voice was relaxed, matter-of-fact. 'You can understand that we're all a bit emotional because it's Donna's last day,' she said to Penners, 'but you're quite right: drinking when the machines are going isn't on at all. If you could give us just five minutes I'm sure we could get things tidied up, Mr Penners.'

It allowed Penners just that semblance of making the decision, just enough to save face. 'Five minutes then, ladies. I'll be back in five minutes to see how things are. It's a wrench to lose a workmate, I can see that, but regulations are there to safeguard us all.' He ran his plain green tie between thumb and forefinger, gave a grimace that he imagined showed forbearance. He was very erect as he walked away towards the stampers, and the uprightness merely emphasised how scrawny he was.

'We'll still be here when he comes back,' said Donna. I think she wanted something settled between them; an incident that we'd have to remember her by. Remember that Donna Moss, we'd say, who put Penners in his place on her last day when she was going off to marry a doctor.

'I think we should just take the bottles and glasses back into the tearoom,' said Mary. 'I don't see why we can't have drinks there after knock-off time.'

'I'm sick of that little prick's officiousness,' Donna said. 'I'm not scared of him, and anyway I'm leaving.'

'But not all of us are leaving, are we,' said Mary calmly. 'The rest of us are back here Monday.'

Donna could see the truth in that. The consequences of anything between Penners and her were likely to affect us when she was gone. 'Yes, well you do all have to come back, I suppose,' she said.

'And so does he,' said Mary. 'Leave him alone. It's too easy.' That's what impressed me, Mary being the only one to consider someone involved beyond ourselves, and someone we didn't like.

So we did take the stuff back into the tearoom, and Penners returned and walked the factory floor. He kept his distance, but nodded a good deal as if to say yes, things are okay now you've decided to do what I want. When time was up we all flocked into the tearoom to have Donna's drinks. All except Susan, whose daughter was having braces put on her teeth. It was something of an anti-climax perhaps, with no *High Noon* showdown between Donna and Penners after all, but we had a good send-off even so. Most of us knew we'd never socialise on equal terms with Donna again: her smock-wearing days were over.

It was Mary, of course, we'd asked to say a few words, and give Donna the lace-top nightie. In the pause before Donna's reply I could hear Penners outside kick, kick, kicking his step-through, as he finished another day.

HAUTE PLAZA NEW YEAR

BRUSCHETTA WITH PRAWN AND AVOCADO TOPPING
WITLOOF WITH SMOKED SALMON AND PEARS
PROSCIUTTO AND CHERRY BITES
FRIED SZECHWAN WONTONS
HORS D'OEUVRE SUSHI WITH WASABI DIP
BABY CITRUS TARTLETS

Such were the perambulatory starters for the New Millennium Banquet at the Haute Plaza, and Simon watched the staff circulating with trays as the guests built up. Some diners found their tables immediately, others stood in groups at the large windows to look down on the Avon, or gathered to talk on the polished dancing floor and the space by the swing doors to the kitchen.

A citrus tartlet suited Simon's mood. Just a few days before he'd had a dream in which he was old, and woke to find that it was true. He would be sixty at the end of the century. There was no revelation in that: the calculation had been plain for a long time. The downer was that he had never before dreamt of being old, and he feared the breakthrough into the perpetual prime of his dreams marked some jolt of emotional significance, an unconscious and final submission.

He had been young and then middle-aged in the twentieth century; he would never be anything else but old in the new one, and have even less of a toehold on the millennium: there on sufferance and looking over his shoulder while younger people had expectations.

He disliked the new millennium even before he had any experience of it. He disliked it in the same way you feel antipathy for a person who hasn't yet arrived at the party, but whose name seems on everybody's lips. He viewed the millennium as the latest idle entertainment for those who had no purposeful engagement with the present, the inexact creation of commercial interests who would blatantly admit error in a year's time and try to sell it all over again. He was weary of the fever of inaugural expectation — the first sunrise, the first song, or prayer, the first birth, the first sparrow fart, vindictiveness and hangover of the new millennium: maybe the first murder, the first cruelty towards a child, the first injustice, betrayal and heartbreak. All of life was to be freshly newsworthy for an opportunist media.

Early in 1999 people he knew had begun to feel quivers — part anxiety, and part excitement. Where should they *be* on this New Year's Eve, a thousand times more significant than any other they had experienced? Whom would it be most advantageous to have as company? What unique novelties were promised that might lift one event clearly above others?

Simon's wife had told him that a cruise ship was to put out from Lyttelton, and meet the dawn of the new millennium on the high seas. Some television celebrities were mentioned, and a diva who might stand majestically at the prow and sing in Italian, or German. Bubbly was to be free all night, and Vivien craftily remarked that there wouldn't be a problem with cars, for presumably the captain would be the designated driver and bring them back safely to port. The Sterlings were almost certainly going, and had said that the ship was in danger of being booked solid. Simon imagined the give-away crêpe hats and streamers, the arrival of Neptune, the balloons and the diva's voice being plucked away by the biting dawn wind, the orchestrated rejoicing as the new millennium came in. Aren't all those occasions when we attempt to celebrate the passage of time essentially sad anyway, sufficing only to accentuate the gallop of our lives towards their end?

People who had barely heard of the Chathams became caught up in a determination to spend a great deal of money to stand on a hill there and see the sun some minutes before other people who stood on hills on the east coast of the North Island. 'But the television will be there, Mr Naughton,' Simon's office junior had said, 'and you might be seen right around the world, eh.' Trudy had streaks of green and purple in her tufted hair, and a darting, avian face. Surely with such thin, hollow bones she could fly to the Chathams, and swoop before the cameras to ensure she was seen right around the world.

Simon caught up with a plate of Szechwan wontons and browsed on them before falling off the pace and looking about for a refill of bubbly. People around him seemed all gross physicality and fatuous euphoria.

RED PEPPER AND CSABAI SOUP

MARSEILLES SEA-BOTTOM CHOWDER

SQUAB AND BROCCOLI CONSOMMÉ

MINTED CARROT AND GOLDEN OAT TROUT SOUP

Simon chose the chowder. He liked to eat substantially at the front end of a menu, but rarely had dessert. And he was heartened despite himself that at least one good riesling was available against the present snobbery in favour of chardonnay and sav blanc. People had taken their seats for the soup, after the maître d' had rung a brass, pagoda-shaped gong to cut through the swell of conversation. The Haute Plaza's main dining room could hold over two hundred in evening configuration. It had many mirrors with deep, bevelled edges. The pillars and walls were of dark marble; ornate plaster wreathes in lolly colours adorned the ceiling; the washer lights alternated with heavy arrangements of white flowers. Simon thought the place resembled the interior of Cleopatra's palace in a B-grade movie.

At the end opposite the kitchen, beyond the small dance floor, was a modest dais for the six-piece band, though rather than band it seemed to Simon more a miniature orchestra: piano, violin, cello, sax, clarinet, trombone. No drums and no guitars. And the musicians were mild, middle-aged, the men with receding hair, and a woman cellist with a hand of impressive rings. From long experience they had become accustomed to being an accompaniment to events rather than a focus. Music was not their main source of income, and artistic hunger seemed a thing of the past also. Sensible career choices had been made. Simon knew the piano player; Selwyn Toomey, who was the court registrar and his occasional golf partner. There were worse ways surely to spend a New Year's Eve than playing piano, especially when the room's attention was elsewhere.

Fourteen was the sum of Simon's party. A number too large for any one person to monopolise the conversation, but not so great that a sense of social unity was lost, or that he couldn't talk with everyone in the course of the night. Their table was away from the traffic route to the kitchens, and close to one of the large, bay windows that gave a city view from the third floor. Simon looked around his acquaintances, and although all were amiable, they seemed to him utterly complacent and conventional. The more dispiriting conclusion was that he must be very much one of them.

Peter Brownlow said it was rumoured that Ansett, or Air New Zealand, had planned a flight to find the new millennium sun — all corporate people by invitation, who would be tall poppies indeed, mile high in fact, as the next thousand years began. Such exclusive vanity was bound to appeal.

Simon had read somewhere that even Christ's birth date was inaccurate, so that there was no cause for celebration on that account, but he was unsure of the source, or details, and wary of his wife's recall in such matters. He decided not to advance it as a debating point until he'd checked it out. He'd been bested on such things before, because he hadn't done his research. Even untested, however, the assumption gave him one more source of grievance. In his work as an insurance broker it was important that all his tables worked out, and any she'll be right arithmetic niggled away at him.

Simon's children, Anna and Paul, both married and both living in Auckland, had plans to attend the gargantuan events that their city thought appropriate to its importance, full of brash vigour and strident confidence: pyrotechnics across the harbour and self-congratulation in a new coliseum. Megastars of the international entertainment industry would be the pied pipers to lead New Zealanders into the third millennium. Simon had rather hoped that if he must celebrate then he could do so with his family. His children showed no such inclination. Keeping in touch wasn't a strong point. 'Oh, don't be such a boring old fart,' Vivien had told him.

The whole business was just a diversion, wasn't it. Something to distract people from the plainness of their everyday years. Something completely fortuitous and unmerited, yet which would provide them with specious claim to fame — having been at the start of the new millennium, celebrated the full turn of some great clock wheel. Maybe it would become more important in time than having seen Halley's comet, or having been present on the field of Waterloo.

Simon had gone along with it all, though, and with a semblance of good humour. He had magnanimously let Vivien choose the form of their entertainment, and resolved that her pleasure, and that of his friends, would be recompense enough for whatever ambivalence he suppressed. 'The Haute Plaza then,' Viv had said. 'The Haute Plaza always has a touch of style, doesn't it? I can't see there being a better place to be in Christchurch on the night. I think we could get a good group up for New Year's Eve there.' Viv knew what Simon would baulk at, and what he could be brought round to. 'What about this then?' she asked, as she refilled his glass with riesling, and Simon's ex-business partner, who had come as a surprise guest, told a story of insurance skulduggery Simon had heard before. Viv rested her hand on Simon's shoulder with casual familiarity. It was a riesling of fruit and balance, and the chowder was thick with scallops and squid.

'They're capable of a good do at the Haute Plaza. I must say that,' said Simon.

'And if we want to, we're close enough to walk to the concert in Hagley Park afterwards: listen to the golden oldies.'

'Sure,' he said, but he thought somewhat wistfully of a New Year's Eve twenty-seven years ago, which he'd spent with climbing friends in a hut beyond Erewhon at the head of the Rangitata. At midnight the moon stared past the scree slopes and onto the greywacke shingle braided with steely streams. They drank brandy from a hip flask and kept their voices low as the new year made no change in the beauty of the old.

The last day of 1999 had held no special augury for Simon. In the morning he washed the maroon Audi and tidied beneath the rhododendrons and azaleas of the drive: in the afternoon he went to the Businessmen's Club where he shared whisky and the complacent apprehension of his peers concerning the economic outlook. He took particular care to keep away from television screens all day, because he wanted no part of the canned millennium celebration that had been prepared for those unable to create an evening for themselves.

CRUMBED NOISETTES OF LAMB WITH BAKED ZUCCHINI, SAUTÉED MUSHROOMS, MINT JELLY AND MIMOSA SALAD

TRADITIONAL STEAK DIANE WITH SCALLOPS EN BROCHETTE, COUSCOUS TABBOULEH, ORANGE GLAZED KUMARA AND RED BEAN DRESSING

PROVENÇAL BRAISED PORK WITH SAFFRON AND TRUFFLE STUFFING, HERBED POLENTA SLICE, BURGHUL SALAD WITH CLEMENTINES

PINE NUT AND CAMEMBERT ROAST TURKEY WITH PHYLLO ASPARAGUS, ARTICHOKE AND FRENCH MUSTARD POTATO SALAD

JACOBIN MONKFISH AND COCONUT SEAFOOD CURRY, WITH BAKED PUMPKIN GNOCCHI, RED ONION RELISH, PARSNIP AND CORIANDER CRÊPE

Simon admitted to the table at large that it was a good choice of mains. You had to hand it to the Haute Plaza — if you were going to give way to the millennium occasion then such a night was painless enough.

Philip Taeb, three to the right of Simon, was a polytechnic hospitality tutor, and lectured the table on the methods hotels used to estimate the mains preferences of a set number of guests. Poultry, he said, was always the most popular and at an all-women function it would run at three to one against anything else.

With trivial and typical perversity most of the other thirteen, without comment, proved Philip wrong by avoiding the turkey. Simon chose the pork, though he grumbled a little at the unknown burghul salad. He drank with it a premium South Australian shiraz. Never confuse patriotism with quality, he told Mary Pratt. Mary was a land agent who specialised in commercial property and made more money than her husband, who was doing research on freshwater crayfish at Lincoln. Simon thought rather less of Peter Pratt because of it — the money thing — without quite knowing why.

Well-cooked pork is a dish that breeds forbearance, and the dark spiciness of shiraz ushers in toleration. If he did need to join in the celebration of this millennium then there were many places and circumstances less pleasant than the Haute Plaza. The décor perhaps was an indulgent and humorous parody, rather than the outright affectation he had considered it earlier, and the irritating chatter from other tables seemed to fade as he became more talkative himself. He gave Noel Eccles a quick run-down on the main consequences for small businesses of the 1998 Accident Insurance Act to such effect that Noel said that he'd like to hear more, at another time. To Mary, Simon confided that he'd been considering leasing new office space, and that if she had a listing of any modern suite with parking he'd have a look.

Simon and Viv had a dance between the main and dessert. The small floor was crowded, so that neither her skill, nor his lack of it, was evident. He disliked the constriction, but was cheered to notice how fat Bernie Sounness had become, and how very bald was Peter Brownlow. An appalling, thin woman in green was dancing double tempo and flicking up her dress around her knitting needle legs. Any abandonment is appealing in a good-looking woman, but plainness and excess don't go well together.

A little after eleven, Viv took the cellphone from her bag, and then came the call she must have been expecting from Anna and Paul. They and their partners were at the Auckland extravaganza, but wanted to tell Simon and Viv that they loved them, and were ringing before midnight so that they weren't thwarted by any telephone overload on the hour of New Year. Simon told his wife that he never doubted they'd be in touch, that they were great kids, always had been, very family minded. He was almost overcome with emotion to hear their voices — voices with an overlay of maturity, but still containing all those echoes and associations of family which rose up within him so strongly that he had to laugh loudly at nothing in particular as a form of release. He was always helpless before the power of such love. Viv patted his shoulder.

'Isn't that thoughtful,' she said.

'It would be Anna's idea.' He didn't want her to think that he'd lost any shrewdness, that he was soft.

'They both took the trouble. That was nice,' she said.

Simon felt increased goodwill towards his New Year companions; towards the Haute Plaza; even towards the concept of a millennium celebration. The waiter correctly interpreted Simon's glance and brought another two bottles of shiraz to the table. 'Good service. Good service at the old Haute Plaza,' said Simon, but the words were lost amid the rising hubbub.

> COINTREAU ICE CREAM WITH CHOCOLATE ORANGES
>
> PROFITEROLES WITH MADEIRA BUFF SAUCE AND CHERRIES
>
> STRAWBERRY MARYLAND TORTE WITH GLACÉ PINEAPPLE
> AND MARZIPAN KIWI ICONS
>
> TANGY LIME AND ALMOND MOUSSE WITH WALNUT TUILLES
> AND CANDIED LIQUEUR TRUFFLES
>
> PASSIONFRUIT AND GINGER ROULADE SWATHED IN LEMON MERINGUE

Perhaps he should make an exception to his custom of not having a dessert: after all it was a special night, a one in three hundred and sixty-five thousand, approximately, and he hadn't blown up over recent years like Bernie Sounness. He could still see his shoes, at least when stepping forward. The strawberry torte reminded him of childhood, and even the rugby and yachting icons seemed inoffensive. He'd always affirmed that the Haute Plaza did everything well. He thought also of the restaurant dinner over thirty-three years before, at which he'd proposed to Viv. He'd borrowed cash from his father to make sure that he'd have enough for the night. And now he was still with her and glad of it, had a business of his own that needed larger premises, two grown children who had rung to wish them well, and was entering the new millennium still with most of his own teeth and hair. So what if he needed glasses, that he had a moderate regime of medication for blood pressure, and a dicky knee.

Simon offered to buy cigars for his wife and twelve close friends. Viv complimented him on his non-sexist generosity and two of the women and four of the men accepted. 'You're enjoying it now, aren't you,' Vivien said.

'Of course.'

'I knew you would.'

Had it ever been his intention to do otherwise? He got up from the table with deliberate mystery and went over to the band, who were between numbers. He shook hands with Selwyn Toomey, was introduced to the jewelled cellist and asked Selwyn if they'd play 'Red Sails in the Sunset' as a favour. What are golfing friends for, after all? Simon and Viv danced to their tune and even though the crush meant they made little progress, they didn't care.

'We've not done too badly, have we, Viv?'

'We'll get by, I guess,' she said.

The various groups within the dining room of the Haute Plaza were coalescing: people intermingling as they bonded from a minute's conversation in the loo, the sharing of a joke against the government, the coincidence of finding they shared a dentist, or had gone to the same school. Happiness is infectious, isn't it? Their laughter and talk rose in volume until the band was completely eclipsed and might have been in mime without anybody the wiser.

DELAFORCE 1985 VINTAGE PORT

TIA MARIA

NAPOLEON BRANDY

BRIE, CAMEMBERT, GRUYERE, BLUE CHEESEBOARD

TUSCAN-STYLE ESPRESSO

BELGIAN CREAM CHOCOLATES

Simon told Philip Taeb that to celebrate the passing of seasons, anniversaries, great events, was a natural human response: that he had always been in favour of marking the new millennium as a special occasion. Life must be pegged out in some such way he said, or else all your experience just runs together. New Zealanders are fortunate people. He gestured with his cigar at the crowded, noisy room. There was nowhere else in the world he'd rather be to welcome the next thousand years, he said, and with slow deliberation attempted to cut a slice of camembert for himself.

Simon was struck with the significance of the occasion. There were only minutes to go and things must be done well. He stood up, seized a passing drinks waiter by the shoulder and asked what real champagne the Haute Plaza had. Yes, yes, they would have the best Heidsieck, Champagne Charlie for the whole table, which by that time included an adjoining Austrian foursome who had been absorbed into Simon's group despite not understanding a word that was said. Jesus, if a man couldn't go out well on the last day of a millennium. What was the point of hard work except to provide for play? 'Now you're in the swing of it,' said Viv. How he liked to see her laughing.

Some of the two hundred Haute Plaza diners had gone out in time to join in the official celebrations, but not as many as had intended to do so. The mirror walls of the large room elaborated a mass of happy people. The dark marble gleamed impressively. Simon and Viv crowded with others before one of the large windows looking out over the city towards Hagley Park. Simon poured more champagne for Mary, Bernie, Philip and Selwyn Toomey who had left the band to be with them. It seemed to Simon that he was surrounded with the very best of friends: people of intelligence, individual charm and affability. He made a resolution to see more of them, to express his admiration more often and more openly. Celebration of life and events had always been very important to him, he told Viv. He couldn't understand people with a sour attitude, wet blankets, never could.

The hotel manager climbed on a chair to hold up a large plastic clock and lead the count down to the stroke of midnight. His kitchen staff, in a disarray of aprons and hats, crowded out of the service area to be welcomed by the guests, all distinction forgone as the new millennium began. The fireworks burst abruptly in vast, coloured sprays in the summer night, but nothing of their explosions could be heard above the shouting and congratulations of the dining room. People's faces shone with sweat and benevolence and joy. All were caught up in a sense of exultant occasion. Simon kissed Viv, Mary and one of the Austrian women. 'Vienna waltz,' he said. A thin, candy striped streamer floated down and hung across the Austrian's dark hair. Simon held his champagne glass high in the air and joined in the shouts that were both welcome and challenge to the next thousand years.

Surely life is marvellous, isn't it? And the new millennium all firm promise, all sunlit uplands? Isn't it?

NEIGHBOURS

My father regarded any new neighbour with wary curiosity. It's not good to be drawn early into a familiarity that may afterwards be regretted. People cooeeing into your kitchen without so much as a knock, borrowing the patio chairs when you are absent at Christmas. People kindly taking the role of emissary to acquaint the town with your achievements and misfortunes. Even the summary jurisdiction neighbours assume over their own premises can be oddly provocative when you have become accustomed to the settled ways of owners before them. The McAllisters had been very tolerant of our silver birch tree branches questing across their boundary, and favoured old-fashioned climbing roses that my mother viewed with pleasure.

When the Gorringes came they brought no tribe of kids. A good start. 'Let's just hope that they haven't a tribe of kids,' my father said when he heard of the sale. One pre-schooler whining on the drive, the squeaking of a worn trike, enough to break the concentration he needed as 'Prodicus' to complete the crosswords syndicated throughout Australasia. In case that suggests a lofty intellectualism let me add that his was a precarious living, and that in itself may have made him apprehensive of any threat to his working privacy.

For my father speech was a vital, but often over-exercised, faculty. He exclaimed with Walter Mitty, I was thinking. Does it ever occur to you that sometimes I am thinking? And why is it, he would say, that most people have no skill to disengage in conversation, but must drag on in a sort of futile and bumbling goodwill?

Mrs Gorringe was white on white: skim milk white, candle white, so that not a wisp of green vein was visible. Her dark hair could only accentuate her skin. She was large, but not at all fat, and in that summer, when her shoulders and knees were visible, they seemed carved in pale soap. Her manner was open and interested, but quite without intrusive curiosity. 'My husband is in futures,' she said. 'A broker.' What part he played in the future I couldn't say, but he barely existed in the present.

We would hear his Commodore leave at seven fifteen, and less often be aware of its return during our busy tea hour. Mr Gorringe was no gardener, his wife cheerfully told my mother, no Titan in his own section, but on very rare occasions he would appear upon the front lawn at twilight, and smoke a small cigar there, almost as if Mrs Gorringe had sent him out to prove to those living next to her that she had a husband, and they a neighbour. He would stand with his feet apart, looking absently beyond his fence, and when the thin cigar was ended he would flick it, tumbling, glowing, into his wife's lavender bushes and consider his exhibition over. Maybe I saw him there twice, three times at most: certainly I never saw him anywhere else but once. He had the large-featured, lined face of an ageing jockey, though he wasn't a small man. He had a capacity for stillness which suited both twilight and cigar smoke.

After a few months my father was confident enough to declare the Gorringes the pick of our neighbours. Mrs Gorringe didn't have a voice that carried, and she appeared to lack mood swings: my father had a horror of temperament. She didn't intrude, but if met at the fenceline she would talk intelligently, and then disengage without awkwardness, and her husband required no conversation at all. When both were invited for a sherry close to Christmas, Mrs Gorringe came, with her equable, candle-white presence, but bearing of him only an apology. My father was delighted with such consideration.

I wasn't a boy when the Gorringes became our neighbours. I was twenty-three and had ditched my doctoral thesis, on the political effects of our gold rush demography, to come home and save money for a working holiday to Europe. So I was capable of seeing Mrs Gorringe in a sensual light at times, even though she was a good deal older. How her pale body might appear beneath the willows of a South Island stream for instance, the broken sunlight and the muted willow green shimmering back from the water on to her skin.

Late in January, an evening extended by daylight saving, I was cutting back the japonica thicket at the end of our section. Maybe it wasn't the ideal pruning time, but the tight, pink flowers were well over for the year, and I wanted to show my parents that I appreciated living at home without payment while I saved for my trip. It must have been more than three metres high and almost as deep. I was well into the guts of it with the long-handled secateurs when I heard my name from the less congested boundary between the Gorringes and ourselves. 'Gordon. May I talk to you a moment, Gordon?' Mr Gorringe said. He held one of his thin, dark cigars — maybe he smoked only outdoors — and there was that sense of stillness again. It was strange to have the neighbour I'd never met use my name. How would he know it? Perhaps his wife told him of all the people living nearby; maybe he heard my parents address me in the section when he was out of sight. 'You've quite a task on, and I don't want to interrupt,' he said. 'The thing is, I've bought a second-hand walnut writing desk and it's too heavy for me to get inside by myself.'

I shook stalks and leaves from my clothes, climbed over the mid-height fence and went with Mr Gorringe to the garage side of his house, where the desk was still on a trailer behind the Commodore. There were several folded tartan rugs which he must have used to protect the desk in transit. If the weight of that solid walnut Edwardian writing desk was any indication of quality, then Mr Gorringe had done well. It had been in a family of lawyers until the line died out, Mr Gorringe told me, but he didn't elaborate because lifting and carrying took most of his breath.

We did a series of short, stumbling hoists up the main passage of the house, and then angled back and forth to gain entry to the study. I'd been in the house several times when it belonged to the McAllisters, but Mr and Mrs Gorringe had made it very much their own. When we'd settled the desk by the bay window, I looked around and realised that the study had become a trophy room: cabinets and shelves of cups and figurines, framed awards and photographs covering the walls.

Mrs Gorringe was a dancing champion, that's what it was. Ballroom mainly, and traditional, though I noticed one large silver cup she'd won at Manila for the rumba, and an extravagant tureen topped with a couple bowing that was the evidence of success in modern medley at a Sydney international event. Mrs Gorringe had been very attractive as a young woman: in one photograph after another her elegance and poise were evident. Some of the shots were posed, but in others she was caught in the gracefulness of dance, her dress and hair in movement, her lithe form in active balance.

Her regular partner appeared in many of the photographs, smiling, close, proprietorial, and it wasn't Mr Gorringe. Nowhere among all that memorabilia was there any sign of him, but he stood easily by the desk as I took it all in. How had such a private man, a futures broker, come to marry a star in competition dancing? But who knows, maybe some other room in the house disclosed a past for him quite as splendid and secret as that of his wife. In time, some other piece of furniture, too much for him to manage without help, might take me there too.

'In our decline,' said Mr Gorringe, 'we'll be able to sell off the silverware piece by piece to sustain ourselves.' The self-deprecating humour was a poor disguise for the admiration he felt for his wife's achievement.

Mr Gorringe made his quiet, restful walk back down the passage with me, and we met his wife arriving at the front door. I stood aside for her to enter her own house, and for her benefit Mr Gorringe said again how grateful he was that I'd helped bring in the walnut desk. No mention was made of the trophies, but as Mrs Gorringe added her thanks in her even voice, a sudden blush came to her face: as if she were briefly that young, dancing woman once again and had been surprised by my approach. It faded quickly from her white skin, with the last tinge going from her smooth, substantial neck.

'I can never understand why she's so determinedly modest about it all,' Mr Gorringe said to me.

I told my father and mother that night about my good turn, and the quasi fame Mrs Gorringe once had as a ballroom dancer. My mother was mainly interested in any changes that they'd made inside since the McAllisters left, but my father, who delights in life withheld, was taken with the possibilities of it. 'Dance, eh — a dancing queen,' he said. 'How wonderful it is that people manage to get from one life to another which is completely different, when there seems no logical passage between them.' My father thereafter considered them even better neighbours than before, though he was less inclined to have contact with them. Perhaps when he was tired of grappling with twenty-seven down, nine letters, the demon huntsman, he would see Mrs Gorringe in her garden, or catch the rare glimpse of her husband, stock still and with cigar smoke curling, in the dusk. He would conjure her as a young champion dancing with a partner quite gone from her life. My father preferred people at some remove, so that there remained an element of mystery: the chance to fashion them in his own imagination rather than be confronted by the reality that so often disappointed.

I never entered the Gorringes' house again: never said more to her than a passing greeting, of him heard only the Commodore. Within three months of helping with the Edwardian desk, I was away overseas and didn't return for almost two years. Mr Gorringe had done very well indeed in futures, my mother said, and they went to live in Wellington where the business was at his fingertips. New people had come whose open intention of ongoing friendship made my father apprehensive as to their suitability.

When I visit my parents and look at that house on our west side,

I think of the Gorringes, even though the McAllisters lived there for much longer, and when I was at an impressionable age, and the Silks are the new, friendly people now making changes as is their right. What stays in my mind is that one visit to the study, the collected evidence of Mrs Gorringe's success as a dancer, and the blush that came on her candle-white, calm face when she knew I'd seen the photographs. What must it be like, to achieve an important goal when you're young and beautiful, and then have the rest of your life a slow journey away from that success, and from that youth and beauty?

THE CORMORANT DEVOURING TIME

'On no account,' says the Head of Department, 'is there to be any alteration or addition to the 306 bibliography without plenary consultation.' Zurvan is the great riddle God of Time. Where the campus dreams had once been lowland podocarp, had since been fescue over-sown with red clover. On terra firma three storeys below the Head of Department — exactly, I mean — a jersey bull had served its purpose, human-like on two rear legs, 7218 days before. In what rapture the clear honey of its drool caught the setting sun; what ring of fire was in its nose.

The Human Cannonball thinks that much of the trouble is a software thing: too many colleagues not using the network to check their disks. What is the use, after all, of establishing a means of communication within the department if there is no disk interface? 'Before you know it,' says the Human Cannonball, 'we'll be back to sticking notes on each other's doors.'

'Has Dr Moriarty rung?' The Head of Department is talking to his secretary on the intercom. 'Excuse me,' he tells the others. 'I just wished to ascertain if Dr Moriarty had rung.'

Elephant Bill is maybe checking his entry on Bandoola:

1897 — November: Born.

1903 — Trained. Branded 'C' both rumps.

1904–17 — Travelling with forest assistants as pack animal.

Even his name was exceptional, being that of a Burmese general who was a hero fighting against the British before the annexation of 1886.

'Though Dr Moriarty isn't with us as yet, I want to move on to the Vice-Chancellor's comments regarding the revitalisation of post-graduate research programmes,' says the Head of Department. The Diva reminds him that she has to leave by quarter to, and particularly wants to talk to the agenda point of overhead projectors in the lecture theatres. She has her hair done in one great glistening and intimidating plait with, at its free end, an authentic Mayan blue brooch given to her by a lover who was once an academic tour guide in the Yucatan. Only the cries and the blood are not there to be displayed. 'Ah, yes. Certainly. You'll be off to Women's Professional Representation: the standing committee on sitting members,' says the Head of Department.

'No. I'm through to the final of the Consolation Plate.' Would that more of us could say the same. Imagine the arc of the heavy, brown plait as the Diva plays a reverse angle boast. Generally her personal vanity is expressed more directly. Imagine the Yucatan by satellite picture: a great spur in the brooch blue Caribbean. Imagine any scene before you as more or less consequential. What a gullet has the cormorant.

1918–21 — Ounging Moo River (i.e. salving logs from sand-banks in it).

1922 — Transferred to Gangaw Forest.

1923–31 — Timber camp of Maung Aung Gyaw.

1932 — Injured in fight with wild tusker. Rested throughout the year. Fully recovered.

In an aside to his friend, Patsy, the Human Cannonball admits that the Diva has one of the best arses in the business. Epigone recalls privately that in this very room after the mid-winter party he discovered a noted medievalist weeping for the loss of a daughter. For an hour he held and comforted the man, gave him of the most mellow philosophy he possessed, and so ensured that both were henceforth too shamed to do more than nod in passing. Patsy, while admitting that it may well be that through a man's eye the Diva has one of the best arses in the business, is also drawn by association of place to memories of the mid-winter ridoto. 'I just can't fathom who it is who shifts the OHPs. It makes no sense at all,' says the Head of Department. As her contribution, Patsy had taken some cannelloni, and sung a madrigal with the Diva. Both had gone down well. She had worn tooled boots, which seemed to charm the medievalist for the first part of the evening.

'No one, I suppose, heard from Dr Moriarty before the meeting?' says the Head of the Department. 'He made no comment about anything cropping up?' Patsy heard the medievalist had some tragedy in his life; something far back that still had the power to overwhelm him.

Merlot's suede shoe approximates the point at which a falcon veering in the sun caught the admiring attention of Wattie Proctor in '54. Where Elephant Bill's shoulder touches the seminar room's wall will be one day a rack of Civil Defence masks. Beneath the Diva's chair at another time, with the carpet gone, will pool the custodian's blood at his own behest. Some glance other than Patsy's through the same window will see the perimeter wire and the caches of black market goods. The dispossessed hold torches and automatic weapons. Always the cormorant is devouring time.

1933 — Transferred to South Kindat Forest, Upper Chindwin River. Allocated to camp of Maung Po Toke.

1934–41 — Fit throughout. Prime Elephant of the forest.

1942 — January–April: Employed on Kalewa–Kalemyo road, before the retreat of the Burma Army.

May–October: Disbanded but kept in secret hiding from the Japanese in side creek of Kabaw Valley by Maung Po Toke living in Witok.

November: Handed over again to Elephant Bill and Harold Browne at Tamu.

December: Enrolled as No. 1 animal, the nucleus, of No. 1 Elephant Company, XIVth Army. Employed dragging timber for bridges.

'Can we take it then,' says the Head of Department, 'that we're substantially in agreement on each of those issues?' Epigone looks from the window and is seized with misgivings concerning what he sees in the night there. Already the gas mortars are striking the baffles of the old university C Block and falling into the loading bays where they loll on the camber, releasing fumes of the most exquisite purple, yellow, Presley pink and Prussian blue. At the perimeter, the sky has filled with the great holographs of the ethnic clan totems, like Daimyo sitting impassively in battle to inspire their warriors.

'How few black market stocks we have left,' he exclaims. Elephant Bill holds the Head of Department's arms behind his back while Patsy forces into his mouth a paperweight of wondrously polished petrified wood. The Human Cannonball swings the Diva into a more advantageous position over the upholstered arm of the seminar room's leather chair. There is a series of tight pleats on the facing, each held by a tack with a convex, brass head. Dr Moriarty, if present, would take the opportunity for a snap vote on the reintroduction of Icelandic Sagas; Ms Hassim in the outer office takes the drumming of the Head of Department's feet on his desk as the commencement of extra-curricular activities and leaves for her class on Windows Millennium.

1943 — March–November: Employed near Tamu collecting timber ready for the return of the Army.

1944 — November–March: Bridge-building with the Army in Kabaw Valley.

Merlot has a sense of anti-climax. It isn't like Moriarty to promise support on an important issue and then not show. It's almost unheard of for a senior lecturer of long standing to have an office on the south side of the block, and for Merlot a grievance almost to the point of death. He allows himself a grimace of boredom and cynicism despite the Head of Department's quick glance, despite the discomfort of the Civil Defence masks in the small of his back, despite the jersey bull's horns nodding hypnotically in his field of vision.

1944 — April–May: Leading elephant in the march out of Burma from Kanchaung to Baladan in Assam.

June–October: Resting in Surma Valley, Assam. Loose for one day in pineapple grove, estimated to have eaten nine hundred pineapples. Severe colic. Recovered.

November–December: Marched back to Burma.

The Head of Department deftly removes the paperweight from his mouth. It is most unbecoming on such occasions if a thread of spittle adheres. As a student he was accidentally struck in the face by a strand of number eight wire when fencing on his uncle's farm at Hororata. Patsy is attracted to the scar, small and very white on his left cheek. It is the one hint of vulnerability, of ill-fortune, she thinks. Because of it he flinches markedly when the gas bomb strikes the parapet of the window and falls in a spiral of cockatoo sulphur to the loading bays, while neither the Human Cannonball, nor the bull with a nose of brazen circumference, is a whit distracted from his ecstatic rhythms. 'Perhaps we had better press on,' says the Head of the Department. 'I must say it is inconvenient that we haven't Dr Moriarty's views on such things, particularly as he is Head of Department designate.'

'I must leave almost directly,' says the Diva. Her voice is somewhat muffled by the leather upholstery.

'Quite,' says the Head of Department. There seems to have been a breakthrough at the north end of the compound. The shooting has increased and Elephant Bill hears heavy armour grinding past on the tarmac in that direction. He raises his voice to suggest that one or two agenda matters be passed over until another time. 'The tutorial load of PhD students, for example.'

1945 — January–March: Attached to Forest Saw Mill Units, R.E., teak-dragging for Army boat-building.

March 8: Found dead, shot by an unknown person near Witok.

'Has Dr Moriarty been rung?' the Head of Department asked Ms Hassim on the Thursday, just to be sure that he would be in no doubt concerning the timing of the meeting.

Patsy is so close to the silken neck of the heifer that she feels the warm exhalations on her forearm and sees the individual tines of its vast, demure eyelashes. Epigone's complaint of course reprographic restrictions is unheard because of the sound of the custodian's body striking the floor. The night sky outside is hung with flares as the counter-assault goes in. Merlot wonders if Moriarty is among the vanguard perhaps, crying for Odin's blessing and holding aloft his Icelandic battle axe.

The cormorant of the riddle God Time has covered the world.

ROCKET BOY

'Mostly she'd come into my room late, and stand in her thin night-dress between me and the bed light, and talk about her work in the animal pound: about the dogs and cats she'd been able to place with good families, and the one day a fortnight when she had to help the vet with the putting down. She'd come close to me and say that it was all life and death, wasn't it, in work of that sort, and take my hand while asking what I was studying, and lean over my work from the technical institute, put my hand up her nightie. Sometimes they got specially odd animals at the pound, like a wallaby once, and one of those lemurs with bulgy eyes. She'd ask me to make love before her husband came home from a late taxi shift. She used to smack her own big thighs. I was young then and took it for granted, but I've never known any woman do that again. She wouldn't have a pet herself, she said, because of all mistreatment she saw at the pound. She didn't like me to ask for it, to make any suggestion: no, we only shagged at night, when she chose to, in the same way each time. Her coming in late when I was working. She liked how thin I was she said. Just chicken bones she said, and she'd wipe sweat from beneath my eyes with her vast, soft tits.'

My uncle was talking about his sexual experiences again. It was always the same when you visited him. He was eighty-six and in the non-denominational Christian retirement home in Hibiscus Terrace. The day lounge there was so hot that even in winter I sat by him in shirtsleeves, and marvelled at the woollen rugs tucked around the knees of the inmates. Uncle Ivan was one of the few men there: mostly it was women with very fixed expressions and their bodies settled down as fine sand slumps in a bag with jostling, or strung with bones as fragile as a kite's.

The skin was drawn tightly over my uncle's face so that it followed every contour of the bone, and dark patches on the surface made him appear like a slightly burnt gingerbread man. Tufts of hair in his ears caught the light from the window behind him, and I saw on the broad path a shrunken woman locked in combat with a walking frame. I gave the frame something of an edge, all things considered.

Mrs Jarvis was the landlady's name, and I'd heard a good many of Uncle Ivan's stories about her part in his education. Like Yeats, my uncle had become obsessed with sex in his old age: his propensity surely in inverse proportion to his ability to perform. Whether his monologue was truth freed from inhibition, or just senile fancy, I didn't know, but my guess was he daydreamed to pass the time. There's no distinction between fact and fiction in the land of living death. My mother wouldn't sit through it, and who can blame her. A woman doesn't want to go visiting and hear all that, especially from her own daft brother.

I went once a month or so, because Uncle Ivan had taught me to fly fish and given me two thousand dollars towards my first car, a Ford Cortina. On all the fishing trips we made he never talked of sex that I remember. He never talked of sex, and he never talked of the war, though he was a sergeant major and won a medal for something or other in Crete. He never talked of the war even in the retirement home: the inhibitions for that must be even stronger than for sex.

'I banged a woman who came collecting for blind people, or crippled chidden,' said my uncle. His voice was husky, but didn't quaver. 'It must have been the late fifties because we were in the Stevens Street house by the domain, and anyway this collecting woman was interested that I'd gone back to Crete after the war. She'd just come back from a trip there looking at ancient ruins. She was sandy, very freckled, which you don't see much in grown women, and had very small, even teeth. It was a cold, windy day and she came in for a cup of tea. While she was telling me about her tour, I interrupted, and said that I'd promised myself in 1940 that if I got through the war then I'd take what joy I could ever afterwards. She got up without another word and walked through every room in the house, then she told me to lock the door and that she had exactly thirty-five minutes before she had to go. With all those freckles on her face and legs and arms it was odd that there was hardly one on her belly, or breasts, and as we did it on the couch she told me about an older brother who was in bombers and bought it over Germany.'

We were sitting chair to chair with four old women, one of whom had fallen asleep with a spoonful of green jelly held in her lap. None of them was askance at Uncle Ivan's litany of copulation: age had rendered them immune, and they nodded as if he spoke of nasturtiums; they interrupted with wild surmise as to the menu for tea; they slept on with the green jelly undisturbed.

A nurse came to us on her peaceful round. She had a light pink smock and a sturdy walk. Her face was plain, but her hair black and lustrous: quite beautiful. 'Isn't it nice to have a visitor, Mr Nolan,' she said and smiled at us both.

'I used to screw a Maori girl who was the dental nurse at a primary school in Wanganui. When she climaxed she used to buck and cry out in Maori, and once she poured mercury into my belly-button. Jesus, we had some good times.'

'He really looks forward to a visitor,' said the nurse. She pushed the pillow a little more firmly between Uncle Ivan's back and the chair.

'I try to come when I can,' I said.

'There was this store cupboard in the clinic. The whole place wasn't much bigger than an army hut. Sometimes if I was between shifts, I'd go round at playtime and she'd let me go into the store cupboard with her. Christ, she was a good-looking woman. We'd stand up against the door, because there were shelves everywhere else, and have a good go. I could hear the little kids squealing outside, just a wall away, and I'd be damn near squealing myself.'

'We know that he's experiencing some recent memory loss, and he had a fall in the dining room last week, but he's pretty good overall,' said the nurse absently. She saw the old woman outside in the walking frame. 'Poor Mrs Fraser's in trouble again. I'd better go out soon,' but she didn't hurry away.

'One day we hammered so hard that her arse caved in the door panel. It was one of those cheap, plywood doors, not solid wood or anything. She just laughed. She transferred to Te Kuiti finally and married a meat inspector. If I'd had any brains I would have married her myself. Christ, she had nipples like clothes pegs, and a kiss like a poultice.'

'Would you both like a cup of tea?' the nurse asked us. I didn't want to be a nuisance, I told her, and Uncle Ivan didn't bother to reply.

'Well, I'd better see to Mrs Fraser,' the nurse said. She leant over Uncle Ivan and straightened his shirt collar. He had no tie, but the stiff-collared shirt was done right up and his neck no longer filled the space. 'You're very patient with him,' she said. 'He gets very repetitious at times. It's just what happens.'

'Rose-anne,' said Uncle Ivan firmly. 'That was her name right enough. Rose-anne. Odd name for a full-blooded Maori. Rocket Boy, she used to call me, and she threatened to tattoo my cock *sure to rise*.' Uncle Ivan lifted his head to laugh, but there was no sound, just his bony head in silhouette, glad-wrapped with the finest skin, and his mouth open like a lizard's.

'It's quite sunny for winter really,' said the nurse, and began her sturdy walk to the glass doors. Her massed, dark hair held the light.

'So it is,' I said.

'You remember Rose-anne,' asked Uncle Ivan.

'Before my time,' I said. He lifted his eyebrows in a brief mimicry of surprise, then clattered his false teeth, which is a habit of his. There's something off-putting about a physical wreck talking of the transports of physical love — his mottled face, his decayed breath, the blue and vermilion veins traced beneath the skin, the tufted ears.

Eroticism is not a wine that cellars well.

'I'd better go,' I said. 'I have to make a valuation of the Llimonds' place in Wybrow Street. She was the principal at Rutleigh School for girls.'

'Vera Llimonds,' said Uncle Ivan. 'I shagged her one election night. It was a landslide for National, and she'd really celebrated at a party thrown by Hec and Trudy Palliser.' It was difficult to change the subject with Uncle Ivan. Anyway, I remembered Ms Llimonds myself: a stern woman with undyed hair, and broad shoulders — both pulled back. She was a nationally ranked bridge player, and I couldn't see Uncle Ivan playing his cards right with her, landslide or no landslide. 'From her bed,' he went on, 'I could see the whole sweep of the waterfront with the massed, sparkling curve of the lights, and then the blackness of ocean beyond. She massaged me with oil that smelled of roses, and said that an occasional man wasn't a distraction from her profession. She'd never had any children and her stomach was just like a girl's. The only thing was, she kept giving me my riding instructions.'

'Well, anyway, I'd better go, Uncle Ivan. I'm meeting a member of the family there at four o'clock.'

'She wasn't a patch on Rose-anne, but I was no bloody rocket boy by then either,' he said. As I left the hothouse room he gave me a wave, but when I came past the windows in the winter cold and lifted a hand again, he didn't see me, although he was facing my way. The dark blemishes on his face and hands were a striking contrast to the pallor of the rest of his skin, as if he had been sprinkled with cinnamon.

Ms Llimonds' niece was waiting for me at Wybrow Street, and we went through the empty rooms. 'This is the main bedroom,' she said, when we were upstairs. 'My aunt used to say she liked being at the top of the house.' I stood within the square made by the carpet indentations of the vanished bed legs, and the view through the window was just as Uncle Ivan had described it, but not lit up for the night — the curve of the waterfront, and then a grey sea stretching to the horizon.

THE PANAMA CONNECTION

It's a rather a dispiriting idea that schooldays are the best days of your life. Even in a happy adolescence most of us have other ambitions we hope to realise when we're more in control of our existence. To reach some peak of achievement, or status, at seventeen, and never do so well again doesn't seem like much to me.

More interesting are the nerdy kids who end up software millionaires, plain girls who fill out as film stars, or fill up as physicists at Cambridge University, drop-outs who discover themselves as a divinity and build up a rapturous congregation on Stewart Island. Even the celebrities, who launch a bitter attack on the schools that expelled them, though why worldly success should exonerate them for bullying, or theft, or obstinate insolence, is never quite explained.

All those kids starting out. Some are achievers all the way, some confirmed failures, some promise much and fizzle out, some, lacking discernible talent, kick on later and astound everybody.

A television programme about Kiwi expatriates brought all that to mind. There was an interview with Dianne Ellecott, my classmate in computer skills for two years, who has now become the chaperone for the daughters of the president of Panama, with a good deal of influence on foreign policy. If I were writing formally then I'd feel the need to follow rules of congruency, and give you a good deal about Dianne as a kid, but what I thought of, as I watched, was her admirer Noel Sutter, far more intriguing as an adolescent at least, and who never had the opportunity, or the gender, to charm the dictator of Panama.

Sutter was a very individual guy, and yet inclined that way I think by the common difficulty of having a more successful and older brother. Andrew Boyes Sutter was tall, dark, strong, fluent and with a quiet gentleness at the heart of all his success which iced his popularity. A lesser student would have been given unbearable stick for having a name like Boyes, even as a traditional family second name, but for him it became an accolade, roared from the rugby sidelines, emphasised with a smile by the principal at prizegiving, murmured with dreamy promise in the senior girls' common room.

Noel Sutter got the trickster's shake of the genes; spiderishly hairy, a sunken chest and classic, case study, acne. His only physical drawcard was double-jointed thumbs that he could spring into grotesque positions. And he was highly intelligent, which was another obstacle to easy alignment with his fellows. Even in intelligence, however, he refused to compete with his brother, and made his identity in ways that avoided rivalry.

Noel became half-clown, half-scapegoat for the school, but even though the other students delighted in his escapades against authority, it was evident that their derision included him as well as that authority. He wasn't of them; perhaps they sensed he wasn't really for them. It was Sutter who rigged up the fart machine under the head's assembly chair, whose sleight of hand replaced the sixth form girls' sex education video with a porno movie; Sutter who challenged the HOD Maths to a duel, and stained the swimming pool purple with Condy's crystals on sports day. It was Sutter found with a distillery in the ceiling of chem lab C, and Sutter who rang the chairman of trustees and, as a concerned parent, claimed the senior mistress and Ms Ignatti had been discovered in the canteen storeroom engaged in naked and mutual flagellation.

Sutter was just as determined in his mockery of all the attitudes, pretensions, cruel hierarchies and vainglorious posturings of his peers. That's why we never took him to our hearts as a champion.

It was Sutter also who fell in love with Dianne Ellecott, and in that one thing he was perhaps just the same as almost every other boy at the school. Intelligence, temperamental isolation, idiosyncrasy, even bitterness, were chicken feed as obstacles to falling for a girl who was to sway a president of Panama. Dianne Ellecott did nothing specific to mesmerise Sutter, she had no intentions towards him: she was just there, and Sutter responded as a plant follows the sun. Her beauty was utterly conventional, but against it Sutter had no defence, despite his successful repudiation of all other convention. Instinct is a Vesuvius that bursts through the surface of life at will, and the sight of Dianne crossing the quad was enough to cause in Sutter a sort of rictus of desire that incapacitated him. It was understandable: once I had a blackout after watching her play softball.

If I were making all this up, then Dianne would, of course, fall for Sutter's golden boy brother, and force Sutter to face the determining situation in his life or, though predictable herself, she would display just enough insight to value Sutter's intelligence and originality so that romance was fulfilled. But reality tends to avoid the symmetries of art. No, when Noel Sutter offered to do her science project for her she refused, and when a few days later he wanted her to go camping with him, she refused with less civility. When he persisted and said he'd managed to get tickets to the Wearable Arts Awards, because that was the sort of thing she liked, Dianne told him to stuff off. When he asked her why she didn't like him, she said he was seriously weird. She wasn't a vindictive girl: she said nothing about his hairiness, his caved-in chest, his acne, or his flaring thumbs.

I wasn't Sutter's friend, or Dianne's unfortunately, but as one of those unassuming, middle spectrum kids I had the neutrality awarded the inconspicuous, and was occasionally used as a sounding board. I thought Sutter's reaction to rejection might be a grand exhibition of weirdness, a gesture of his own disregard, but instead he had one of those switches of fixation that youth accommodates. From Dianne he turned to the stock market, and within one month had made more for the school's student business association than it had achieved in the three years before. That created jealousy in Pitma Rasouse, the economics teacher who advised the association, and Sutter resigned without a murmur. In the world of finance he seemed to have lost the need to draw attention to himself, though I thought the change was more directly due to his unrequited love for Dianne Ellecott.

I saw him occasionally at Otago University, but there he was a very unspectacular student: his fierce and flamboyant crusade against the world faded with his acne. He kept his thumbs furled, and his hollow chest swathed in scarf and jersey. He got a good degree in some branch of economics, and took a job as investment adviser for Tower Insurance. I never saw him again. He faded into a successful institutional career, moved to Christchurch and married, built a discreetly impressive home in Sumner.

They have exchanged roles in life — Dianne Ellecott and Noel Sutter — without discussion, but perhaps on Sutter's side some awareness of irony. He has given himself up to convention, and she is ambiguous in the entourage of the president of Panama.

SPRING WITH THE SUMERBOTTOMS

I'm here because of Elvis Presley. The guy has a long reach, not just beyond the grave, but from the other side of the world. Here, in this small town hemmed in by dairy cows, is the Elvis Presley Memorial Record Room, reputed to have the most extensive collection in Australasia.

My editor told me to get up here and do a feature for the weekend leisure and arts section. She knows I don't much care for Presley; that adds to her enthusiasm. So I'm at Morrieson's Motel, which is just off the main street. I'm in unit nine and listening to the owner, Clarry, go on about the memorial room. Clarry's a retired dairy farmer, of course: perhaps that's why he doesn't want to put down my regulation pottle of milk and leave me to unpack. Clarry tells me the Elvis Presley room is private and do I realise that? That I'll need to make arrangements to visit and so on.

I've been to this town once before, nearly twenty years ago. Maybe even before Elvis Presley came. In my first university year at Massey I lived in a hostel, dutifully following the advice of the school counsellor. The theory is that students become friends with a wide range of peers and maintain contact with them throughout the rest of their time, even if subsequent years are spent in flats or boarding houses. Presumably that prevents them from becoming emotionally isolated, or bonding too closely with inappropriate folk.

When I left the hostel after one year, I took considerable care to avoid a good many of the people I'd met there, and in some of them I noticed a similar disposition towards myself. A colony of late adolescents is a restrictive introduction to adult life. That careers counsellor, however, who was also a collector of Antarctic memorabilia, was indirectly the reason I met Andrew Sumerbottom and his family. Andrew's room was in a different block, with a better view to the campus, but he was doing a couple of the same units, and was one of the few guys with a reasonable game of tennis. He had a strong baseline game with few unforced errors and a heavy serve, but he wasn't comfortable at the net.

He was blond, cheerful, slightly overweight and apparently took no offence at the fun made of his absurd name — sun bum, spring arse, wintertop. Within the hostel he had a reputation for clownish amiability which passed as popularity, but few of us, I think, progressed from acquaintances to being a friend. His good humour deflected those enquiries intended for a heartfelt response. Games and rituals he liked: activities of agreed and predictable routine. I noticed in his room books on career success and personal development, but he said it was just stuff that had been there when he moved in. He had a gorilla suit that was famous in the hostel, and even his regular clothes were better than mine. In the winter I noticed that his coat was special. It had a blue lining and suede lips to the pockets. Ready cash was always a problem, though, as it was for almost all of us.

In the spring, before exams, but after lectures had finished, he invited me to go home with him to Taranaki for a weekend. We had been working late in the library, and he gave the invitation awkwardly as we walked back to the hostel. We both knew it was something rather different in that time of tennis, shared tutorials and casual company. Maybe with the end of the year in sight he felt able to open up a bit.

Mrs Sumerbottom came in to collect us on the Friday afternoon.

'Call me Miranda,' she said. I imagine the invitation was less natural informality, and more the wish to avoid being called Mrs Sumerbottom. Miranda was blonde like her son, but underweight in comparison. She was attractive in a slightly desiccated way, and had a tremulous intensity that hurried her words and caused her blonde bob to quiver. 'Such a delight to meet you at last,' she said. Her wrists were showing from her Country Road shirt and the tendons on the underside stood out parallel and pale beneath the skin like brittle spaghetti. 'I never get accustomed to the city traffic,' she said, as Andrew and I put our bags into the ageing Toyota. Miranda sat forward and very upright to drive, her unobtrusive chest almost brushing the wheel, as if that way she could gain a fractional advantage to deal with emergencies. The gear lever she treated as if it were electrified, her hand making apprehensive sorties towards it, then giving the stick a sudden wrench, and releasing it as she felt the shock. 'Now tell me all about yourself, Hugh.' My name was pronounced with positive emphasis, maybe so she could the better remember it, and she swivelled her head in a quick flash to make eye contact. Then, before I could begin to reply, there was just the back of the trembling, blonde bob again.

The Sumerbottoms lived here, in this dairy town. Mr Sumerbottom used to have a thriving dental practice in Wellington, but someone in the hostel told me that there'd been some professional misconduct, largely hushed up, and the family had come down in the world in both economic and demographic terms. If that was true, then the house they'd bought was appropriate: one of the few grand, older homes, and it stood near the edge of the township, on a section that must have been over an acre. Full-grown oaks, pines and sycamores shaded the rough lawn and the gravel paths almost claimed back by the weeds. The trees crowded the two storeyed weatherboard house, even on that section, so that it was almost always in shadow. It was a property that had a sense of past gentility and future potential, both of which must have appealed to the Sumerbottoms, but there were the failings of the present also. The last paint job had been a cheap one, and the high guttering left rust trails down the weatherboards. One of the small, stone lions that guarded the front steps had lost a paw, several of the hall lead-lights were damaged and the furniture was a menagerie of styles.

'We're taking things one at a time,' Miranda said as she gave me the tour. 'You need to live in a place a while to know what's best for it. We're almost sure the flooring is kauri.'

I followed her up the worn carpet of the stairway to the room where I was to sleep. It had a small, black iron fireplace blocked with a flap of breakfast food carton. 'You'll love the birdsong,' said Miranda, 'but we found that they sometimes come down the chimneys for some reason.' It was an ugly, small room with bare boards that may have been kauri for all I knew. One light hung from a fabric-coated cord, and the bed had Flintstone transfers on the headboard. 'Such a marvellous vista,' she said, and so it was: a powerful oak to one side and on the other a view over a scatter of houses towards Mount Taranaki.

One patch in the wilderness of the lawn had been roughly mown, and on it was a new trampoline, its bright, commercial colours at odds with all about it. Miranda told me they'd bought it for the children of home-stay guests. That was how the Sumerbottoms planned to make a go of it all: an elegant, patrician home-stay property for wealthy people from the cities. At that small window of an upstairs room, I realised that my view was not at all what Miranda looked upon. She saw the complete and ideal restoration, and allowed hopeful deceit to blind her to the truth that she didn't have the money to achieve it. She bought a new patio awning, a gate sign with heraldic device, rimu kitchen furniture from a restaurant foreclosure, a cheap red and green trampoline, while all the time beneath such cosmetics the antiquated plumbing system boomed in malfunction, the slate tiles cracked and slid, the massive tree roots heaved up the brick wall at the front gate. I didn't have the heart to ask her how many families they'd had to stay. I excused myself from her fixed optimism and went to find Andrew.

The Sumerbottoms had a daughter much younger than Andrew. Diedre would have been no more than eleven or twelve, and she came home from school with the same vulnerable eagerness of her mother. She took a shine to me and wanted us to play swingball together. 'Don't go bothering Hugh,' her mother told her indulgently, and so Diedre and I stood in the long grass not far from the trampoline and used purple plastic bats to keep the yellow ball going.

'Andy never plays with me,' she said directly, and Andrew, sitting on the verandah steps, gave a smile clumsy with embarrassment as I acted out my role as guest. Diedre had a pony-tail, and as she jumped and twisted to hit the ball, her pale hair, her thin arms and legs, were caught in the dapples of late afternoon sun through the confining trees. 'Play properly, play properly,' she shouted if I seemed to be holding back at all. I hardly knew her, most likely we'd never meet again, or recognise each other if we did, for she was growing quickly, and her gender allowed an easy escape from the name of Sumerbottom. I wondered how much longer she would retain her easy, unquestioning affection.

Mr Sumerbottom returned in the stillness of late afternoon, bouncing his small car over the roots at the entrance, and apologising, after meeting me, for holding up the meal. 'Another session with the accountant. Jesus,' he told Miranda, and to Andrew and me, 'Wait till you have to deal with GST and all that carry-on.' He was well dressed, well groomed and he flapped his hands in front of him as if warding off a flurry of financial paperwork. He tried an easy smile, but it twitched at the corners, and Miranda's head trembled. 'Anyway, anyway,' he said, 'What have you people been up to?' and he left to wash before the meal. Mr Sumerbottom was darker than the rest of the family, but just as lean as his wife and daughter. I wondered where Andrew got his round face, his heavy arms and legs. Mr Sumerbottom moved and talked in bursts, and had times of almost dummy-like passivity in between.

We had tea in the big kitchen with the attractive foreclosed furniture, and fine, old, white and blue porcelain tiles above the sink. Only a few were badly damaged. The meal was of that variety to which I became accustomed, but not reconciled, during my time there: largely uncooked, cold and vegetable. We ate potato salad, bean sprouts, salsa bread, pasta and nuts, couscous, tomatoes, rocket and lettuce. True, there was the smell of salmon, but the pale, fragmentary substance of it was elusive among the greenery. Andrew's addiction to burgers during the academic year, and the gracile frames of the rest of the family, were sufficiently explained.

Unlike his wife, Mr Sumerbottom wasn't sensitive about the family surname, and never volunteered a Christian one. Without prompting he told me that the origin was the old English word, summer, meaning a large, horizontal beam used in construction.

'So there you are then,' he said, as if satisfying my query. 'We're builders from way back, from Warwickshire in fact. And we certainly need to be builders in this house.' He leant over the table towards Diedre and began to sing, 'We're builders, builders, builders. We're builders, builders, builders.' After each repetition his voice went up an octave. 'We're builders, builders, builders.' Diedre began to sing too, and Mr Sumerbottom then made conducting motions to the rest of us as a sign to join in. Miranda took it up immediately, and then Andrew and me. 'We're builders, builders, builders.'

So we sat amid the salads, and sang the extempore Sumerbottom genealogy. Diedre enjoyed it immensely, Miranda was seized with febrile gaiety, Mr Sumerbottom seemed delighted with his improvisation and broke off several times to cast his head back and give a machine-gun laugh. His dark, soft hair was thrown back from his forehead when he did so, but then he was suddenly still and silent while the rest of us were left chanting. I didn't look at Andrew.

He and I helped with the washing up, and then walked down to the pub. After a term drinking in the same city bars full of students, I found it strange that Andrew and I were such a youthful minority among the regulars there. The locals looked up as we came in, and were baffled to find they didn't know us, as people are in very small places. We took our beer on to the verandah and sat in the dusk facing a Wrightsons store across the road. A window full of gumboots, drench and slick parkas. Andrew said nothing about his family. We talked about varsity and the hostel, with all the more freedom because the year there was almost over. Both of us, it turned out, had decided to go flatting for our second year.

Andrew was hoping to go in with some ex-private school girls, he said. The parents of one of them had bought a house close to Massey to rent out. My own plans weren't so promising: two guys from the same rugby team who said a room would be coming up in their flat, which was a jerry-built addition to an old dump in Pitt Street.

The bar was just starting to fill up when Andrew and I left. We walked back to the Sumerbottom's section, and warily made our way through the extra darkness of the trees to the house. There was just one outside bulb on an arched bracket above the front steps, and its buttery glow had little penetration. The stone lion with missing paw matched its twin in an Assyrian pose, and Miranda's thick, Trade Aid door mat was jaundiced in the artificial light.

The Sumerbottoms weren't downstairs. 'I should say goodnight to your folks,' I told Andrew, but he said it was okay because they'd be watching television in their room. So I said goodnight to him at least, a courtesy we never bothered with in the hostel, and went up to my room with the Flintstone transfers and the narrow, black fireplace blocked with cardboard to keep the birds out.

On my bed was a matching towel and flannel set. The flannel was folded in a way that made it stand up as a small pyramid on the towel, and the pale blue of the set was repeated in an individual round soap no bigger than an egg yolk. I imagined Miranda's absorption as she searched the shops for such trivial, but achievable perfection, while all the time the borer had the old house by the throat, and the guttering rusted out. And in an airing cupboard somewhere, she would have a dozen matching powder blue sets awaiting the rich people she dreamed of as guests.

I took the towel along the top hallway to the bathroom, and when I turned on the upright, chrome taps a cacophony of snorts and hiccups began far away in the plumbing. The eventual flow and temperature were in inverse proportion to the noise that heralded them. The lavatory was on a lead sheet base, which was cool enough even then to make me wonder how it would be on the feet in winter, but the cistern was new and its gilt handle gleamed.

Later, as I lay with Barney Rubble and Bam Bam on the single bed and watched the tip of a fir tree against the sky, I wondered who had built the place, and how many families had been part of its glory days and then slow decline. I saw the first proud owners carting water to the oaks and sycamores that now were higher than the house, and the workmen rolling out a resplendent fleur-de-lis carpet strip down the kauri hall and crimping the sides with brass. Old houses retain something of the lives within them, even when the people are dead, or gone: smells most of all. Home-made quince jelly and apricot jam, damp gabardine and galoshes at the hall stand, a reek of mortality from the room where the old woman is dying. Sweat and tobacco and mutton fat and yellow laundry soap as hard as cracked cheese. And the favoured perfumes: the lavender sachets, talcs and pot-pourri jars. By the favourite possie in the sunroom may linger the living smell of the black Labrador buried long ago beneath the macrocarpa. White roses in the front room, and the fragrance of happiness floating in with childish laughter. Why should everything of experience be lost just because people don't remember any more.

The next morning there was nothing cooked for breakfast, of course: I'd twigged to that. Halves of grapefruit, muesli, yoghurt, juice, croissants and toast in a chrome rack with a ring to carry it. A fine show on the crisp tablecloth, and I saw Miranda look back from the bench in innocent appreciation of her own artistry. Everything in her life was seen as if it were a magazine layout, and judged that way.

Miranda had development plans for the day, and we were the workers she had in mind. She had begun the creation of a patio outside the sunroom door. There was large heap of used bricks crushing a yellowed rhododendron, and a few tentative lines of bricks set in the lawn immediately beside the steps. She had at first carefully removed all the old mortar, but then become more impatient. Andrew and I took out turfs and levelled an area, laid some bedding sand, and chose bricks to put down. Mr Sumerbottom made a show of assistance, mucking round with pegs and string to mark out the final boundaries, but well before eleven he went off with his golf-clubs and a wave as he bounced down the drive. 'It's so important that he has a complete change of pace from the pressure of his weekday surgery,' Miranda told us. 'People don't realise the level of accountability in the professions these days at all.' She had new gardening gloves to protect her hands, and carried bricks one at a time. 'When the trees are topped,' she said, 'this will be one of the warmest spots on the section, and it could be set up for barbecues, maybe Devonshire teas.'

Andrew and I could see that there weren't nearly enough bricks to reach the string with which Mr Sumerbottom had sketched his wife's ambition, and we didn't grieve. The patio of used bricks would become yet another of those stalled improvements that were apparent everywhere in the place: The wainscotting half stripped beneath the stairs, the pink primer on the worst of the window frames, the new garden plot by the road gate which had become a riot of twitch, the laundry tubs lying on the floor and the pipes to which they'd been connected plugged with corks. After a month or two the weathered string would be broken, and the sand pile scratched out by cats and dogs, while Miranda searched the small ads, if she remembered, for more bricks.

Diedre had a friend to play, to show that she had equal rights of hospitality within the family no doubt. The friend was a solid, freckled girl, all smiles, heavy brows, the complexion of an unripe strawberry, and just a year or two from the devastating realisation that she was plain. At our healthy lunch, when all the bricks had been placed, both girls were happy and talkative, and there was just one early moment when the friend surveyed the table, that her face allowed a fleeting but poignant bewilderment at all the glistening greenery, pale vegetable flesh and vinaigrette.

Andrew and I planned to play tennis at the high school courts in the afternoon, but the Telfers arrived soon after the meal. A massive, four-wheel drive gleaming in dark blue, and towing a jetboat. Mr Telfer came part way up the rough drive, and then realised that he wouldn't be able to turn because of the trees, and he just switched off there. He and his wife came smiling towards the verandah, sure of a welcome although they had given no warning of a visit. Wealth and affability are conducive to social ease, and besides they had been close neighbours when the Sumerbottoms lived in Island Bay. Mr Telfer wore a red linen shirt, pale trousers and a half smile as if a successful joke still lingered in his mind. Mrs Telfer was taller than her husband, more stylish, but less handsome, and careless of her arms and legs so that they always seemed to be reaching, flexing, crossing — blocking the passage of other people. 'Miranda, how wonderful,' she said, and claimed her with a long, silvered arm.

'We thought we'd drop in on the off chance,' he said. 'We're going boating for a day or two.'

Andrew got a beer for Mr Telfer, who sat smiling on the step next to a lion, and showed both interest and knowledge concerning university courses. He was a member of the vice-chancellor's industry advisory panel at Vic, though he said modestly that he couldn't figure out why they wanted him.

Miranda took Mrs Telfer on her tour of the house and grounds, and we heard their voices advancing and retreating as the two women wandered through the rooms, and then over the large section. Diedre and her friend followed for a time, attracted by the novelty of Mrs Telfer's extravagant arms and legs, but then they tired of the long stops during which Miranda outlined her plans, and went to watch television. 'Of course,' Miranda would say, 'there's just so much to be done, and you can't get the tradespeople you want at a drop of the hat out here. I'm determined not to rush it. I want to do it just the once, and do it right. I've had a really good landscape person recommended, who used to write regularly for *Contemporary* magazine.'

Mrs Telfer was entirely diplomatic and encouraging in what I heard of her replies. She marvelled at the trees, patting the great trunks as she would have the old Labrador — 'Money can't buy a hundred years of growth,' she said. She agreed with Miranda's hunch about the floorboards, one foot roving and tapping to check resonance — 'It must surely be the period of kauri flooring.' Yet when they came back to the verandah, when she held a glass of chardonnay, and after she had contained herself to some extent

within a basket chair, there was about her just a touch of conde-
scension that friendship couldn't repress. To see friends reduced in
circumstance arouses sympathy, but also a small human satisfaction,
celebration almost, that for the moment it isn't us.

I liked the Telfers. They were intelligent and conscious of the
feelings of those about them: they knew that their own lives were of
less interest to others than themselves. They were accustomed to
success and so believed, even with a touch of cynicism, in the benevolence of the world. And best of all, there was still tolerance and
humour between them after years of marriage.

When Mr Telfer stood up to leave there was a stain of lichen, or
bird shit, from the steps on the seat of his cream trousers, and
Miranda was full of apology. She was about to rub it with her small,
folded handkerchief when she realised that was too intimate and
drew back. 'Don't worry about it,' he said mildly.

'He's just a complete grub,' said his wife.

We all walked with the visitors to the car, and continued along-
side it as Mr Telfer backed slowly to the entrance, not an easy job
with the crowding trees, and a boat trailer behind.

Mrs Telfer gestured with one sinuous arm out of the window,
and carried on the conversation with Miranda, while Andrew and I
made up a sort of chorus of fatuous goodwill. Even Diedre and her
substantial friend had appeared, their interest in the Telfers renewed
by their departure.

And as the Telfers drove away in a panoply of expensive
machinery they would commiserate with the Sumerbottoms, voice
their apprehensions concerning the ambitions Miranda had for the
property, speculate as to the soundness of the marriage beset by
stress, shake their heads at the lapse that had cost Mr Sumerbottom
his professional reputation and savings, and then, refreshed, press
on to their boating recreation.

Miranda was stirred to even more activity and brightness by the
visit. Her eyes glittered, and her laugh became more frequent and
more brittle. She disappeared upstairs briefly and came back
wearing a silk top. 'I should have had it on earlier,' she said. 'Wasn't

it just a lovely surprise to see them. You were very friendly with Chris in Wellington, weren't you, Andrew?'

'He was okay.'

'Chris was only a year older than Andrew,' Miranda told me. 'He's doing medicine at Otago now.'

'He was okay,' said Andrew.

'They had a covered swimming pool,' said Diedre. She used the information to awe her friend, who nodded and smiled with acquiesence children often show when away from their own territory.

The Telfers took something of the afternoon's gloss with them: the sky clouded, the tabby vomited on the trampoline when the two girls tried to make it bounce, and when we inspected our work on the brick patio, there was less done than we'd remembered, and the surface was clearly uneven. Miranda responded by throwing herself into preparations for tea, and making Andrew scrape the front steps that had soiled Mr Telfer's trousers. 'It's too late now, Mum,' he said. 'And anyway the birds perch on the overhang there. It won't do any good.' But he did it all the same.

Miranda made an asparagus and blue cheese quiche, and chilled a bottle of Marlborough sav blanc. We held off until half past six, but then ate without Mr Sumerbottom. Even I knew it was a good quiche and I told her so, but that was one small thing against the day's tide of circumstance.

Andrew and I had brought swot books with us, and for an hour or so after the meal we made some effort to prepare ourselves for the coming exams. Diedre, bereft of her friend who had given up the wait for tea, completed her homework with greater success, and then wanted me to play swing-ball. She and I were playing in the half-dark when Mr Sumerbottom came home. He dragged his golf bag from the back seat and waved in answer to Diedre's calls. For a moment it seemed that he would walk over to us, but then he waved again and, tilted against the weight of his clubs, went inside.

I let Diedre win the last game: not difficult after the yellow ball caught me a blow on the left eye in the dusk. She looked up at the first of the stars. 'Yes,' she said fervently, 'I am the champion.' When she went inside, after giving me an innocent, friendly hug, I walked through the trees to the road gate, and on towards the town for a few minutes. Quiet, dark farmland was behind me, and the strung lights ahead. I'd been with the Sumerbottoms for less than two full days, and already the family disconcerted me with its vulnerability. My own people were wary, humorously pessimistic, and kept a shield of emotional reticence against the vicissitudes of life.

At that turning time before full darkness, there was complete stillness in the world. Few cars came down the road that led to the main street, no people looked in the windows of the few closed shops ahead of me, no music sounded from the houses whose lights were yellow lamps. The trees and shrubs were dark masses as steady as the buildings and all the birds had gone to roost. The town at night was swamped by the fragrances of all that countryside around it: pine windbreaks, hay sheds, turned soil, the cloying drift of dairy effluent. At the pubs there would have been some leisurely talk and movement, fried food, but I didn't walk that far, instead turning at a transport yard and walking back to the Sumerbottoms. Long before I reached the place I could see the dark towers of its trees, higher than any others around.

As I came through those trees on the dark, uneven drive I saw that the Sumerbottoms were inspecting our morning's work on the brick patio. The side door was open, and Miranda and Mr Sumerbottom outlined there in the spilling light. 'Oh well, it's a start,' he said. I stopped to listen, and ran my fingers through the soft leaves of a sycamore.

'We need to get a lot more demolition bricks,' Miranda said.

'We need to get out of this place,' Mr Sumerbottom said with sudden bitterness. 'I'd like to ditch the whole idea of a fancy bed and breakfast, and go back to Wellington. I can hardly believe that we've ended up like this. How's it happened?'

Miranda didn't say anything for a while; maybe she was deciding whether she wanted to get into all that. She came out on to the freshly laid bricks and looked directly back at him. 'The Wellington life's gone now,' she said. 'I realised that again when the Telfers were here this afternoon. All that's gone.' There was no accusation in her tone, just finality.

'You know, after golf today I stayed on drinking and talking, and I knew I should have been getting back here for tea, and I didn't want to. Not you, of course, but this house and all the stuff to be done, and no bugger comes here anyway, despite the advertising. We'll go bankrupt soon: I just know it.'

'We're only getting under way though.'

'And I don't even like most of the guys at golf here, yet I could've sat with them all night. We're in a tail-spin. I can see us going bankrupt.'

'Home-stay tourism's what everybody recommended. It's a boom thing, but you have to give it time to take off.' Miranda went back into the doorway and stood close to him. Her stance, her voice, her lifted face, were all part of a positive attitude she didn't dare let go.

'We're coming down in the world. After all this time I'm working for somebody else,' said Mr Sumerbottom. Maybe the drinks in the golf club had allowed him to release his regrets and fears. 'I know — Jesus, you don't have to tell me why it's all happened, but it's hard isn't it, coming down in the world.'

'It must, must, work out, though,' she said. Her voice was lower than before, yet with greater intensity. It barely carried through the night to where I stood beneath the sycamore.

'No, but we are. We're down-sizing on everything, including our opinions of ourselves.'

Miranda closed the door then, and although I could still see them through the glass, I couldn't hear any more. They were both slender, nimble, and at that distance could have been two much younger people starting out together. I waited among the night trees a while longer before going up between the lions to the front door. I didn't want the Sumerbottoms to suspect they had been overheard.

I wanted the next day to be there already. I wanted Miranda to have dropped us off at Massey and to be driving away like a jack-in-the-box at the wheel of the Corona. I no longer wanted to be an observer of the family. Some people are born sport for the fates. I could pick a future for them. Andrew would press on under the guise of amiable laughing stock, innocent Diedre would have something terrible befall her in the park on the way back from music lessons, Mr Sumerbottom must suffer increasing humiliation because of his own weakness. Miranda, worst of all, would pit her bright desperation against the odds in an anguish that is more than pain: that becomes a bewilderment of suffering.

Maybe all that and more has happened. Just an hour ago I looked for the Sumerbottoms' place, and found six squat town-houses on its site. 'Do you remember a family called Sumerbottom?' I ask Clarry. He laughs, then realises I'm not joking. 'Years ago,' I say, 'they had that great big tiled place in Powys Street, but it's been replaced by townhouses now.'

'It was the homestead of the Wattlington estate,' says Clarry, still holding the milk that is rightfully mine, 'but I don't ever remember any Sumerbottoms having anything to do with it. There's no local family called that.'

So Elvis Presley lives on here, from beyond the grave and the other side of the world, but I seem to be the only one who remembers the Sumerbottoms.

ENDSONG

Everything they did was observed, everything they said was overheard, by the fat woman in the other cubicle bed. Frank had become accustomed to it over many visits, as an actor in a small theatre becomes accustomed to the front row audience.

'You'll need to have the roses pruned,' said Frank's wife. 'Have you got Lloyd's number? It should be in the blue pad, but if you can't find it ring Michelle. She'll have it because he does some work for her too.'

'I could give it a go myself maybe.'

'No. Better to get Lloyd in. It's only a couple of hours.'

The fat woman's dark eyes were fixed on him, and she was plumped up on three pillows. She had visitors of her own sometimes, Frank's wife told him, but he'd never seen anyone. She was a successful florist with cancer of the spine.

'Geoff and Helen Wittem called in,' said his wife after one of the long silences they had become accustomed to. 'They were coming through to a wedding in Christchurch, and Mary had told them I was bad again.'

'Oh, that's nice. He'd be retired now?'

'No, he's got a new job as an auditor for some top accounting outfit. He seemed pleased about it.'

Frank recalled them as near neighbours when they lived in Nelson. Their main connection had been to babysit each other's children. Helen was a mad jogger, and used to go out white and come back flushed as a tomato. Frank remembered that, although he couldn't bring her face to mind. Was it enduring sympathy, or morbid curiosity, that caused such old neighbours to visit after twenty years indifference.

'What was the youngest one called?' his wife asked. 'I've been lying here since they went trying to come up with it. Do you think I can.'

'One was called Roderick.'

'No, that's not the one. And the older girl was Margaret.'

'Has Dr Williamson been round.'

'No one says anything. They come round, but it doesn't mean you get told much more.'

'That's them all right,' he said. He didn't want to see how thin his wife's arm was, lying like a piece of old vine on the cover. The fat woman, who he knew quite well was Mrs Secker, swayed from side to side cautiously in an endeavour to get comfortable in the bed. Her face creased with the pain of it, and her dark eyes turned up to the ceiling. Frank and his wife paused in their conversation until she was settled again. Proximity conveys certain rights, even though she had no place in the conversation.

'Is there anything you want brought in?' he said. She shook her head, but moved a finger towards a supermarket bag of her washing. 'I suppose I'll be on my way then,' he said. He gave her a kiss on the cheek while she looked listlessly towards the corridor. The sound of laughter in the carpark seemed removed in time rather than space. There were floral scents in the ward, but despite the evidence of true flowers, the smell was rather of a canned freshener. Frank gave a wave at the doorway, and the fat woman, who must have known all about false flowers, relaxed back on her pillows as if his visit had been a matter of endurance for her. His shoes gave a soft squeak on the lino which seemed to have been rendered supple by constant applications of polish, or maybe late at night patients gnawed at it as Inuit women did seal skins.

All their lives this place and condition had been waiting for them. Through good times and bad this destination had remained constant though they had no knowledge of it, and that ignorance was a guise of mercy.

Frank decided to get a Chinese takeaway on his way home, but drove past the shop thinking of his wife's loss of weight. There were still hours of daylight, and after he had put a small load of washing through, and made himself ham sandwiches, he went into the garden and carefully anointed dock leaves and twitch grass with the weedkiller stick that was so selective he could stroke enemies nestled beside the most tender of flowers. It was such an indirect and blameless act of execution, wasn't it: the weeds remaining prosperous and full in appearance even though a sure end had been dealt them. Frank found a satisfaction in it that went unquestioned. The evening sun was warm on his stooping back, and helped him to straighten with just a couple of pauses for the kinks of late middle age.

He put the weed stick in the chest of drawers that stood at the back of the garage. The dark chest had been part of a wedding bedroom suite from his wife's parents, gradually demoted through the years to less important rooms in the house, and finally evicted altogether. The brass handles had been reused for rimu furniture many years before, and Frank had clumsily fashioned substitutes of number eight wire. The dark top was scarred, ringed with lighter paint marks. Stacked plastic plant pots, secateurs, wizened bulbs and discarded labels bearing the Latin names of plants, lay where once there had been delicate doilies to protect the gloss, and photographs of their children in silver frames. Frank had just the faintest frisson of all that as he closed the drawer and went back to stand in the sun at the garage door.

His neighbour walked nearby with only the low box hedge between them, and hesitated as if wanting to give some support, but then just smiled, lifted a hand and went on into his own house. Three years ago the neighbour and Frank had a falling out over an elm on Frank's property which was squeezing the fence, but since the illness of Frank's wife all was peace between them.

The evening air was ripe with autumn scents, and reminded Frank of the cricket practices and games he'd had at such times: bat and ball and laughter until the first two were ended by the dusk, and then they'd turn to beer.

Cricket was long past, but he could still enjoy a beer, couldn't he? He went inside for his dark sports jacket and then drove to the King Dick by the bus station. An older pub: weatherboard sides, dark interiors and red Formica, no dance floor and no tables on the pavement. Frank wasn't a regular at any pub, but when he did go it was usually there. It didn't get too crowded and wasn't fashionable enough to be a dating place. He thought that he'd have just a beer, but heard himself order a whisky chaser as well, and he sat on one of the bench seats by the window and watched the people in the street and at the bus station opposite it. As well as unmistakable Kiwis, there were a few strong backpackers in shorts who sat on the steps at ease with their foreignness.

'Hello, Frank,' said Marie Farnley. Her wheelchair took up almost all the space between his window bench and the bar stools.

'How's Anne at the moment?' Her face tilted to the side in sympathy. Her blue jeans looked as if they'd been stuffed tight with straw, and the black boots at the end of them were square on the footrests.

'Oh, you know. Not so good — much the same. I suppose the chemo's the best thing, but it knocks her around.'

'I'd go in even more often if it was a bit easier.'

'I know. She enjoys your visits.' Marie was almost family, had worked with his wife at the reading recovery centre, and had often come round to the house to play bridge, or discuss the programmes they used at the centre and the exasperating attitudes of their bosses.

'Let me get you a drink,' he said, and when he'd done that they shifted into the body of the bar so that her wheelchair didn't block people coming past. 'So how are things with you?' he said.

'Don't ask,' she said, but then went on to tell him of the atrophy problems, her children wanting her to sell the house, the bosses at the centre being no better than when Frank's wife left.

'One or two of the recovery people have been round to see her,' said Frank. 'Last week there was this very tall woman who'd missed out at school because of something.'

'She was dyslexic,' said Marie. 'Isn't that nice she went.'

'And a kid with a baseball cap on back the front.'

'Can't think who that would be.'

'Part Maori I'd say, and trousers way too big for him.'

'No, can't pick him at all,' said Marie.

Marie's drink was white wine, and Frank switched to that when he got another for her. That would do him then. He'd never been much of drinker, and his wife wasn't either.

'Anne quite likes a chardonnay,' he said.

'She does,' said Marie.

'God knows what I'll do with all her things. She never could throw anything out. It might come in useful, she'd say, but the trouble is with that you end up with so much stuff you can never lay your hand on the odd thing you do want to find again anyway.'

'She told me you've been marvellous throughout everything.'

'Did she?'

'It made her think about how strong you'd been years ago, she said. I suppose she meant those times when Ben should have died of asthma.'

'He's come through all that now. Doesn't have much trouble at all.'

One of Marie's boots had moved to be half off the plate, and she leant right down with surprising agility and moved it back with her left hand so that the heel clicked over the back. 'Will he come over again?' she asked.

'He's flown over twice. Anne says it's not fair and she doesn't want him to be phoned again, but I'll probably let him know when the doctor says it's all up. He should be able to make up his own mind. After all Michelle's quite handy, it's all right for her.'

Frank wondered if Marie had come to the pub alone, or if she was waiting for friends to arrive. Maybe they were there already, but as he looked around the room he didn't see anyone likely. 'I'd better get going,' he said. 'You okay?'

'A maxi-taxi comes to get me whenever I'm ready,' Marie said. 'It's got that attachment thing for the chair. All part of the service.'

In front of him, she wheeled out into the darkening carpark. 'Oh, it'll do me good to get a breath of air,' she said. Frank wondered how come the legs of her jeans seemed so tight if atrophy was a problem. Maybe the circulation wasn't so good and she had to wear some layers to keep her legs warm. Frank didn't get into the car immediately. He stood beside Marie and they both looked out across the carpark to the bus station on the far side of the street. It was well lit there, but obviously nothing was due to come or go soon, because there weren't many people, and those that were there looked settled for a fair wait. One backpacker lay stretched on a seat apparently asleep. 'I don't know what to say really,' Marie said.

'You've been through plenty yourself.'

'I'll get up sometime this week. One of the things is that fat woman in the room with her. It's so difficult to talk with her there.'

'She's a florist with cancer,' said Frank. 'And the odd thing is she never gets brought any flowers.'

'It's such a thing for you both to go through, isn't it, but she really did tell me that you were strong.'

Frank put a hand on Marie's brown, smooth hair and stroked it. 'You always did have lovely hair,' he said.

'I used to have good legs too.'

He took his hand away and opened the door. 'Here you are worrying about Anne and me, and God, what about the stuff you have to put up with.'

'All in all you've been a bloody good husband to Anne,' said Marie. 'Don't you worry about that.'

'Do you ever hear anything from Paul?' he said.

'Not a bloody thing. He could be dead for all the kids and I know.'

'The whole thing was too much for him. He couldn't bear to be around after that I reckon.'

'You tell Anne I'll be up before Friday for sure,' she said.

Frank remembered to put on his lights as he drove away. He wished he'd been able to give more support to Marie, say something that would be meaningful, but grief made him selfish and sapped his energy as well. He drove towards the hospital rather than home. He felt he was on a long, hard journey with nothing to look forward to at the end of it. Sometimes, depending on the nurses, he was allowed in for a while even quite late at night. Sometimes the fat florist was soundly sedated, then he and his wife could talk as if alone, or be quiet together without being watched.

TRUSTY AND WELL BELOVED

Neither of them had sought a career in the armed forces, neither had been fired by adolescent cinema hunger for two-fisted heroism. Charlie Tan was set to complete a degree in engineering, enjoyed surfing, Garrick Swanson had a BA in geography, tinkered with photography. They had been brought together as twenty-year-olds by the birthday lottery National Service of the sixties, and selected for officer courses after the months of basic training not by reason of outstanding aptitude, but because of their academic backgrounds. Maybe it was the hangover from the British system that had automatically awarded pips to the chinless wonders of the public schools and universities.

Charlie was from Auckland, which needs no further identification. Garrick was from Moa Creek, which is an expanse of tussock at the top of the Ida Valley in Central Otago. People die of frostbite there, rather than pollution. They had barely met during basic training at Waiouru, but were together for the FACC — first appointment to commission course. Both instructors and members squeezed a good deal of humour from the acronym. God knows, any source of humour was scarce enough.

Thirty-two began the FACC, and six were bumped before it

finished for a variety of reasons, including concussion from a swinging log on the confidence course, endemic lack of a team ethic and the enervating effects of persistent masturbation. Garrick and Charlie passed out in the undistinguished lower quartile, but they passed. There was a special parade at which they received their commissions from the full colonel in charge of Waiouru, and the ramrod CSM, who had been persecuting them as cock-suckers and morons for weeks, shook their hands and called them sir with a sneering civility.

There was a social get-together after the passing-out parade, with the twenty-six new second lieutenants already withdrawing from the enforced intimacy of the course back to the stronger confederacy of families, friends and lovers. Most were anxious to leave, rather than stand in the C Block gymnasium on a grey afternoon eating regulation scones and lamingtons from the trestle table, and drinking urn tea out of the officers' mess second-best china. In a place so ingrained with fretful routine, and forced, anxious diligence, Charlie, Garrick and their fellows felt little exhilaration in their new status. For them the wall bars still creaked with effort, the trussed high ropes signalled exhaustion, and the whole barn-like space reeked of physical exertion.

Most of the course departed with family, or friends, but Charlie and Garrick were to be taken by Landrover to the station to catch a train south. Charlie wanted to visit a girl in Wellington, and Garrick was set to see his parents at Moa Creek.

They went back to the barrack room to get their kit bags, and sat on the step, each with his beret on a knee, and waited. The beds had been stripped and the room cleaned and regimented. Everything was commonplace and well used, but the wooden beds and kit boxes were exactly in line, and the faded windowsills had not a speck of dust.

From habit, Garrick passed his handkerchief over his glistening number one boots, and then, to pass the time, read the opening formalities from his commission scroll. 'ELIZABETH THE SECOND, by the grace of God of the United Kingdom, New Zealand and her other realms and territories Queen, Head of the Commonwealth, Defender of the Faith. To our trusty and well beloved GARRICK NORMAN ASHLEY SWANSON —'

'Norman Ashley,' said Charlie. 'Jesus, I didn't know that.'

'So what's yours?'

'Charlie Liang Tan,' said Charlie, without bothering to unroll his scroll.

'Maybe you'll be our only fucking Chinese officer in the whole Kiwi army,' said Garrick, settling back on his kit bag.

There was a cock-up in the travel arrangements: it wouldn't have been the army otherwise. No Landrover came for them, and when Charlie and Garrick walked down to the orderly room with their kit bags a weight on their shoulders, the corporal there said that transport had stuffed up again. He seemed oblivious to their newly achieved rank, and treated them the same as he had always done. 'I dunno,' he said. 'Those useless bastards. God save us from the transport if there's ever a war.'

'So what now then?' said Charlie.

'You'll never make the train now,' the corporal said. 'I can jack you up billets for the night I suppose.'

Garrick and Charlie didn't want to spend another night in Waiouru: a two-person remnant of a course officially no longer in existence. 'I've got an aunt in Taihape,' said Charlie. 'Maybe we can stay there.'

'You've never been there during the course.'

'Well, she's not really an aunt. One of those family friends you call aunt because it's simpler. Aunt Rita was the bakery supervisor in Mount Eden years ago, and my mother worked there for a year or two. They kept in touch and visited and that, and Rita married a master baker much older, and they shifted to Taihape. My mother's been telling me to ring her up.'

Charlie did get in touch. He used the orderly room telephone and rang Rita. Garrick and the corporal could hear Aunt Rita's every shrill word; the excitement in her voice at hearing from the Tan boy, the declaration that it was no bother to have him and Garrick for the night, her determination to drive in right away and pick them up. 'See you soon then at the main gates,' said Charlie. He knew what a rabbit warren the camp was to civilians. 'Thanks, Aunt Rita.'

'I could get on to transport for someone to take you out to the entrance,' said the corporal.

'Don't bother,' said Charlie.

'You're right. Pack of dozy pricks the lot of them,' said the corporal, and he watched the subalterns settle their bags for balance on their shoulders and walk steadily across the parade ground. It was six o'clock on that grey day and the camp was surprisingly quiet — no jogging squads, tanks, high-pitched parade commands. Training was over and most soldiers would be smartening up in their barracks for mess parade. Charlie and Garrick walked past the rows of similar wooden buildings, falling into step from habit. Their jungle greens were well matched and the kit bags slightly lighter in colour.

Taihape isn't far away, but Charlie Tan and Garrick Swanson sat by the main gates for a considerable time before an Austin 1100 did a U-turn and drew up beside them. It was a dull military green itself, the paint almost furry with neglect, and had a list to the driver's side. Aunt Rita's bulk was the explanation, and in her tent-like floral dress she almost filled the interior, with little distinction made between front and rear seats. That model was naturally a low car, and further depressed by Rita. Her bun face was at the level of their knees, and she peered up cheerfully at Charlie and Garrick, while they bent down to be polite. 'You haven't changed a bit, Charlie,' she said, looking at Garrick. 'Not a bit since you were just a whippersnapper.' Garrick had developed a good tan during the course, but he didn't think that he'd turned into one.

'This is my friend Garrick Swanson,' said Charlie.

'Oh, I do like a man in uniform,' said Rita, and convulsed for a moment in an effort to get her arm out of the window to shake hands. The manoeuvre was beyond her, but in the struggle she stamped on the accelerator, became flustered when the engine revved to a scream, and shouted above it, 'Hop in. Hop in and we'll head away.'

Garrick and Charlie almost had to get on their knees, but they did hop in, Charlie in front as befitted his accredited relationship with Aunt Rita, and Garrick in the back, which he shared with both kit bags. Rita worked her way through the gears until, in top, they were doing a vibrating sixty-three ks down the Desert Road. The two guys leant to their left in an unconscious effort to even up the weight distribution, and watched the succession of eye-level hubcaps as other vehicles overtook them. 'Fancy becoming an officer,' shouted Rita. 'Why, it's just like a title, isn't it. I saw on television you have ceremonial swords and pass the port to the left. Have you got your swords yet?'

'Not yet,' said Charlie.

'Why not?' she shrieked as a stock truck passed, the draught almost blowing the Austin from the road.

'Pardon?'

'Why not a sword then?'

'We haven't joined a corps yet,' said Charlie. Rita nodded: corps was an impressive military word and she was happy to accept it as an explanation.

Garrick had always thought of Taihape as a series of false fronts on the main street, a sort of grotesque movie set you saw fleetingly from car, bus or train, but in which no one had to live. He realised he was wrong when Rita turned into the side-streets, and a three-dimensional reality emerged: houses, correctly dwindling in perspective, a large birch tree flexing in the breeze, a small girl with a clamped, pugnacious face, glowering from her pushchair.

Aunt Rita's house was weatherboard and painted cream. It had sorely tested geraniums at the front entrance, and a stag etched on the frosted glass of the door. A Morris Oxford and a Vauxhall Velox were parked on the dual concrete strips to the garage. Rita pulled up behind them. 'My Scrabble partners are here today,' she said. 'It's a lucky chance that we can all be company. Bertha and May their names are, but you'll meet them inside. We're regional finalists,' she said. Charlie and Garrick wormed their way out of the car, and waited while Rita got her legs steady on the concrete, then heaved herself upright. She leant a little into the wind which bore on the considerable expanse of her floral dress so that the gargantuan physical topography beneath was clear. 'How is your mother?' she asked Garrick kindly. A nondescript spaniel came trotting from the yard and clasped Charlie's leg with orgiastic fervour. 'Oscar Wilde gets excited with visitors,' said Aunt Rita. 'Take no notice.' Charlie gave the dog a back kick as Rita turned to head for the door.

'Jesus,' said Charlie quietly.

Amorphous, fluctuating colours could be seen behind the etched stag, and when Rita opened the door there was a greeting line of three people in the narrow hall. May was first, probably because she was very short and the others could easily see over her. She had straight dark hair, a diminutive smile and a line of cardigan buttons that stretched from top to toe. Bertha was very upright, had her hair in a bun and was incessantly cocking her head like a yard chicken. '

And this is my husband, Rudolph. Rudy we call him,' said Rita of the last in the line. For a moment Garrick thought he must have misheard. No one was called Rudolph, surely. Rudolph stood, almost invisible behind Bertha, in the half-crouch of old age, as if fossilised in some long lost judo posture. When Charlie and Garrick shook his large, unresponsive hand, he repeated his own name in a strange, hollow and whispered courtesy that was the remnant of his former charm.

There was something of a jostle in the narrow passage to move into the living room, and there it was realised that they were one short. Rudolph was found patiently stymied between the door and the passage wall, and Rita brought him in and sat him like Abe Lincoln in a long-armed, wooden chair. 'He's not so old,' said Rita. 'He still sometimes goes to the bakery. You never lose expertise, you know.'

'Knowledge,' said Bertha.

'Wisdom,' said May.

'Yes, skill always remains,' said Rita.

'Understanding,' said May.

'Lore,' said Bertha.

Over half the world's population was female, thought Charlie bitterly, and yet here he was — a newly commissioned officer bursting with hormones — with his mother's fat friend, and May and Bertha. Life seemed to lack some natural fitness and justice.

While Rita had been picking up Charlie and Garrick, Bertha and May had been to Ted's Takeaways and brought back tea. It was a special treat to celebrate the threesome's selection as regional Scrabble reps and the visit of two of Her Majesty's officers. The feast was in the oven, and scents of shark, paua patties, hot dogs and chips were strong everywhere. The newspaper caught fire, but the brief flurry to extinguish it created a sort of febrile gaiety rather than consternation, and Rita brought plates of the unharmed food to the red formica table that separated kitchen from living room. 'How appetizing,' shrilled May, whose bobbing head barely appeared above the table level.

'Toothsome,' said Rita.

'Palatable,' said Bertha.

'Beer, Rudy. We need beer,' said Rita. Rudolph was still in his chair, and his only preparation to join the others already standing at the table was to begin the transference of his weight by leaning forward. Obviously the efficient manner of providing beer to the table was for Rita to fetch it, but she deferred to this last male prerogative in a way almost touching. When Rita and Rudolph had married in Mount Eden the age difference had given him a certain authority in their partnership, but time had reversed their roles, and now he was just a cypher dependent on her goodwill. To Rita's credit that goodwill persisted.

Rudolph made his way out across the tame carpet with the caution others might show on the Matterhorn, and after time enough for anyone else to walk the block, reappeared with a full flagon clutched in both arms. Charlie and Garrick moved aside to allow him a path to the table, and he successfully positioned the flagon on the formica by the six spotted Marmite jars, staggering back slightly when the release of the weight affected his equilibrium.

'Nectar,' exclaimed Bertha.

'Elixir,' followed May.

'Quintessence,' said Rita, and Rudolph gaped and whispered as the cynosure of their admiration, while his quivering hand sought to gain purchase on a pattie wonderfully glistening with fat. Ted was unsurpassed as a chef in Taihape.

The warmth of the feast broke out on their glowing features, and the draught beer had just that cutting astringency draught beer should have. Rita made a toast to old friends, of whom Charlie was the token, and to all the brave army lads who would stand firm against the yellow peril. Given Charlie's skin colour, Garrick could hardly believe Rita intended no irony, but her face and tone bore no hint of it. Charlie told a story about the grenade range, Bertha described a radio documentary about Gallipoli. They swayed and ate and drank; even Oscar Wilde desisted from advances long enough to steal food from Rudolph's hand each time it sank at the call of gravity.

At Waiouru Garrick and Charlie had begun to smoke small, dark cheroots — perhaps expressing an unconscious desire for some trivial idiosyncrasy in a uniform society. Rather to their surprise, Rita and Bertha accepted one also, but not May, who was already conscious of stunted growth. Rudolph took one, but the evening wasn't long enough for him to get it lit, what with his duties as co-host. 'Beer, Rudy,' said Rita, once the flagon was three-quarters empty, and he began his trek to the laundry again, pausing in the doorway with the gravitas of Captain Oates, and reappearing not much sooner with another flagon.

Because May's head was only at the level of the young men's waists, she was much struck by the highly polished brass of their web belts. 'I can almost see my face in the buckle. My goodness, what a burnish,' she said, and undid a mere half-dozen cardigan buttons in the heat.

'Gloss,' supported Rita.

'Lustre,' said Bertha. 'The army's the making of a man, I always say. Always say it. Rudy was in both wars of course: Kitchener, Rommel, the Desert Rats, over the top, Peter O'Toole, all of that. Weren't you, Rudy?' Rudolph was back in his chair and feeding

Oscar Wilde a chip. Rita loomed over him and shouted, 'Weren't you, Rudy? War, Rudy.' He cast his eyes up imploringly at the sound of war, and his mouth stretched open silently to show a mixture of Ted's paua patties and chips. 'Don't talk to Rudy about war,' said Rita emphatically, as if he had explained all in a glance.

'Men are instinctively belligerent,' said Bertha, her head quick and alert. It was a topic that seemed to galvanise the team.

'Adversarial,' said May.

'Antagonistic,' said Rita.

'Combative,' said Bertha.

'Pugnacious,' said May.

'Bellicose,' finished Rita.

Rudolph said nothing at all, Charlie and Garrick competed for the shark in batter as was the nature of their sex and Oscar Wilde put his paws on the red formica and lapped quickly at a puddle of beer.

It grew very dark outside, but Rita didn't draw the curtains, and May and Bertha made no move to leave. Garrick wondered if all of them were somehow to spend the night in the same small house, and was drunk enough to be reconciled to sharing with anyone except Oscar Wilde. 'Now we'll sing "Hang Down Your Head Tom Dooley".' said May firmly, and they did. The longer they were together, the more they drank, the less each of them was inhibited by being very small, or very fat, very old, very yellow, very rural, or having hair in a bun — or even by being born a spaniel. They sang and yapped, Rudolph fell into a perfect sleep despite the din, and the darkness pressed on the window like velvet.

Garrick fetched his commission scroll to display the impressive seal, and read from it on request. 'We, reposing especial trust and confidence in your loyalty, courage and good conduct do by these presents constitute and appoint and recognise you to be an officer in the said territorial forces of our New Zealand.'

'Oh, from Elizabeth herself,' called Rita, and she lifted her Marmite jar and proposed a toast to the sovereign. What a comfort such loyal subjects would have been to Elizabeth the Second if she had seen them. Then Rudolph was temporarily woken so that he could stand as a veteran of two wars for the singing of 'God Save the Queen'. Garrick shook his leg free from the libidinous Oscar Wilde to do likewise, and May, even though upright, thought to remain so low was somehow disrespectful, and stood on the white kitchen stool. They sang heartily in the small, bright room, while the darkness lay over the Desert Road and all the world spun on its hub — Taihape, New Zealand.

NATURAL SELECTION

LECTURER IN HUMANITIES, vacancy C108, the advertisement said; postgraduate qualification expected and experience in teaching at tertiary level an advantage. And a job description had been available on demand.

'It would be fair to say,' said the dean, 'that the college is looking for a candidate with specific strengths in New Zealand history, although outstanding geographers should feel at no disadvantage, and with a national review of social studies syllabi imminent the relevance there is obvious. In fact we have a high level of flexible expertise within the humanities department.' The dean was taking the rather unusual step of talking to the shortlist candidates as a group before beginning interviews. He considered it the fairest way to achieve a level playing field, and save time, though Ronald Prydam, who represented lecturing staff on the dean's panel, had expressed doubts concerning confidentiality. Not every candidate perhaps wanted to sit en masse.

In a literal sense the eleven candidates gathered for interview were already conscious of the level playing field: it stretched away below the second floor of the Judkins Wing and from it came the clock, clock of the ball on hockey sticks as a group of secondary trainee art historians had the second of their twice-weekly PE rec periods.

'In a very real way,' the dean was saying, 'you have already succeeded by being accorded an interview, and the college will be the loser in that it is unable to offer more than one of you a position at present.' To the west of the games field was a line of silver birches and then the rather practical central brick block of the college of education.

'It is a long time since we on the interview panel have perused such an impressive collection of CVs.' Beneath the second-storey windows of the Judkins Wing a gardener was working the rose beds. He had a handcart with spoked bicycle wheels for the weeds and a transistor hung on one of the handles. 'Don't dream it's over,' sang Crowded House. 'Let me assure you all,' said the dean, 'that we are committed to being an equal opportunity employer.'

At the conclusion of his introduction, the dean asked for any queries from the eleven, before ten of them went off to pass the time before their interviews, and one waited to be invited in to see the panel. An Australian with a bow-tie confirmed the dean's initial dislike of him by asking searching questions concerning salary and superannuation.

By 11.20, two of the short-list had already been interviewed. Besides the dean and Prydam, the panel comprised Mervyn Sisley from senior management, Rebecca Hadlow from the council's appointments committee and Pia Greer from whanau and equity.

The third interviewee had played netball for New Zealand and thereafter done occasional television commentating on the sport. All those on the panel were aware of that, but no one made mention of it. Nevertheless, for the first time Mervyn Sisley took some notes. Sisley was one of two deputy principals of the college and represented the chief executive, whom he knew to be very interested in obtaining staff with a public profile. In the end, the chief executive always told Sisley, everything is political, and everything that is political is concerned with perceived advantage.

Following Prydam's questions concerning academic achievement,

Sisley engineered an opportunity for the applicant to mention the positive comment from Massey on her research diploma and the breadth of experience concerning young people that had occurred from a tour as manager-coach of a youth development squad. 'So much depends on rapport in instruction,' said Sisley. 'So much in motivation is the provision of a role model.'

'Exactly so,' said Ms Hadlow.

'Young women united in successful endeavour and at an international level,' said Pia Greer.

'Quite, quite,' said the dean and he asked the candidate whether she thought that the history of Pacific rim countries was sufficiently represented in existing prescriptions.

The dean had begun to realise in the last year or two that his star had passed its zenith: that while he held undisputed intellectual sway within his humanities, nevertheless, philosophies of management and macro-education foreign to him were pervasive throughout the college as a whole. Even his *New Zealand and the Twentieth-Century World* no longer bestrode the senior school syllabus like a colossus. And no longer could he appoint staff from a CV comparison of their academic distinctions alone. Everything seemed subject to recommendation and review. And so much time was taken up in committee which could be better spent in solid lecturing, or wine and reminiscence with friends.

The fifth interviewee had briefly worked at the college before, and then secured a place at the Braisely Institute, which had turned out badly through little fault of his own. The light cynicism of professional ambition was turning to bitterness, and he made a tart remark about feminist perspectives which wasn't representative of his beliefs, but which cost him all the same. Prydam felt sympathy for him, and part of that sympathy was a recognition that he could himself have made one career move that proved treacherous and found himself chasing shortlists for positions formerly his as of right.

Pia Greer marvelled at how easily a man considers himself victimised, how much of his ego is always on display. She thought of all those women who had encountered not just bad luck in their profession, but habitual discrimination and persistent, casual dispar-agement. Let the wheel turn a little, perhaps. 'No, no I'm very interested in your frank expression of view,' she said. 'Let rip by all means.'

Rebecca Hadlow, too, considered that there was an underlying sense of reproach and grievance in the applicant which would only add to the sum of such feelings already sufficiently developed among the students at the college. On the other hand, she appreciated the man's ascetic features: Rebecca Hadlow had an almost intestinal dislike of flab in man, or woman, and bitterness has an astringent effect in most cases. The interviewee's face was narrow, sharp and the tendons of his neck a supple gantry. Despite herself, Rebecca made the comparison with the bison shoulders of the dean, Sisley's well-fed cheeks, even Pia Greer's self-accepting amplitude.

She wouldn't have lunch at the staff club, Rebecca decided: all those hot, savoury dishes in the warming trays. Instead she would drive home and have a cucumber and pear open sandwich, ring her dying mother, clean the tiles of the en suite bathroom and be back in time for the afternoon interviews. She was pleased that she had chosen to wear the lightweight ruff blouse, for the interview room caught more and more of the sun as the morning wore on.

The gardener in the rose bed gave a loud belch, or such it was assumed, and the panel smiled at such a human interruption to the bitter candidate's account of his paper on teaching strategies for inte-grated learning delivered to a plenary session of a Brisbane conference. 'Quite, quite,' said the dean, to get things going again.

Ronald Prydam developed an antipathy to the next candidate after being picked up on an error concerning the drop-out rate of teacher trainees. Prydam gave no outward sign of animosity, however. The candidate had an excellent CV and references, but he wore green corduroys, and had a very bald head with freckles. The last two features would certainly outweigh the first two in a compet-itive field, although, of course, in any general panel discussion they wouldn't be mentioned. Prydam knew that the chief executive wouldn't countenance such a man as an ambassador for the college.

Rebecca Hadlow was aware that baldness was a hereditary trait from the distaff side, but nevertheless had always an illogical but persistent feeling that it was brought on by minor and complacent self-neglect. Pia Greer, on the other hand, found herself in unlikely alliance with the dean in somewhat encouraging the corduroy man, not so much because of his Newcastle PhD and numerous publications, but because of the total lack of any macho self-awareness. Such a man would be a comfortable addition to staff: a man whose collegiality would be more in evidence than his gender. Greer doubted, however, that he could ever be a potent factor in advancing college netball.

The dean enjoyed his lunch: some pan-fried sole with buffalo chips and a local riesling. Sisley needed to spend some time in his office, and Hadlow said that she wished to check on her mother's health, but Ronald Prydam and Pia Greer sat with the dean in the staff club and listened to his anecdotes of past hard cases on the staff — all male, Greer noted.

Prydam was only mildly attentive, for he was a mathematician and so not immediately within the dean's sphere. As lecturers' representative, he had come to see where the pump was best primed for the future. He wondered if it would be too obvious to go to Mervyn Sisley's office, and ask if there was anything he could assist with before the afternoon interviews. A quick check of budget forecasts perhaps, or a perceptive comment on the computer teaching-space allocations. Maybe Sisley hadn't noticed the Newcastle PhD score with the student drop-out figures.

The three of them walked back through campus to the Judkins Wing. There were small trees in concrete pots to ameliorate the stark parking area, and on the lawns the students grouped to lounge, laugh and wave their multicoloured sneakers in the air. The dean joked with Pia Greer about the women's studies course, and wondered with a first apprehension if he would ever finish his book on the influence of personal First World War experience on New Zealand politicians and politics. Greer watched the students and wished that she was with her third-year group as scheduled rather than her present company. Prydam maintained a jaunty air, but thought of the state of his marriage and could see no way forward. He gave a fierce laugh as a response to one of Pia's comments, and the tears gathered for a moment in his eyes.

The first candidate the panel saw after lunch was the principal of a school of over nine hundred students. She had as much profile, both literal and figurative, as even the chief executive could possibly require and came from a family that featured prominently in the dean's research for his projected history. In fact, he was for an instant tempted to take advantage of the position to ask her if she had any store of family papers. 'A signal service to secondary education, I feel bound to say. We have your students represented in our intake in a conspicuous way,' was what he said eventually, however.

'Certainly the administrative experience is impressive,' said Sisley.

'I admire what you have achieved in a patriarchal system by dedication and sheer professionalism,' said Pia Greer.

'I see that you have had fellowships at both Massey and the Tuffnell Institute,' was Prydam's contribution when the woman's eye came to him in turn. But Rebecca Hadlow, who had been a prefect and debating captain at the very school, said nothing and hoped for once not to be remembered.

The dean did, however, feel obliged to allude to the lack of recent classroom experience and the inevitable sacrifice of scholastic modernity to the demands of day-to-day administration. And there was the increasing friction with her board concerning her power of decision, though no mention was made of this any more than to the candidate's age. Were there other motives perhaps, to move her from such a pinnacle to college vacancy C108? The dean had a feeling that she was too much like himself to be comfortable within humanities.

Rebecca Hadlow decided that it would be a continuing embarrass-ment for both her former principal and herself to be closely associated with the college. As Pia Greer asked a question regarding single-sex as opposed to co-educational schools, Hadlow recalled some scathing personal comments she had received from the principal after the senior dance, and the justice of the observations didn't serve to diminish the resentment with which they were remembered.

Mervyn Sisley paid considerable attention to the ninth candidate for interview, because during a lunchtime phone call, dealing mainly with projected roll figures for overseas students, the chief executive had mentioned that there was one application on the shortlist who was a nephew of Sir Lyall Bernes. 'I deliberately refrained from making the connection before the dean's panel decided on its shortlist,' said the CE, 'but it is significant to see him coming through on his own merits, I think you'll agree.'

The dean thought the ninth interviewee's thesis topic of little relevance to the teaching programme within the college. Marine biological presages of tectonic plate tsunamis were not of pressing concern to the humanities department, or its students. Ronald Prydam had been told in confidence the day before by an activist within the lecturers' association that there was a nephew of Lyall Bernes among the applicants, and to be on the lookout for any undue influence in his favour. Prydam was opposed to anyone from a private school background in any case. He took the defence of egalitarianism in academic appointments very seriously.

'I'm interested,' said Mervyn Sisley at one point, 'in your fluency in Japanese and Russian.' He knew that Rebecca Hadlow had a hobbyhorse of integrated studies drawing on expertise across departmental divisions. The nephew had other attributes that recommended him to the council representative: he was a trim, athletic man with tanned forearms and slightly tousled, dark hair. Not a sign of sloth or fat.

'Quite, quite,' cut in the dean on the discussion of language between Hadlow and Sir Lyall's nephew, 'but if we could come on to the matter of teaching experience. You recall the specifics of the job description.'

'There is,' said Prydam firmly, 'no substitute for experience.'

In the short break between the tenth and eleventh interviews, Rebecca Hadlow rang her partner to confirm the restaurant meal before the Polish chamber music trio, Pia Greer enthused to Prydam concerning progress in her plans for solo adoption of a Bosnian orphan, Prydam prayed to God that his wife would not that night wish to talk about their relationship again, and Sisley and the dean knowingly sounded each other on a recommendation. The sun had lowered and so stretched through the interview room to the far wall. The gardener and his transistor had not returned, but the cart still stood by the rose bed and from the playing field rose again the clock, clock, clock of the same ball on the same sticks in different hands.

The last of the shortlist to be interviewed seemed to be a token local entry, and coming as he did at the end of the line and of the day, whatever merits he had were, in the panel members' minds, set against the accumulated achievements of the ten before him, so that he lost in comparison on every count. He seemed to sense the futility of his application himself, and spent a good deal of time talking amiably about the part-time and untenured positions he had held in the college over several years. 'You know from experience how important it is to match specific department needs to specific expertise,' said the dean kindly. How else could he tell him that he had been tried and found not wanting, but merely adequate.

'How pleasant to see you again,' said Pia Greer, who remembered striking the man in the face during the final of the faculty volleyball competition. Sisley wrote assiduously during much of the final interview, but it was all concerned with earlier candidates. He wished to be well prepared for the final discussion on a recommendation.

Before that took place, the panel members had a brief respite and a cup of coffee. Sisley slipped away to check with his secretary in case something important had come up, the dean scribbled down a few procedural points which he hoped would ensure a quick resolution in discussion, Prydam, Hadlow and Pia Greer stood with their own preoccupations at the window overlooking the roses and the playing field. The eleventh applicant granted an interview was already a diminished figure at the carpark, but no one was thinking of him, or any of his predecessors.

AN INDIRECT GEOGRAPHY

They're gathered up: met here to travel south to help me celebrate my ninetieth birthday, but I couldn't wait any longer. Such decisions are made for us, and death has released me to accompany them on the journey to my funeral. Better they don't know the change of plan.

They cluster ready for departure in this summer morning. Donald's my eldest, and become pompous, though he's family minded and reliable. It's his car they're using and his Aaple Motels they're leaving from. Nigel isn't his, of course. He's Ruth's youngest, and she's my youngest — only forty-six. I never know what to make of Nigel. I can't understand what he says. He talks in an adolescent mumble while he turns his face away. Andrew's my second son. His father always said he was the deep one, but his brains don't seem to have made him happier than anyone else. 'All aboard who's coming aboard then. We'd better be on the road,' says Donald. It's his car and he's the South Islander on his own ground. Nigel asks if he could drive for a while, but Donald says maybe later, on a quiet stretch south of Ashburton perhaps.

'Oh, make no promises that bind us all as passengers,' says Andrew. 'All life hangs by a thread.' He's right there.

'I told Mum not to expect us until this afternoon: that we'd have lunch on the way down,' says Ruth.

'But she'll still be expecting us earlier,' says Donald. 'Whatever time I arrive she says she thought I might have been there earlier. One day I'll come at daybreak.'

'Mum will have the bed turned down from the night before,' says Andrew.

Ruth will have organised the boys. She will have said they should be coming down to be with me on my ninetieth. She and Nigel flew down to Christchurch yesterday morning and Andrew on a later flight. To be honest, their talk has often bored me, but I think about them a lot. I've had close, special things to say, but rarely said them when the opportunity was there; instead fallen back into the old pattern of trivial, nothing, everyday talk. Sometimes the more you care for people the less risk you take with them.

It's nice, though, that they're gathered up, that they're coming as a family to see me.

Ruth makes herself comfortable in the back with Nigel. It's a long time since she's driven from Christchurch to Oamaru. Her mood is one of family reminiscence and reflection. 'I had a dream about Mum last night. We all gave her our birthday presents, but she wouldn't look at them. She said she wanted to buy back the farm so we could live there again, and she took sets of false teeth out of her mouth one after the other as she talked.'

'It wouldn't take much to buy it back today, by Jesus. I'm glad I got out when I did, that's for sure,' says Donald. Nigel mumbles something about getting out with a packet too, and Donald complains that he can't understand a thing he says.

'All those false teeth in your dream,' says Andrew, 'one set after another, you said. That's an odd thing. Maybe it's a repudiation of age: going back to the good old days of personal virtue and the horse.'

'For all your fancy notions, the age of the horse may well be in front of us as well, the way things are going. Don't write horses off.' Since boyhood, Donald has been impatient with his brother's departure from practical considerations.

So they talk of horses! What do people know or care of horses now. Today they're on the race track, or they're runts of ponies for children to ride. Ralph and I worked in the breath of real horses — draughthorses of strength and even temper, and riding hacks of a decent size. There were drays and traps, waggonettes and sledges. As a girl I went to town on wet days in the gig, when my father couldn't work outside.

The Depression kept horses on, Ralph used to say. Most of us couldn't afford tractors for years and kept the horses going through the thirties. A working horse sweats a lather like sea foam, and at the large concrete troughs, big almost as country swimming pools, they'd stand to drink, and you could hear the water rattling by the gallon down their throats. And after winter work the steam would drift from their great bodies as if they were gradually smouldering away.

Andrew passes the time by gently ragging his older brother. 'When technology fails, you could corner the market in horse transport. You should start secretly now, breeding Clydesdales, and make a killing when the world is desperate. There'd be jobs for all of us too. Nigel as a pooper scooper, for example. A sort of human dung beetle.'

'Keep it in the family, you mean,' says Nigel. He smiles, but continues to watch the houses thinning into the flat farms and orchards south of Christchurch.

It's strange that the ordinary circumstances of your life become novelties with the passing of time. We used to go on school picnics to the top crossing in a wagon. People were admired for skills that aren't known or understood today. Ralph was thought to be the best stacker in the district. He used to go all over the place, from farm to farm in the early days, stacking oats and wheat. Who knows anything of stacking oats before threshing now? Who cares for the skill of the ploughman, the smith, or the water diviner, like Wally Nind who found over forty good wells with a branch of willow.

There was nothing glamorous about it all, God knows, but there were skills that gave livings and personal satisfaction then, that are nothing today. Time gives things a sense of quaintness, and the quaintness disguises the same serious business of living that's always there, so that even your own children are cut off from your early life. In the end you find yourself part of your grandchildren's projects on women in the Great Depression, or the aftermath of the First World War.

They pass Burnham, and Andrew and Donald swap anecdotes of the National Service as eighteen-year-olds. The barracks and the AWOL trips to the city: the regular instructors and the platoon hard cases. They weren't there together, but the experience seems much the same.

Before that there'd been a real war, of course. My young brother, Clem died at Maleme airfield in Crete, May 1941. Ralph and I had a radio in our bedroom. It had a varnished case almost as big as a grandfather clock. We were tired in the evenings after the farm, but sometimes we would listen for a while, particularly during the war, for news of how things were going.

Ralph would fall asleep before me, especially in the winter. In the winter too, we often lit the fire in the bedroom. The fire would die down during the night. I remember waking up now and then late at night, because there was a sudden last flame behind the guard which lit up the room with flickering patterns, so that the wardrobe would bob, and the varnished radio case and tongue and groove ceiling would glimmer. The last brief flame would soon be exhausted and the dark return, and I'd lie in the warm room waiting for sleep again. There would be the call of a morepork perhaps, or the wind in the woolshed pines like an ocean close at hand, or the rattle of the chains as the dogs slunk in and out of their kennels.

I used to wonder what other people were doing all over the world. I felt for people who were up against it in some way: up against war, or famine, pain, or loneliness, up against sly old age itself.

They're coming to Dunsandel on the plain, and Donald decides he may as well fill up there. He reminds the others that it's the place Ken Avery wrote the song about, and sings a line or two — 'By the dog dosing strip at Dunsandel . . .' Andrew joins in. 'A dead and alive place really,' says Donald afterwards. 'I remember coming potato picking here one May school holidays, and Dad thought I should have been helping at our place.'

'That's a while now, Donald,' says Ruth.

'Nineteen forty-nine it would be. One of the guys had beer hidden in the water tank, and when he climbed up to get it he gashed his hand, and had to be taken to hospital. Old man Keen told us he'd get lockjaw.'

'Did he?'

'He may have for all I remember. Old man Keen said, "He's a goner, lads, with lockjaw and he's brought it on himself, you see."' Donald pulls up at the pumps, and leaves his story to get out and talk with the pump attendant.

Andrew asks Nigel what job he wants now that he's leaving school, but Nigel is uncommunicative as usual. Andrew looks out at Dunsandel and wonders what makes Nigel tick. His own adolescence is so far behind him. *I guess Nigel still thinks there's some special life in store: opportunities to make the changes he dreams of, but won't talk about. He's about to join the dole queue, but won't be doleful either way. Youth is never completely daunted by circumstance.*

Keep moving, Nigel. That's the secret. Keep moving. Too many weighty considerations and you're through the thin crust of things and into quicksand beneath. All those supposed meanings, motives, spiritual assessments and the paralysing self-consciousness that nails you down. Keep moving, that's the story. Keep bobbing and weaving, and don't ask for any reason with your rhyme. Keep moving and talking inside: fast talking, sweet talking, soft talking, smooth talking, tall talking. Keep moving, talking, so that the reflex hit men at all the doorways of life don't grow bored and tighten their trigger fingers in their boredom.

Nigel begins to sing what he's picked up of the Dunsandel song, and Andrew joins in more confidently. 'Stop it. They'll hear you,' says Ruth, but she laughs anyway.

'Shut up,' says Donald from outside. 'A couple of bloody humourists,' he tells the attendant. So Andrew returns to his thoughts.

You need to be a humourist here in Dunsandel on the plain. I can't see anyone with lockjaw despite Donald's story. There's no railway station any more; just the compacted gravel and weeds of the yard. just the ramp facing the line. The tracks are rusted on the sides, yet worn shiny on the top despite so few trains passing.

Two garages and the yellow, roughcast tearooms. There's an antique shop, and a thin grey spire of the country church sticks up for its beliefs above the Honda sign, but proves, as it comes closer, to have been taken over for antiques as well. For a young country we are stuffed with antiques.

I look out at Dunsandel, but I'm thinking of Wolverhampton, and the rooms I shared with two art teachers. From my top-storey window I could see the canal's trapped water with its blowfly blue on the oily surface, and an unofficial cycle track among the rubbish on its banks. A quiet Canadian girl and I made love by the window of that view on a wet Monday. I think the dingy threat of the visible world urged us to make a show of defiance: to mimic creation in all that expanse of decay. Lying with her, and just a few post-impressionists, for company, I looked out and saw the rain on the blue-bottle water of the canal and streaking the fences, and the cartons thrown away. She talked of winter in Alberta Province, and I talked of summer in the Mackenzie Country. The two of us drawn close in disillusion with Old England — and camouflaging it as love.

There are Wolverhamptons everywhere, of course. You need to be strong in the Wolverhamptons of Taihape, Gore, Cannons Creek or Remuera, because they're hard on ideals and pretence. You have to pack in all your own spiritual supplies to such places, and not rely on any renewal while you're there.

Ruth is saying that they should take me out to the farm tomorrow, as part of my birthday. Other people own it now, but she thinks they won't mind a visit. I'm quite pleased it won't happen. Other people muck your place around, no matter how pleasant they are. 'If she's well enough,' says Donald. 'You haven't seen her for ages and don't know how frail she's got. You'll find Mum's gone back a lot.'

Of course I've gone back. Who wants to spend their time as a ninety-year-old widow? I've gone back in ways Donald wouldn't dream of. Now I'm free to go back altogether. I don't need any permission now, or any help.

Recently I've never talked much about the past. It's tiresome when you have to keep explaining things that everybody used to know. Like tin-kettling and first-footing. In our district we went first-footing after midnight on New Year's Eve: farm by farm and some of the men getting the worse for drink as it went on. At Tolligers once before the war, the men shifted the outdoor loo into the vegetable garden. Ray Tolliger lost his rag and threatened to push one of them down the exposed long drop. At least two of those men were killed overseas not long afterwards: killed in places where first-footing in the small hours had greater dangers even than Tolliger's long drop.

Our fun was local and inexpensive. Card evenings, tin-kettling, woolshed dances, A and P shows, weddings and send-offs, were the big things. Ruth talks of progressive dinners, ethnic restaurants, barbecues. I've never been to a barbecue in my life. I waited too long to have a decent kitchen around me, to want to go outside and cook without it.

I worked hard in country schools before I was married, and we slogged on the farm afterwards. Every fine Monday morning for years I lit the copper at six o'clock to heat the water for wash day. The electricity came to the district in time, of course, and I had a washing machine afterwards. Years later Ruth said she'd like the old copper bowl for her plants, and not long before he died, Ralph broke down the concrete casing and took out the copper, and patiently scoured it clean for her. She had a wrought-iron stand made for it, to display her indoor plants. When I visited her in Wellington I sat and looked at that gleaming copper full of dark foliage in her lounge, and I thought of the hundreds of Mondays on the farm I'd stood in the lean-to and stirred clothes in that copper with a broom handle. There it was, after all that time, among Ruth's polished furniture and crystal. I admired the burnished curve of the copper in its stand, and the fronds she cleaned with milk which hung over the sides in green contrast. What's all that in the process of time passing, I wonder?

'I'd forgotten coming down the Showground hill into Timaru like this,' says Ruth. 'I've always had a soft spot for Timaru. Let's have our lunch on Caroline Bay and see what changes there's been.' She sees it all as Donald drives on down and parks by a wooden table on the grass. Recognition mixed with small shocks of change, arouse her recollections.

A lot's still the same. The phoenix palms on the median strip — pineapples we used to call them. The way Donald and Andrew sit waiting while I set out lunch is the same too. The same as Dad used to wait for Mum to provide his food.

The Benvenue Cliffs are still hung with ice-plant and its glassy flowers. There used to be sand dunes between the lawn and the sea, and unpainted, wooden changing sheds. There used to be lupins, marram grass, gorse even, ridges in the dunes and hollows where sunbathers and lovers lay. And in the carnival afternoons there were acts in the sound shell. You sat high on the concrete steps built in the cliff while some local boy sang 'How much is that doggie in the window'.

'We used to come here often in the long holidays,' she tells Nigel, but it's Donald who answers.

'People don't come the same now. They head inland more, to the lakes.'

'Well, there's no surf here,' says Andrew. 'You need a beach with a good surf, or lakes for water-skiing to get young people today.'

'Young people today!' Donald says. He improves his posture to address a topic that provokes him. 'I'm sick of hearing about young people today, as if they've grown another head. Listen, young people today are the same as young people yesterday, except they've been allowed to get away with too much. After a boot up the jacksie young people today behave a good deal more like the rest of us.'

'Perhaps it would work in reverse,' said Nigel, mumbling, his head turned away to watch the swimmers. 'A boot up the jacksie to make everyone more like young people. A neat experiment, eh.'

'What's that?' says Donald, but Nigel's said all he wants to, and gets up and wanders off over the sand.

'Don't go far,' his mother calls. She starts to tidy up and remembers being on the bay as a girl. *We had our last family holiday in Timaru when I was seventeen: Nigel's age now, but I was so much older surely. Girls are, though. For New Year's Eve I wore a full-patterned cotton skirt with a stiff petticoat — they were all in then — and stockings, not pantyhose. And clip-on earrings. I'd met Selwyn Holdaway who had an ivy league shirt which looked great. He used to fold the sleeves up to his elbows, and his brown skin, the muscles moving, the silver watch strap on his wrist, made me think of sex.*

You can trust your body at seventeen. The back of your neck isn't wrinkled, your legs don't have swollen veins, and your togs don't ride up over a second crease in your bum. My friend Barbara and I used to wear togs under our dresses to walk down from the motel and we'd stand in the warm, white-grey sand to undress.

Selwyn Holdaway could talk — he was a great talker. He was fun to be with, and if his legs were slightly bandy it didn't matter because they were brown, muscular legs. He was deputy head boy, or proxime accessit I think, one or the other, and he was going to Canterbury to be a lawyer he told me. On New Year's Eve at the top of the Benvenue Cliffs we stood with a soft bush between us and Barbara and her boy, for privacy. There were still people swimming as the New Year came in, some couples on the anchored raft, the ships' hooters, and a lot of noise from the other side of the bush as Barbara got shirty with her boy.

Between kisses Selwyn talked of going to Canterbury. We agreed to write to each other. He sent me one letter early that year, after he'd started varsity, and I wrote back, but that's all I heard. I blamed still being a schoolgirl. I remember that in his letter he said he'd found great freedom in being away from his family.

If the others weren't here I could walk up the track on the cliffs and look out over the bay again, though it was dark then of course that New Year night, and Selwyn Holdaway told me how he was going to write to me about all the things that happened afterwards. He didn't, but all the things happened afterwards just the same.

Nigel has taken off his shirt: his shoulders are red with acne but he doesn't care. Ruth should have him using some of that antiseptic soap, and no chocolate. It's been a long time since Ruth and the boys have been on Caroline Bay, and Andrew is wondering where the years have gone. 'I still feel the same as these young people around us,' he says. 'I could stand up and join in, receive the same quick glances from the girls, but then I see my old, white feet on the sand, or pass my hand over my head and find I've grown bald. "I grow old, I grow old, I shall wear the bottoms of my trousers rolled."'

'You're old, but you never act your age,' says Donald. 'Never had to work hard enough, that's what.'

'Don't start with the bullshit, Donald.'

'Oh, come on you two,' says Ruth.

There they are with the glitter of the sea behind them and the noise of the summer beach around them. The four of them in bright sunshine, which is only a memory of warmth for me now. They wouldn't find it flattering, but they're precious to me because they carry something of Ralph with them as much as for what they are themselves. Donald walks like his dad, and his large, oval thumbs with white moons on the nails are just the same. His shoulders are adopting the same slump of habitual labour. Andrew and Ruth have Ralph's eyes: the blue irises oddly small so that a full circle of white can often be seen. But Ruth has my skin. The women in my family had wonderful skin.

I look at the four here, and see other characteristics from both sides of the family. A bit of my Uncle Lee in the way Nigel's hair sticks up from the crown, and the thin McCallum lips as Andrew smiles. As my children and grandson walk on the beach I see others, more distant, come forward for an instant through a look, or gesture, signal, then fade away. I've a feeling that the outlines of Donald, Andrew, Ruth and Nigel aren't completely set. There's a jostling aura behind them of generations who want some recognition. And now I've joined them.

The four have a last walk on the sand before they leave, and Andrew and Nigel break into a brief race that only accentuates Andrew's loss of powers. 'Silly buggers,' says Donald amiably.

'Can I drive now?' asks Nigel, as if his winning sprint has made him more competent for the task.

'Oh God,' says Andrew, 'and I'd hoped for just a few years more.'

'Maybe later.' Even Ruth shows no support.

'Maybe on the way back, when you're familiar with the road,' says Donald.

'I could get a bus back, I suppose,' says Andrew.

And so they pile in and drive back to the main road past the phoenix palms again, and close to the cliff track where Ruth stood on a New Year's Eve with Selwyn Holdaway. Donald lectures the others on the regional downturn. 'Listen,' he says, 'I don't know if you realise it, but local government reorganisation and ongoing centralisation will drastically affect places like Timaru. It's make or break for heartland New Zealand over the next few years. Mark my words.'

'Nigel, mark your uncle's words,' says Andrew. 'About three out of ten will do.'

'He really gets into all that stuff, doesn't he.'

The mumble stirs Donald to justify himself. 'Now look, look, you should realise what's important in the long run, and it's not sport, or art, or saving whales, or getting in touch with your individual consciousness, but economics, which means resources, and politics, which means who controls resources. People who think that's boring and can't be bothered with it are handing over their lives to others.' That's Donald's way: as the eldest he's always taken on a role that is practical and responsible. He talks a sort of layman's politics and economics based on newspapers and current affairs programmes, and he picks out those things that agree with his own experience. Things are always cut and dried for him: sometimes he seems cut and dried himself. His thoughts are full of firm, undoubted principles.

I wish they'd have more common sense. Listen, I'd say, there are too many people who want to talk for a living, and not enough prepared to roll up their sleeves and work. Too many people spend their time discussing gender roles, creative dance, post-natal depression and macramé — and then expect someone else to fill their bellies. They scoff at the routines of work, at those who get up each morning, smother their temperament and give a fair day's work for a fair day's pay. Winter and summer, wet or fine, time of the month or change of life, feeling up or feeling down, it's important just to get on with it. Nowadays there are too many people riding on the back of the solid middle class. It's routines and routine people that matter in the end, get things done, not the media ponces, investment counsellors, would-be pianists, solo mums, Maori and lesbian activists. Andrew never understands that.

It's us who carry the can, and get nothing but sneering derision for being fool enough to do it. My old CSM told me that there are two ways in the army: the easy way and the hard way. The easy way isn't easy and the hard way's bloody hard, he said. It's like that for a practical man in New Zealand now, I reckon. The easy way isn't easy and the hard way's bloody hard.

The road south of Timaru is never far from the sea, along the edge of the downs. Ruth and Andrew talk to bring their lives up to date: they've not seen much of each other for years. Nigel sprawls in adolescent languor, a captive in the presence and purposes of his elders.

Glenavy, where the Waitaki is bridged, prompts Andrew to tell Nigel another family story. 'Your Uncle Donald fell in love with a girl here years ago. She had such magnificent knockers that she found it difficult to remain upright. Well, that was one reason.'

'I can see that we're going to have another session of your damn imagination,' says Donald. He's resigned to it.

'Donald told Dad that he was needed on the other farm to help with heading, but he came over here and took Amelia up the valley for the afternoon. Wild oats rather than heading, eh.'

'Yeah?' Nigel begins to show an interest.

'The next day Dad found her bra under the rug in the back seat. I can see him now, bringing it in at morning tea, and Donald's face.'

'It's an old family story,' says Ruth, but laughs all the same.

'You know we'd been swimming and sunbathing, that's all,' says Donald, 'and she kept her togs on to go home. You know that.'

'We know what you told Mum and Dad. Your brain was quicker in those days, among other things.'

'Dad didn't say much, but he seemed impressed by the size of the bra,' says Ruth. She, too, has always played a part in ribbing Donald.

'She was a sizable heifer, certainly, was Amelia,' admits Donald.

Beneath his denial, as always with this story, is a certain embarrassed pride which the others play on. I remember how his father enjoyed the story too; how each of the children starred in their own family anecdotes, as much a part of the family record as the photographs and the collections of small trophies from schools and clubs. Ralph and I would often go over the stories when the children had all gone: a small way to keep them in our lives.

The closer they come to Oamaru the more Andrew is in the grip of the old life, the more what he sees is populated by the past.

We never do completely outgrow our country. Education and travel only make our memories of home more powerful. Not the helicopter views of mountains and waterfalls, but the plain quiet shingle of the Waitaki, say, with the shot of rabbit droppings in the scrapes, or the sight of rugby posts above the fog in winter parks. The corner dairies with the papers piled on the counter, a stainless steel pie-warmer, and a Coca-cola ad a glossy world away. Uniformed kids on the way home: the greys, blues and greens, the Latin blazer mottos that neither Pakeha nor Maori can understand. Easy country roads through hills contoured with sheep tracks. The long summer beaches with a fragrant breeze coming in and few people to breathe it. The twitch ever creeping out from the fences in to the dry, suburban gardens.

Above all, the committees that meet in community halls and schoolrooms, conference centres and modest boardrooms, vestry rooms, lodges, club lounges and pavilions, civic chambers and staff quarters. The Rabbit Boards, Neighbourhood Watch, Red Cross, Squash Rackets and Indoor Bowls Clubs, PTA and Friends of the School, Women's Auxiliary, RSA, Jaycees, Katherine Mansfield or J.K. Baxter discussion groups, Cactus and Succulent Society, Progressive League, Rape Counselling Centre, Acclimatisation Board, Rotary, Playcentre Management Committee, Guild of Main Street Businessmen, VSA Steering Committee, Federated Farmers, Toastmistresses, Masons, Working Men's Club, Friends of the

Takahe, Compost Society, Small Bore Rifle Club, Colenso Textile Brass Band, Civil Defence volunteers, Forest and Bird Society, Trampoline and Gymnastics Promotion League, Avalon Marching Cub, Repertory Society, Girl Guides' Management Seminar, Embroiderers' and Potters' Fellowship, Alzheimer's and Korsakov's Psychosis Support Group, the committee to organise the Ransumeen family reunion.

All that mister and madam chair, and rising to a point of order, and taking the right of reply, and wishing opposition or abstention to be recorded in the minutes.

Who said we are a taciturn people?

All those hobby-horses ridden assiduously in a hundred rooms and halls of nodding boredom, while outside beneath a leering moon a stray dog savages the sheep in the domain, or glue sniffers twitch in the doorways of the main street.

And they drive on, coming closer to Oamaru. They talk mainly of their own lives, sometimes their conversation is of the places they pass, sometimes of me. Nigel remembers that as a small boy he was promised one of his grandfather's guns, and Donald acknowledges the debt and says there's a good Hollis that would suit him down to the ground. Andrew wonders if Ruth and I will be closer than he ever manages with me. 'Maybe Mum opens up more to you, Ruth, because you're a woman.'

'It isn't any easier,' she says. 'Why should it be easier? Mum was never able to talk to me about being a woman. She was just more afraid for me, and her fear made her angry at times and stopped us becoming close. Being mother and daughter isn't any guarantee of understanding you know.'

She's right. I wanted more for her than I had myself, even though I had everything that mattered. Too much emotion, hope and love is an embarrassment. True feeling for all the family became overlaid with minor irritations and trivial preoccupations — mine and theirs — so that when I should have been grateful for Donald's occasional trips from Christchurch, instead as he talked I was thinking it was time for my television programme, or noticing the dirt from his shoes on the rug.

I should have forgotten sometimes that I'm their mother: put it aside and just talked to them as a person without special responsibility. I should have risked more, but you become more and more aware of the gap between what you feel, and what you can hope to express.

They're nearly home. Cape Wanbrow can be seen above the town, and the downland is pressing towards the sea. The plains are over and cabbage tree country begins.

There'll be no birthday party for me here after all. Let's leave them now before their disappointment, their grief, or their relief. I've recovered all my life now. Still, they're coming to see me — that might still be true. They may come to see me more truly now than they ever have before.

MR TANSLEY

Small-scale heroes are enough when you're a kid. Sometimes just conspicuous possession could do it — the man who drove a Ford V8 Custom Line; sometimes just conspicuous loss — the man who lost an arm in a combine harvester. The fish and chip shop owner seemed to me the most fortunate and successful of businessmen. The government deer culler who regularly got sozzled at the Gladstone pub surely had a life of greater excitement than the rest of us.

Mr Tansley was the caretaker at the gasworks, that collection of dark, smudged buildings with storage domes that could rise and fall like cakes in a fitful oven. He rode a black Raleigh bike. When he went to work he wrapped his lunch tin in the jacket of an old pinstripe suit, so the wire spring of the carrier would grip it safely. He took cold tea in a corked beer bottle, which he dangled at the handlebar in a grey woollen sock as he cycled. He pedalled carefully, intent on the road, as if his lunch box, or bottle of cold tea, was at risk. It was no use calling out to him when he rode past on the old Raleigh, because he wouldn't respond, always intent on the road and his slow, persistent pedalling.

He lived in an army hut behind the Loan and Mercantile building, and close to the river. He had a wooden kitchen table with turned legs outside the door of the hut, and there every morning he had his wash and shave. At head height above the table he'd banged a fair-sized nail into the hut wall, and each morning he brought out a metal-framed mirror and hung it up. Also an enamel basin, a green towel, an army mess tin with his shaving gear, and so he'd set up there because there wasn't enough light in the hut, I suppose. The first thing, though, that came out of the hut's security, was his Raleigh bike, and he would press his thumb into the tyres as a test, and always lean the bike in the same way, on the same corner of the shed. I knew the inside of Tansley's shed, and always wondered how he fitted the bike in there last thing at night.

From my bedroom window I could see him most mornings with just a singlet above the waist and his braces hanging beside his trouser legs. In the frost, or drizzle, things were done quick time, but on a fine morning his wash and shave became almost an indulgent ritual, and I sometimes went down before breakfast to join him. He used a cut-throat, and would lift his chin high to tighten the skin of his neck, then slide that long, narrow blade down, and wash the soap and stubble from it in the water of the enamel bowl. The handle, with its split for the blade to fold into, was of ivory yellowed with age and use, and smooth as a horse bit.

'To be clean shaven is a sign of self-respect,' he said once. 'And a man with no self-respect hasn't any respect for others.'

Tansley had been awarded a medal in the desert, fighting against the Desert Fox, my father said. He'd reached the rank of sergeant, but then lost his stripes because he disobeyed an order. My father said that Norman Beal, who was the manager of the Loan and Mercantile Agency and had been an officer in 23 Battalion, maintained that Tansley was morally right, but they broke him to private all the same.

Tansley must have been an older soldier than most, because even allowing for the view of childhood he was surely nearly seventy when he lived in the army hut twenty years after the war. He was a big man, pale despite service in the desert. The muscles of his chest and arms had begun to loosen. The hair on his large chest was grey, and darker hair grew over his shoulders and down his back. Because he spent so much time in his own company, he carried on a sort of conversation with himself at times in a quite unself-conscious way. 'Reckon so,' he'd say. 'I don't doubt there'll be rain before the day's out', and he'd fling the used water from the basin into the river, and stand and look at the sky to find intention there.

On summer evenings he'd sit on the wooden step of his hut and read the afternoon paper — even that's a thing of the past now. 'I see old Joey Wadsworth's dead,' he'd say, or 'Look how they advertise these Jap cars, by Jesus, bold as you like.' You might expect me to say that he and I formed a special bond, that he passed on some principled wisdom to me, and I provided company that mitigated his loneliness, but there was nothing like that. He talked to himself exactly the same whether I was sitting with him or not. From my bedroom window sometimes I could see his lips move. He didn't dislike me; he never told me not to come around; we shared bread and strawberry jam: he just didn't recognise children as the same species as himself.

He had a chrome cigarette-making machine, not much bigger than a tobacco tin, and I often got a glimpse of the simple mechanism when he made one up — rollers and a strip of dark canvas. We're quicksilver as kids, and to me all his actions seemed slow and clumsy. I wondered if his movements had been more adept in the desert when he won his medal. He put a half-choke grip on the loaf to laboriously cut himself a slice, and to do up the buttons of his fly after a piss on the bank was a business of lengthy concentration. The Loan and Mercantile let him use the lavatory at the back of the building, but for just a piss he didn't bother to walk those few yards.

Many afternoons after work he'd walk down Seddon Street and across the bridge to the RSA. He'd have a drink there because I could smell it on him afterwards, but he never came home drunk. It was the company he wanted mainly, I suppose, though he always left his mates behind and came back to the hut alone. There was another man in the town who'd won a medal, but I never saw them together, which surprised me, because I imagined that they would have a lot in common. Mr Lineen the dentist was the other man with a medal, and his left forearm had been hit by mortar fragments, my father said. In summer when he rolled his sleeves up you could see how pitted and thin that arm was.

My father once suggested to Mr Tansley that he apply for a state house. 'This hut here will see me out,' Tansley said, and I heard him say much the same another time about his bike. He was getting ready to go to work at the gasworks, putting the lunch box on the carrier, slipping the cold tea bottle into the grey work sock. He lifted the Raleigh by the centre of the handlebars and spun the front wheel to check for any wobble. 'She'll see me out okay,' he said admiringly.

The bike did see him out, and it wasn't even a close thing, because Tansley was hit by a truck one winter evening when he was biking home in the half dark from his job at the gasworks. He was one day in hospital and then he died. My father said he talked about nothing but locomotives before he died. It seems that as a young man he worked in the railway workshops.

Because my father was both a neighbour and a returned soldier, and Tansley didn't have any family as far as anybody knew, he helped clear out the shed and was a pallbearer. There wasn't any money to speak of in the shed, and no record of a bank account. Someone at the RSA said Tansley used to send all his money in postal notes to Italy, but there are always those stories, aren't there? And how much money do you make as gasworks caretaker anyway?

The town and the RSA didn't care about Tansley's trade, or his lack of savings. The community hadn't forgotten Mr Tansley had won a medal in its service, and so his death deserved to be marked with respect. There were plenty of contributions to do the right thing by him, and the long piece in the paper gave him the rank of sergeant, made no mention of the court martial, and published the citation in full for his military medal. He'd rushed a machine-gun post after its fire had killed two of his mates.

At the funeral Norman Beal of the Loan and Mercantile spoke, and Mr Lineen the dentist who had the other medal in town — the military cross, which was the officers' version of Mr Tansley's medal, my father said. There was a bugler, and it took place in the special RSA part of the cemetery. It all seemed a long way from the old man in a singlet and hanging braces shaving himself outside his shed with a cut-throat razor, or pissing into the river as he debated the day's weather with himself, or setting off on the Raleigh with his lunch box on the carrier and a bottle of cold tea in a sock.

CLAUDE ENTERTAINMENTS

Claude Sturmer was in an ice-block when I last saw him, wearing just a black and yellow close-fitting thermal, and staring out through the ice. The sides had an odd, magnifying effect, so he was lumpenly misshapen. He had a ridiculous Old Testament beard, and the bit of face you could see was blue with cold. But he was smiling because he was the centre of attention, and that's what Claude needs. There must have been over a hundred people looking into the refrigerated truck where he sat in the ice-block raising money for the salvation of the wild horses of the Volcanic Plateau — and a cut for his expenses no doubt. His PR girl, in tight skirt and white blouse, was handing out leaflets that promoted him as well as the wild horses, and there was a new van painted to advertise his company, Claude Entertainments.

Most of us decide to play life by the percentages, I reckon: choose conventional ways to reach a position of independent means, status, some freedom of choice. You want some qualification, like a law degree, pharmacy or software, which gives a reasonable shot at such things. And the illegitimate world is just as much ruled by such practicality, maybe more so. Cannabis, prostitution and wound-back cars are a few reliable things. Who wants to go for the long shot and come a cropper anyway? You're better to forget notions of being a big Hollywood star, or robbing Fort Knox, give up ideas of inventing something that runs on water, or becoming the underworld king of Marseilles.

Claude Sturmer is a dreamer who never learnt that, and it affected his whole life, I guess. His family lived near mine in Aranui, and we were kids together. Claude's mum worked at the airport cafeteria, and his dad had a diseased hip that kept him at home most of the time, where he bred budgies and made garden frogs for income. Sometimes on a fine Saturday Claude and I would take a cage of budgies and a bag of frogs, and go round a suburb flogging them off. If we had a good day his dad would give us enough to go to the pictures. There were first-class frogs and second-class frogs I remember. The first-class ones had no blemishes from the mould, a coat of sealant over the paint, and cost extra. The budgies had no class distinction, though some were green and some were blue.

Friendship, like ambition, undergoes a sensible contraction. When I was a kid it included things and ideas: the glimpse of sky through the sycamore leaves, a talking elephant in a picture book, the reassuring whine of the refrigerator at night. Later I realised there should just be people, and even most of them weren't cool.

Claude and I were friends of convenience, living that close to each other and going to the same primary school. Out of a swarm of rib-punching, casually intimate kids, we had the same direction to walk home together, and often met up in the weekends. We were at Aranui High together too, but we hung out less then. Most of my friends were keen on sport, while Claude was mad on music and the drama club. I got sick of his dozy ideas, and more and more I'd dodge him in the weekends.

I was a prefect in the seventh form, and on sports day, when I hadn't made any finals, Jetarse the senior master asked me to make a check of out-of-bounds classrooms. It was a pain, but Jetarse was always on about the obligations of leadership. I found Claude and that Dougal Campbell, the Presbyterian minister's son, looking at slides in the art room. They'd climbed in the window, and when I did the same they carried on discussing the paintings. I told them if they didn't knock it off I'd cop them, but Dougal went all smart, said I should loosen up, it was a victimless crime, and so on. They were looking at a slide that had a green donkey upside down in the sky.

'Chagall,' said Claude. 'This stuff is legendary.'

'Iconic,' said Dougal Campbell. He was a useless runt who didn't play sport and said grace over his sandwiches.

Just for a moment it was all there in the glance Claude and I held: the convenient friendship as kids, the budgies and frogs, a history of personal things we knew about each other. It was all there, and when Claude chose not to leave the art room and I chose to cop him, it was gone and there was nothing between us that was private, nothing that could be used by one to hurt the other. Jetarse said I'd done the right thing, no doubt about that.

I joined the city council next year as assistant in the Culture and Public Amenities Department. Claude went to varsity doing philosophy, sociology, stuff like that. He got into protesting about spy satellites, student fees, dolphins, refugees, corporate fraud, party drugs, ecology wetlands and free condoms. Several times he had his photo in the paper over some grievance. He could have passed a degree in protesting if they had one, but he didn't do enough work to get one any other way. He was big in the Students Association and the varsity newspaper, and even got paid a bit. Occasionally I'd see him at the King Dick, or the Dipper, which were student pubs. We'd say hi as Aranui old boys, and make no references to any history between us. We'd say good to see you, and not care if we did again.

A career in protest shaped Claude into an exhibitionist. He had a red velveteen jacket and a varsity scarf so long that when wound round his neck several times, the ends still brushed the ground. I wondered what his hard-working mum and handicapped dad made of him grown up. He didn't live at home. The thing I couldn't understand was how he could afford to have a place of his own and run a car as well, with just the money from his Stud Ass jobs. Not a bad car either. A hatchback Corolla he kept in a rented garage by the park. I found out later he lived in the garage with his car, and no one knew. He had a palliasse under the garage bench to sleep on, and used the public toilets in the park. So he could cut something of a dash during the day, and yet live on the cheap by sleeping under the garage bench and ducking into the park toilets with a towel.

His car and his protests gained him the company of some quite good-looking women. You wonder, don't you, what the hell women see in some guys. The council gave $5000 to an organisation he led called Youth Freedom. I put in a memo to my boss about it, but it made no difference. It pissed me off, because I knew the only youth to gain freedom from that money was Claude.

He was banned from the campus finally: he didn't pass anything, and was usually heading up some bolshie bunch giving the varsity aggro. Even the students stopped backing him. Protest is a youth thing, and new groups coming through had their own firebrands. They didn't need some guy in his late twenties with a velveteen jacket and no feeling for the latest music.

So Claude had to reinvent himself. He set up his own theatrical company, Claude Entertainments, and touted himself around the schools and shopping malls. He had the cheek to come to us and ask for a contract to run summer shows for kids in the city centre and Soone Park. I was given his proposal, and had an interview with him about it. When you boiled it down, what he did was dress up as a giant kiwi and have the kids do crayon competitions, learn a couple of Maori haiku and pretend to be figures of history. He sat in the interview room and told me this in a way that made it sound like a new play by Shakespeare. We didn't talk about our friendship as kids. I told him straight out I couldn't recommend his proposal as a sound use of ratepayers' money, that his show had no artistic credibility. There's far too much liberal, PC crap supported at taxpayers' expense in this country, that's for real, but I didn't say that to Claude. I'm too professional for that. Maybe next year, with a different programme, I told Claude. Pigs might fly too.

He took it well, I have to say: uncrossed his legs, fingered a pewter earring and thanked me for my time. He said he admired those people who could stick to a clerical job day after day, but it

wasn't for him. He went over my head, though, and got an appointment with my boss, who reckoned the kids would love the giant
kiwi suit that Claude brought in, and was impressed that 114 Maori
words were included in his show. So my recommendation was
ignored, and Claude Entertainments was awarded a summer
contract for $12,000. Claude sent me copies of the programme and
itinerary in a letter addressed to The Prefect.

I had it out with my boss, who was a smarmy young prick with
a BA. What was the point of me making recommendations if they
were never followed, I told him, and he talked about the democratic
process and issues of transparency in decision-making. Two weeks
later he and the mayor were on the front page with Claude as giant
kiwi and a heap of cheering kids. The council awarded Claude a
scroll as honorary provincial cultural ambassador. Just a publicity
stunt, but Claude was able to play on it to get loads of work in the
city and beyond. I was told the council was impressed with him, and
that I should extend all courtesy and assistance: be a sort of liaison
person for him. The boss and some of the others in the department
started calling me Prefect, and that could have come from only one
source.

Why should you take being put down all the time? I told Human
Resources I wanted to be transferred to another area, and that I was
overdue for promotion. That's how I ended up as Noise Abatement
and Dog Nuisance officer on reduced pay. It's not an exciting job, but
it's regular and makes a contribution to the welfare of citizens.
Absolutely. I bide my time, and when I see Claude prancing with
some celebrity in the paper, or read some hype about Claude
Entertainments expanding to Auckland, I know he'll come a cropper
soon enough. He'll be back to a palliasse under a garage bench
somewhere, while I have a solid job and rent fully paid up. He'll find
out in the end you can't go through life in a giant kiwi suit, or staring
out of an ice-block.

WAKE-UP CALL

Hector Jansen came regularly to Singapore on business. He had his own familiar track through it, but all else remained totally foreign. He knew Changi airport well, how to get to the taxis quickly, how to use Andrew Shih's bank for a decent rate of exchange. He knew several downtown hotels close to the Soong Corporation building. He knew the zoo and Sentosa Island for snatches of relative privacy and the feel of grass beneath his feet rather than concrete. He knew a couple of escort agencies recommended by Andrew Shih. If he kept to his track in the city he seemed quite adept there, but he realised how superficial and restricted his experience was, and that the only thing of significance he had gained over all his visits was some personal credibility with Andrew Shih, and Mr Liang and Mr Yuan-jen at Soong.

On several of his recent visits, Jansen had taken Mervyn Linkiss with him. Jansen had suggested it, and the CEO had wholeheartedly agreed. 'We need you there, though,' said Tony Alexadis. 'I never feel happy about things at that end unless you're on the spot, Hector. You've got the touch with those people.' But they needed to groom someone up for the Singapore side of things. Businessmen there don't like abrupt changes of contact, don't respond well to a strange face over a contract. And Mervyn Linkiss was personable, intelligent and someone Jansen wanted to do well in the corporation.

On the latest trip to Singapore, Jansen felt unwell on the night of their arrival. All his life his health had been good. A passing sickness is soon forgotten, anything that doesn't come to a threatening conclusion, although at the time it worries you. A decade ago Jansen had had evening chest pains over several weeks, which his GP couldn't account for, so Jansen picked up pamphlets on angina and heart irregularities, the cardio-vascular benefits of exercise, and indigestion. But then while he was very busy organising middle management professional development, the pains didn't come any more, and later he hardly remembered why the pamphlets were in his drawer. Even earlier there had been the loud ringing and sharp, spasmodic pain in his left ear while he was holidaying in the Hokianga, so that for several days he didn't go swimming, and rang up a doctor in Whangarei for an appointment. The noises and discomfort stopped suddenly in the night, the appointment was cancelled and recently he had filled in a medical insurance form saying in all sincerity that he'd never had any trouble with his hearing. On his standing CV he described his health as excellent.

The Singapore pain was different, though: it was very central, deep-seated, located somewhere level with the lower ribs, and seeming to need some physical space of its own, so that existing organs there were displaced. When Jansen first woke he thought it was some nausea caused by the heat, but the first movement made him give a sudden cry of distress. Sweat pooled in the hollows beneath his eyes as he lay and wondered what was wrong. He was panting, and gave a small aah with each quick exhalation, which seemed somehow a comfort. With his left hand he reached cautiously, searching for the light switch in the unfamiliar room, then he forgot that in his concentration on his pain. There was enough light from the street anyway, even though the room was several storeys up. It was very early, but already there was traffic noise, particularly the waspish whine of scooters, which for Jansen was always the sound of Asian cities. The hotel was an older one, though still favoured, and the furniture was of massive hardwood. Elephants, surely, must have been needed to move the logs from which such timber originally came.

Jansen straightened himself gently in the large bed, pushed out his legs, so that his stomach had as little constriction as possible, but if anything it made it worse. He remembered the twinges he'd had on the long flight the day before: the sense of his guts being compressed by all that sitting, despite the advantages of business class. The pain flowed and ebbed. It was an acidic pain if such a thing existed. Jansen remembered Mervyn's room number. He had that sort of mind — could still remember the seat numbers of their Singapore flights, and the names of the perfumes he was to buy for his wife, and the exchange rate of the New Zealand dollar against the Euro, the greenback and four Asian currencies.

'Yes?' said Mervyn, his voice husky with sleep.

'It's Hector. I'm sorry to bother you, but I'm feeling really crook. I've just woken up with it and it's giving me absolute gyppo in the guts.'

'I'll come right away. Is your door unlocked?'

'I'll do it now,' said Jansen.

'Okay.'

'Mervyn.'

'Yes.'

'What time is it?'

'Half past five,' said Mervyn.

'Jeez, I'm sorry,' said Jansen.

He found crawling the least painful form of progress, and pulled a face and hissed as he reached up to unsnib the door. He was on all fours back by the bed, gathering strength to climb in, when Mervyn came and helped him. The thin sheet Jansen pulled over himself was unnecessary in the heat, but even with such pain he wanted the decorum of a covering for his grey-haired chest and pale shin bones. He could feel the sweat of sickness and anxiety trickle through the hair above his ears: each pulsebeat flared an aurora around the light source windows.

'Hell,' said Mervyn. 'We're not mucking around here at all. I'm calling the desk for an ambulance.' Jansen gave a tight nod. He didn't say anything because he was afraid of what might come out if he tried. He concentrated on keeping the pain from taking over altogether. The last thing he remembered was his colleague talking forcefully on the telephone, and at the same time patting down his spiky hair with his free hand. Mervyn was a good guy to cope with an emergency. He did have very peculiar hair in the night, though. 'Mr Hector Jansen, Room 453,' said Mervyn. 'Right away. As soon as possible. Whatever emergency procedure you have here. You understand?' He spoke loudly and very distinctly to ensure his English was presented in the most accessible way.

The pain in Jansen's belly was overwhelming.

They'd taken him to a Roman Catholic private hospital close to the harbour. He had his own room with recessed ceiling lights and cream walls. High on the door was a clean, square window through which staff, or visitors, could look in from the corridor. He recognised his suitcase in a corner. Mervyn sat on the only chair in the room. 'Okay, Hector?' he said. Jansen waited a bit to assure himself the pain was much less, and then nodded slightly. Even that movement was enough to make him aware he had a tube up his nose. Mervyn drew his chair closer: it hadn't been seemly somehow to be peering into Jansen's face when he was unconscious. 'You had an emergency operation for something that burst in your stomach,' said Mervyn. Jansen thought of a reply, opened his mouth, but couldn't find the strength to speak. 'I've told the Soong people we'll get back to them tomorrow,' said Mervyn.

Jansen talked to his wife by telephone when he was awake again four hours later. She had been speaking to the doctors and knew a lot more about his condition that he did himself. 'I haven't seen anyone at all,' he said. 'Just Mervyn and flowers sent from Mr Yuan-jen.'

'The doctors have been there, but you've been out to it. They say you'll be fine now, unless there's infection from material that's escaped into your abdominal cavities, but you'll have to stay there several days before you can fly home. I can get tickets to fly over tomorrow, or the day after.'

'No,' he said. 'Thanks, but if everything's okay it doesn't make much sense. You'd just get here and then have to turn round again.'

His wife went on to reassure him that their adult children were fine. It didn't seem inconsiderate to him at all. It had been their way ever since becoming parents. Whatever happened in their own lives was immediately evaluated in terms of its impact on the children. Would his acceptance of promotion disrupt their schooling, or enable them eventually to attend university without taking student loans, or both? Would his wife's absence at the week-long on-campus fine arts course prove a trauma too much for them to bear? And now that both Greg and Samantha were quite grown up, and insistent on their parents pleasing themselves at last, it was too late to alter the focus of their lives. 'Sam wanted to come over and stay with me until you got back,' his wife said, 'but I wasn't having her driving by herself all that way while she's pregnant.'

'No. Quite right,' Jansen said.

'I don't want her to worry in her condition.'

'Quite right,' said Jansen.

'They're both waiting to ring now you're awake more,' his wife said.

Tony Alexadis rang too, saying Jansen was to forget all about business, that the firm was happy to pay for his wife to fly over. He said to pull the plug on the Soong talks for now. They could tee them up again later in the year. Jansen didn't agree. He was sitting up, supported by pillows, and the pain was reduced to a level that allowed him to think about other things if he concentrated. 'Mervyn can handle it with help from Andrew Shih at the table, and me briefing him in the evenings,' he said. 'And Mervyn's been up here several times now, remember. He knows the Soong team, and if we don't get something rolling now we're going to lose a whole year, maybe the project itself grows cold.' The CEO wanted the meeting to go ahead, but only with Jansen's agreement. It was a ritual to show the regard between the two of them, and after a few minutes talk it was decided to carry on, and it had the appearance of being Jansen's decision, though both men knew what the business reality was.

When Andrew Shih came to the hospital, Jansen said the worst thing was being fed by fluids and that he wouldn't have anything near solid for at least another twenty-four hours. Andrew had some misgivings about continuing the talks without Jansen — remember the management faction in the overseas department of Soong working through Mr Hau tong, he said — but Jansen persuaded him that Mervyn was up to it, with their assistance. 'No one's indispensable, Andrew. You know that.'

'Soong like continuity of representation during a deal.'

'So the three of us are still here,' said Jansen. 'It's just that I'm not able to sit at the table.'

'You are able to continue to call the shots though,' said Andrew Shih, pleased with his command of the idiom.

'Tony Alexadis and the board will call the shots. You know that, but we can do a good job at this end.'

'I think you are right,' said Andrew. They had known each other for more than ten years, and done business together in Singapore for several weeks in each of those years. Andrew Shih specialised in assisting overseas firms, and was a model of confidentiality. Jansen knew that Andrew also represented Bridgeport of Australia, Randra and PSR, but never had Andrew said anything to him about the business dealings of those companies, or any others he acted for. Jansen had seen Andrew drunk, heard his best jokes repeatedly, seen him naked with a Thai girl after the 98 deal, but not once had Andrew divulged anything at all. Jansen liked that, and so did Tony Alexadis. 'The best lawyers know when to hold their tongues,' said the CEO.

When Andrew Shih had gone, Jansen rang Mr Yuan-jen at Soong and thanked him for the flowers. Also he apologised for being the cause of the delay in the talks, and said he and Tony Alexadis had full confidence in Mervyn. 'Yet we have become used to your voice on behalf of your board,' said Mr Yuan-jen solemnly.

'Thank you,' said Jansen.

'I know the Catholic hospital. My wife's father had his heart operation done there. All of the doctors are very good. Excellent in fact.'

'Thank you.'

'Yet we will miss your voice,' said Mr Yuan-jen.

Mervyn was excited when Jansen asked him to represent the company at the meetings. The excitement showed itself in the rigorous calm he imposed on himself: the slightly lower and more deliberate speech. It was the response that Jansen expected from his knowledge of his colleague, and it reassured him. He gave Mervyn his own briefing papers, thick with handwritten annotations. 'Perhaps you could spend a couple of hours looking through this,' he said, 'and then come back and we'll go over it. You know it'll all be positioning on the first day anyway. I'll try to sleep for a while, and you come back about eight tonight.'

'I'll put it together with my own notes,' said Mervyn.

'If you can read my writing,' said Jansen.

As he rested, aware of the minor dislocation of having no meal times to mark out his day, he tried to remember his own feelings when he had first taken charge of offshore negotiations for the company. It was unusual for him to search his memory for anything that wasn't strictly applicable to the business needs of the present, but he found the recollection quite clear. He had been sent to Hong Kong to sit in on the preliminary two days of supermarket access talks, with the aim of being able to brief the then CEO when he arrived later. Instead of arriving, the CEO had rung and told Jansen to carry on alone; that they had full confidence in him. Jansen had hardly slept for two days, working on agenda papers until five or six o'clock in the mornings.

It's what Mervyn would do after their talk. He'd go away and cover one hundred percent of everything just to make sure he had the five percent that would come up. That's how a good executive begins, and then with time comes the confidence and judgement which allow selective preparation and some sleep.

When Mervyn came down, he'd read all Jansen's notes, and he asked good questions and was attentive to Jansen's advice. 'Never hesitate to ask for some time to talk to Andrew Shih. Time by your-selves as an extension to lunch, for example. Andrew's so good on the close legal stuff, but also he's great at picking up on any change of tack. And watch Mr Hau tong: that's where any trouble will come from.'

'Maybe I should call in here on my way to Soong tomorrow,' said Mervyn.

'No, you'll be fine. Give me a call when it's all over, but have a cold beer and take off your tie first. And make sure Andrew doesn't send a girl to your room. He's a bugger for that.'

Jansen had a snooze after Mervyn left, and then met his doctors for the first time, including the surgeon who had cut into his stomach. Jansen had come to admire the intelligence and skill of the Chinese: he had no doubt he was in the best of hands. He decided to send the surgeon the company's prestige assorted pack of cheeses. He said how much he appreciated the air-conditioning in his room, and talked with the doctors a little about the amount of snowfall in New Zealand. The Chinese doctors of Singapore found the possi-bility of a white and frozen landscape interesting and exotic. 'Tomorrow,' said the surgeon, 'you will be able to take some mild food orally, but please don't eat anything visitors bring in without checking with staff. In particular, no fruit. Fruit is in composition bad for you at present.' When they left, the younger doctor looked back through the window in the door, and gave an informal wave and a smile, as if farewelling Jansen at an airport.

He slept less well that night than the one before, and guessed it was because he wasn't so doped up. Twice he eased himself out of the high bed to use the commode, which had a motor for height adjustment. The central heating wasn't calibrated with South Island Kiwis in mind, and even the coolest setting was barely doing the job. He lay on the cover and let his mind wander. It took him to personal things, rather than anything to do with business. The Soong talks seemed a long way from his concern, and instead he began to wonder where he and his wife should live when they retired. They hadn't talked much about it. Jansen thought that was because both sensed that it would prove a sticking point, and in their marriage they preferred to avoid serious disagreement. She enjoyed the opportunities offered by the city: he, although a city man all his life, had a yearning to end up in a small place, by the sea perhaps, or one of the southern lakes.

He knew that it was a notion unfounded on any experience of life in such a place, and not sensible in terms of proximity to the facilities they would increasingly rely on as they got older.

Yet, lying there almost naked in the private room of the Catholic hospital in Singapore, the idea was stronger in him than ever. He told himself that it was just a reaction to the business pressures over the years, this pipedream of a village life with both simplicity and solitude. Maybe even some explicable response to his stomach pain and the operation, which would pass. In the morning common sense would thrive again.

It was a novelty to use a spoon again at breakfast, and, despite the pap, the tastes were strong after being fed intravenously. Even the sensation of food passing down his gullet was briefly unusual. The nurse who brought his tray was youthful and very small. He had a fancy he could see light through her slim hands, and in her presence he felt clumsy and stolid.

Several times during the day he remembered the meeting going on at Soong: Mervyn Linkiss and Andrew Shih working so carefully to secure the right deal. He found it surprisingly easy to move on to other things, however, or just lie and think of nothing much at all. No doubt the pain, and then the operation and drugs, had broken his concentration on business. It occurred to Jansen that all over Singapore there were meetings that were crucial to those involved, but in truth had little significance. All the world was an ant-hill of industrious communication with decision piled on decision, and corporations waxing and waning like the Medes and the Persians.

Despite Jansen's advice, Mervyn came straight from the meeting. He had about him still the whiff of battlefield powder, and went through the happenings of the day with barely suppressed eagerness. He wanted Jansen's advice for the next day, and only just remembered at the end to ask about his health. 'Go back to the hotel and relax for a while. Take it easy,' said Jansen.

Andrew Shih rang soon afterwards to give a more succinct account. Mervyn did better than okay, he said. Tony Alexadis was also in touch. 'I'll give Mervyn a ring, of course,' he said, 'but I wanted to get your feel of things.'

'Andrew Shih says Mervyn's doing fine. And he's been at Soong meetings with me before, remember. I reckon he'll handle it well.' said Jansen.

'You've always been very supportive of him, Hector,' said the CEO. 'That reassures me a good deal.'

For his evening meal Jansen was given sweet fish rice and soft vegetables. The prospect attracted him, but part way through his appetite left him, and he lay back, conscious of pain. The nurse said that he would probably have such discomfort for a few days, but that it was important that he have solid food passing through the digestive tract as soon as possible. She later changed the dressing on his stomach incision, sprinkling a white powder like icing sugar on the stitched wound.

'How's it looking?' Jansen said.

'Is excellent,' she said.

His room had a television on a swivel bracket, but he didn't turn it on, although he knew there were English-speaking channels. There was also a remote, which dimmed the light in the room, and he used that until there was a soft, half darkness. Activity in the corridor outside decreased as the night went on, and Jansen lay on top of the bed with the air-conditioning at maximum coolness. The pain in his stomach was somehow the pain of recovery, and not the fearsome thing he'd experienced in the hotel room — was it two, or three, days ago? He had not the slightest inclination to dwell on the Soong talks, or Andrew Shih and Mervyn. Thoughts about his boyhood, his time at university, his two and half years in Canada were insistent and clear. It's having the scare with the operation and everything, he told himself in the soft dimness. He'd heard others talk about the effects of such a shock: the reassessment of your life. That's what it was.

Until he'd gone to Canada he'd played a lot of badminton, represented his province even, but he'd never picked it up again on his return. His job had early begun to push other things from his life. In his mind's eye he saw the shuttlecock in a perfect arch, and his quick, athletic leap to meet it. He remembered a men's double partner who used to bite his own arm to increase concentration, and a mixed doubles one as expert in blasphemy as in the game, despite her schoolgirl looks. He was listening to the whispering of the air-conditioning and trying to remember her full name when Samantha rang. She wasn't sure of the time over there, she said, and hoped she hadn't woken him. Jansen was more interested in her health than his own. 'Oh, Dad, stop worrying about me. I'm pregnant, not sick. I wanted to go over to Mum's, but she says she's fine. Concentrate on getting better yourself, for goodness sake. What's the latest from the doc?' As he reassured his daughter, Jansen wanted to talk about her as a child: the years when the four of them were the corners of the family square, and almost everything was shared. He'd experienced a measure of power and responsibility in business, but not with the gratification of love that accompanied them in fatherhood. He just avoided any sentimental mention of that by a switch to badminton, which seemed even to him somewhat random.

'I used to play badminton a lot, Sam. Did you know that?'

'I remember some of your racquets we used to play with as kids. They had very narrow metal shafts, didn't they?'

'That's them. It was my main sport before I went to Canada, and then for some reason I gave it away. Busy, I suppose.'

'Well, you won't be playing badminton for a while now. Are you okay? Are you sure you don't want Mum or Greg to fly over?'

'I'll be home in no time,' said Jansen.

'You're not being bothered with any business stuff while you're in hospital are you?'

'None at all.'

Jansen dozed for a while after his daughter's call and was woken by the slide of his cellphone from his relaxed hand onto his neck. He recognised his surroundings immediately; was not at all disorientated. Mervyn at the Sheraton would be still working almost for sure, but Jansen had no curiosity about that.

Other things had gained in importance since his illness. Sixty-four was an age at which it seemed some balance began to tip, triggered by the failure of his digestion. His father had been chief economist for a bank, but in retirement spent all his time and energy, and a good deal of money, in ridding offshore islands of rats so that native bird species would have a better chance. In old age he derided the profession in which he'd spent most of his life, and which had provided well for him. Economics is a dead language and smells of it, he told his son. And later, when he was diagnosed with Parkinson's disease, he reminded Jansen that old age rarely comes alone. Hector Jansen had loved his father, his mother too, and in thinking of them with a tenderness that surprised him, he drifted off to sleep in the darkened and private room of the Catholic hospital in Singapore.

His pain, if anything, was worse the next day, and both his doctors came back to look at him. His temperature was up a bit. The surgeon said that there was a moderate infection and that they'd go back to intravenous feeding and give him antibiotics. 'It's a dirty operation once the wall of the duodenum has been perforated,' he told Jansen. 'Infections are unfortunately quite a common consequence. You should monitor your own discomfort carefully, and we'll take another x-ray.'

'Will it keep me here any longer?' Jansen asked.

'In another twenty-four hours we'll know how things are,' the Chinese surgeon said. He was a very thin man, and the skin of his head followed the bone structure so closely that he had a slightly mummified appearance.

Andrew Shih rang at the end of the day to say that the second day of talks had gone well. He and Mervyn were on their way to informal drinks with Mr Yuan-jen of Soong. The invitation was a good sign. 'Mervyn did very well again,' said Andrew. 'You'd be proud of him. After lunch Mr Hau tong ambushed us with some in-house memos he'd got hold of, setting out retail margins, but Mervyn was hardly ruffled. He's very well prepared, and has a good rapport with Mr Liang too.'

'That's great, yeah,' said Jansen.

Andrew Shih put Mervyn on, and, during the conversation, Jansen could briefly hear Andrew telling the taxi driver the best way to Mr Yuan-jen's executive club. Jansen had been there several times himself, and remembered the long verandah festooned with wisteria, and the Second World War photographs behind the bar: the thin British general surrendering to the Japanese, and then later the Japanese officer in his turn handing his sword to the British and Americans.

'How are you, Hector?'

'A bit groggy today,' said Jansen.

'Maybe I won't bother you by coming in tonight, then,' said Mervyn. 'Let you get a good rest.'

'Andrew says the day went well. Good on you.'

'I think we're making sound progress. It's a constructive atmosphere, apart from Mr Hau tong, and Andrew's really on the button.'

'Maybe I should give Tony a ring,' said Jansen.

'Actually I've done that. I thought I'd better check in. He especially asked about you, wanted me to pass on his best wishes.'

The circle was closing without him: not with any deliberate exclusion, not with any particular intent, just the pressure of business and the need for the main players to be in direct touch. No one's indispensable. Commerce is a broad pond and the circles form and reform constantly on its surface. Jansen felt only a slightly cynical relief after the call. He hadn't felt up to talking business with Mervyn anyway. Isolated and ineffectual because of his illness, Jansen felt only a benign apathy concerning his career. For the first time he saw past his work to some equally worthwhile life beyond. Sixty-four's not old, not as such, he told himself. He traced with his fingers the perimeter of the dressing on his stomach; massaged gently to test the pain.

Jansen had a vomiting session in the afternoon, bringing up bile and a little blood. The lesser doctor took out the tubes and asked him to sip a thin, white liquid every ten minutes or so. 'This will give you a lining,' he said cheerfully. Jansen saw on the blue name tag that the doctor's name was Lowe. Without the eminent presence of the surgeon, Jansen was more aware of the individuality of the younger doctor. Dr Lowe was darker than most Chinese, and his face was pock-marked from the eyes down. He had an easy, natural smile that made his face attractive despite his complexion. His voice was deeper than most of his fellows: more European in timbre. 'A wash is a pleasant thing after the discomfort of vomiting,' he said. 'I'll arrange it immediately, and just ask if you want something for the pain.'

A male nurse gave Jansen the sponge bath, and recounted his backpacking experiences in Queensland and the Northern Territories. He said the sky was bigger there than in Singapore.

'Has the air-conditioner any cooler setting?' asked Jansen. The nurse looked at the dials carefully, and said it didn't.

Jansen slept for an hour and woke feeling no worse, but for the first time he had the thought that maybe he would die in Singapore: that the end of business for him would be the end of everything. He was angry with himself for not considering the possibility earlier, for not being more searching in his talks with the doctors. He rang the buzzer — he'd not used it before — and when a nurse came, said that he'd like to see Dr Lowe as soon as possible.

Dr Lowe came within fifteen minutes, and his smile was untroubled. He sipped from a white cardboard cup, and pulled the one chair closer to Jansen's bed. 'So,' he said, 'there is something?'

'I'm worse today than yesterday,' said Jansen.

'Yes, you have an infection as we said, and with that a slight fever. It happens quite frequently with acute admission cases such as your own. The abdominal cavity is difficult to cleanse of all intestinal material.'

'But I'll recover, right?' said Jansen.

The young doctor smiled so broadly there was a slight ripple in the dark, bristly hair above his ears. He leant forward, holding the cup loosely on his lap in both hands. 'Would you deal in absolutes in a Catholic hospital?' he said. 'We must remember our fallibility, but what we can say is that nothing in your condition since the operation changes the opinion that you should make a good recovery. Low level post-op infection is quite common in cases such as yours.'

'You'd say if there was real concern?' asked Jansen.

'Yes, absolutely,' replied Dr Lowe. 'You will go back to the snow of New Zealand certainly, I think. Maybe no skiing for a while, though.' He stood up and yawned, and shrugged his shoulders right up to his ears a few times to ease the muscle tension of a long day.

'Thanks.' Jansen wasn't a skier, and he rarely saw any snow, but why bother to challenge the image that Dr Lowe and the surgeon had of him and his country. Dr Lowe leant over and squeezed Jansen's wrist quickly, and he paused outside the door again to look back through the window and wave, as he had when leaving with the surgeon. He had forgotten his cardboard cup, and the small, pale cone of it was left on the flat of the chair.

Jansen used the dimmer until he was lying in semi-darkness. He still had pain, but accepted it and began to plan the changes he would discuss with his wife. Maybe a trip to begin with — lots of places where he wouldn't need his laptop, his cellphone or his briefcase, where he could wear shorts and a garish top, and even the trivial administration of meals, travel and accommodation would be left to others. He knew that his response to all that had happened was quite predictable and conventional, but accepted it as authentic nevertheless. He had a wake-up call in Singapore, his friends and acquaintances would say: a heart attack, or food poisoning, or something, and nearly died. A mixture of vagueness and exaggeration is typical of such second-hand accounts. And he gave it all away, they'd say, and resigned just like that. Why not, good on him, some would say, while others would consider he wasn't going to get right to the top anyway, not at his age.

Maybe his wife was right, he thought. An inner-city apartment with no lawns and the only plants those in pots on a patio that had a view of the harbour. Sam was pregnant, and for the first time he thought not only of her health, but of the child she carried and what part in its life he might play.

Jansen was surprised to feel tears on his face, but without any sobbing. He put it down to the trauma of his illness. The hospital smell of his private room masked the sour base of recent vomit and his crusted dressing. The waspish whine of scooters was at a distance, and the whisper of the air-conditioning close at hand. Life was fragile and there seemed the beating of wings in the tropical night. Home was the thing: Hector Jansen wanted to go home.

THE TRIUMPH OF HISTORY

This is my uncle's story, but he's dead now. He told it in various ways over the years, and when he was too old and sick to remember it, I sometimes told it to him, to pass the time as we sat in his untidy sunporch on my visits there. Telling a story alters it, so this is my uncle's story, but now it's my story as well. The thing that interests me is that no matter who tells the story, or how it's told, at the heart of it is something that happened: an actuality, a meeting of people and events over fifty years ago which gives it a pulse even today.

My uncle fought in Italy as an infantryman during the Second World War, but his professional training was in accountancy, and immediately after the war he was asked to join one of the teams working for the War Graves Commission. The job of these people was to go back to the war areas and to establish the fate of Allied soldiers whose remains, or graves, had never been recorded. My uncle's team worked in north Italy where he'd fought. He was there for nearly two years, and although the work was often sad, he liked the Italian people and kept in touch with some families for years afterwards.

The two others in my uncle's team were a Scotsman who had worked for the British Museum, and an Australian whose father was

Italian. In the winter of 1947 they were in the alpine region of northern Italy, at Collinanera, where some Allied soldiers in hiding had been betrayed to the Germans and shot. My uncle said the winter was hard, and they were in a small hotel on the outskirts of the village. It had been a hunting lodge, and had a suit of armour, a bear's head, crossed halberds and several petty dynastic banners in the entrance hall. The War Graves people were the only guests, and they didn't go out for days at a time because of the weather.

Roaming dogs were a big nuisance in Italy at the time. In places they still are: I've had to climb a wall in the streets of Pompeii to escape them. The packs at Collinanera were made desperate by starvation, and besieged the habitations looking for trash. Only a few weeks after the shortest day, the hotel owner and her daughter were attacked on the drive while they were walking back from the village with provisions. My uncle and the other men ran out and managed to get them up the steps and inside. The owner was badly bitten in the face and hands; the girl was even more severely mauled, and was losing a good deal of blood from her head and legs. Both of them were hysterical, and my uncle said that their shrieks inside the hotel, and the crazy crescendo of the dogs outside, almost unnerved them all.

The phone wasn't working, which wasn't unusual after a snowfall, and the half Italian Australian, who was a big man and an artillery veteran, said he was going down to the village to get the pharmacist who acted as doctor. He and my uncle took alpine sticks, but got no further than the bottom of the steps before being overwhelmed by eight or ten dogs stirred into a frenzy by the proprietor's lost bread and sausages, and the taste of blood and submission. They were lucky to fight their way back to the door without being borne down.

The young girl was in a state of shock and still losing blood despite the pressure bandages made from towels and sheets. My uncle said that none of them knew what to do next — except the third member of his team; Menzies, the one who had been a scholar at the London Museum. 'Get me that effing suit of armour,' he said.

The Australian pulled it out of the hall corner, and tried to dismember it. Menzies was the only guy small enough to have a chance of wearing it, and they had to pour cooking oil all over it before any of the joints would flex. The Scot got most bits on, although there were gaps at the tops of his thighs, and part of the stand wouldn't detach from the back of the torso, and he had to wear that too, like a hand-rail on his back. My uncle said that the helmet was oddly snoutish, and that there was a section over Menzies' groin like a Venetian blind. The Australian and my uncle weren't sure if their colleague should give it a go, but Menzies told them that the Scots and the Swiss used to be the best mercenaries in Europe. He had a rather individual sense of humour, my uncle said.

So Menzies, taking a butcher's knife in each hand, edged through the door and stumbled down the steps into the snow flurries of the winter afternoon, and the dogs were upon him immediately. The dogs got the better of it for a while, knocking him full length several times and almost covering him from the view of those in the hotel. But they couldn't hurt him, that was the thing. He may have been covered with olive oil, but he wasn't going to be an easy meal for them, my uncle said. Menzies got to his knees finally, and fought there clumsily and systematically with the one knife he hadn't lost in the first assault. More and more often the snarls and barks were punctuated with yelps, until the dogs drew reluctantly away, and Menzies rose unsteadily to his feet, and with the dogs circling and snarling at arm's length, he moved down the dirt drive in a series of wary and cumbersome pirouettes. His armour was very black against the snow, and the bitter clamour of the dogs could be heard long after he and they were out of sight.

My uncle said he and the others at the hotel heard shots and howling within twenty minutes, and knew the villagers were on their way. Then out of the drifting snow and mist of the winter evening they saw the local poliziotto, the pharmacist, other men from the village. There was not a dog to be seen, or heard. My uncle said it was a tableau that never left him: the lacerated women sobbing with pain and relief, the armed villagers walking in purposefully from the tree-lined drive, and the little Scot behind them, indistinct in the twilight and the silent, falling snow, an emblematic apparition in full, black armour and a snoutish helmet.

CHANGING SEASONS

The firm opened a branch that spring in Rutledge, an inland Canterbury town. The reality was a single room, behind the New Zealand Post Shop, which was staffed each Tuesday after appointments had been made at the main Christchurch office. The partners of Wycombe Tolley Davies considered there was rural business to be gained there. 'See if you can build it up,' Rhys Davies said to Brian. 'And there's a surprising number of well-heeled people retiring there now, and you're good at investment advice. We'd like you to go rather than a younger solicitor. It's a place that expects maturity and some connection with the land, we reckon.' Brian's only connection with the land was his father's position years ago as the regional Dalgety's manager, but he made no objection. He'd been long enough in the firm to be drawn to a novelty.

So each Tuesday he drove to Rutledge to meet his clients: family trusts and wills, conveyancing, minor litigation. And Rhys Davies was right, as well as farmers there were quite a few retired people who were prepared to pay for an hour or so mulling over their non-stock portfolios. Older people were glad to be spared even the trip into Christchurch.

The room had one large window, and from it there was a view of the carpark and some fully grown English oaks and chestnut trees beyond. In summer and autumn he enjoyed eating his lunch alone in the room, and then having a stroll among the trees in the park. Sometimes, not often enough, there was a decent gap in his appointments, and he could get ahead with his town work in pleasant solitude.

In the third week of April, during such a break in his afternoon at the Rutledge office, he went across the carpark and into the park for a breather. Acorns were thick on the ground and he picked up a handful and flicked them one by one with his thumb into the spent garden plots as he walked. There was no one else.

Who used parks in such small places when everybody's home, gardens and lawns, were within walking distance? He found a fallen chestnut still half in its horned case, and the brilliant burnish of it reminded him of his father's best brown shoes.

Was there no one else? From a rank of rhododendrons came the sound of retching, and Brian didn't know whether to turn and go away, or wait and see if he could help. He stood quietly until a woman came out onto the crushed gravel path. He remained still while she walked to a tap, the exposed upright pipe of which was supported by a small post. She rinsed her mouth, without seeing him, and by the time he was walking again towards her around the slightly yellowed rhododendrons, she had a handkerchief to her face, and wouldn't have realised that he had heard her vomiting.

That's how he met Angela Slee, who was subject to severe migraines, sometimes clusters of them, and on that occasion had been forced to stop the car by the park when overcome with nausea. She was very white and her hands trembled: she was barely able to be polite. When a student, Brian had occasionally suffered from migraines himself, and recalled how sickening they were. He led her back to the Post Shop, whose staff he knew, and Liz Wells took her into the small rooms at the back to wash and rest a while.

Brian had two more interviews, and in his concentration almost forgot the woman from the park. As he was leaving his room he met Liz going to her car. 'It's Angela Slee,' she told him. 'You know the

Slees.' It was the confident assumption, rather than question, that marks small town identification.

'No,' said Brian.

'One of Dr Slee's daughters.'

'So how did she get on?'

'She lay down for a couple of hours and then Ron drove her home.'

Brian had the feeling that Liz was keen to use talk of Angela Slee as a springboard to more general conversation, but he didn't want to encourage a tendency that might interrupt the quiet lunch hours of his Rutledge days.

The very next week, however, he was interrupted by Angela Slee herself. She came to his room to thank him for his help, and sat on one of the high-backed chairs by the window. 'I must have seemed very rude,' she said. 'I would have come in before I left last week, but I guessed you were with a client, and I was still pretty grotty.'

'People think a migraine's just a headache, don't they, but it can be utterly incapacitating.'

'So you get them?'

'I used to, years ago,' he said.

She was a tall woman, perhaps mid-forties. She wasn't thin, but rather flat-chested. Shapely legs and neck, though, and a direct, quiet gaze. 'I didn't realise your firm had opened up here,' she said.

'Just last spring, and just one day a week.'

'Anyway, I won't take up any more of your lunchtime. I imagine it's the only time you get to yourself in a busy day. I just wanted to thank you for last week.' She stood up, and paused to look from the one, large window. 'A wind's come up,' she said. 'The leaves are flying.' There was a special pleasure in the way she said it, or so Brian thought. He, too, always felt an exhilaration in the autumn when a wind came up and sent the dark leaves away like a flock of birds with each gust. The two of them watched from the window the crests of the great chestnut and oak trees tossing above the park fence.

'Have a quick cup of coffee with me before you go,' he said, and opened the cupboard door that looked like all the others, but hid a basin, zip and fridge, all of a pigmy scale. 'Why don't you turn the chair to look out over the park,' he said, and she did. 'My clients face this way, but sometimes when they're talking I feel I can glance past them to the trees.'

'And you lose track of what they're saying?'

'No,' said Brian, 'the legal part of my mind keeps going, but that's just training, not a gift.'

Neither of them made any more conversation for a time. He made coffee; she relaxed by the window. A ute came and parked quite close to the room. It had cases of apples and pears in the back, and the driver, a blonde girl with a pony-tail, delivered two cases of each to an unseen destination, striding away with a box and running back unencumbered. She had chunky blue and white sneakers with laces so long that they were tied and gathered like a spray. Her youth was a radiance and, as she climbed into the vehicle to leave, she saw Angela at the window and waved in goodwill.

'You know her?' asked Brian.

'No.'

'Liz Wells said you were local: that your father was a doctor here.'

'But I went away to boarding school,' said Angela, 'and I never really lived here after that. I've only been back a few years. My partner and I bought an old orchard block a few ks out and we're doing up the cottage.'

'A country GP's life seems rather pleasant from the outside, but most professions are less idyllic the closer you are to them, I suppose.'

'My father was very busy, and people expected him to be a civic spokesman as well. Fly fishing was what he loved, and he was quite mischievous in his own way. There used to be a local paper owned and run by a very orthodox, but under-educated man. My father suggested he call the rural section "Country Matters" and supported it with the quote from *Hamlet*. The editor never realised the real connotations, and my father had a smile each week when he turned to the column.'

'Your father's gone now?'

'Years ago.'

They talked easily, looking out from the quiet room to see the strong wind in the trees, and then Brian's one thirty appointment arrived, and Angela left. 'Thank you,' she said at the door, so the incoming client would assume her visit had been business.

They met again within a month, at a charity auction in Christchurch. The proceeds were to go to the Cancer Society. Brian had been visiting his mother, and went to the afternoon auction because he'd had contact with the society. He bought a Victorian silver-topped inkwell, and noticed Angela when she was bidding for an early sketch of Butler's Mesopotamia Station. She sat well, calm and still except when making a bid, and when she had withdrawn from the competition in favour of a final, determined buyer, Brian went and sat beside her. 'Hi,' he said. 'Bad luck.'

'Oh, I'll get something or other. I don't want anything big, that's the thing,' she said.

'I'm the same. An inkwell won't dominate a room, and I can easily carry it away.'

'Duty done,' she said. 'So who did you lose?'

'My wife.'

'My father.'

'The doctor who was interested in Shakespeare's country matters.'

'Yes.' She was surprised that he remembered; surprised to recall she had told him something so personal.

'Will the things we buy remind us of wife and father, do you think, or will we have forgotten where the hell we bought them in a year or two?' In the seat behind a couple argued over their bidding limit with subdued bitterness.

'Well, it's a good cause in any case,' said Angela.

She bought lot 147, which was a small, inlaid box the auctioneer said was originally used for visiting cards. The inlay was a four-leaf clover in creamy jade. 'It's cold here,' said Brian, 'This place is like a barn. Why don't we go somewhere warm and have a coffee.' They drove separately into the city centre, and went upstairs in a café at the Arts Centre. He asked if she had time for dinner, but Angela was to meet her partner at five. They talked of university days, not cancer, because the stone buildings around them had been the original site of the varsity, though both of them remembered only the new buildings at Ilam. They talked of places they had visited on trips overseas. They talked of Canterbury and Rutledge. They talked equally and easily, and each of them was aware of interest and relaxation, and of the other's knowledge of it too. They liked each other's company, and were entitled to it.

When they were about to go, and he was putting on his overcoat, he found the silver-topped ink well still in his pocket, and she took the card case from her bag and unwrapped it. They admired both pieces, which seemed to gain lustre from being owned, being separate from the welter of auction bits and pieces, being placed together on a small table in a warm upstairs café, having been close to Brian and Angela as they talked. 'Let's swap,' she said with sudden decision, and they did so immediately, each feeling somehow the better for the transaction.

'Come and have lunch with me soon in my room,' he said.

'Give me a ring then,' she said.

Often he allowed the main office staff to arrange appointments that left him with only half an hour for lunch, but he told them to make sure he had a full hour on the Tuesday of the second week following the Christchurch Cancer Society auction, and he rang Angela. It didn't worry him that her partner might answer, for there was nothing to be guilty about. He was even a little curious, but it was Angela who answered.

'I've got a decent lunch hour on Tuesday this week,' he said. 'How about calling in and we'll have sandwiches?'

'Actually, I'm flat out this week. I'd love to, but we've got all this tax stuff for the business. I just have to get done.' He hadn't spoken to her on the phone before, and her voice had an cool evenness he hadn't noticed when with her. Maybe it hadn't been there.

'You're okay, though?' he said. 'No migraine or anything?'

'No, I'm fine — just busy. I'd like to keep in touch. How about I contact you when I'm on top of things more.'

'Sure, that's fine.'

Tax return time brought pressures for lawyers too. Brian didn't have much time to wonder if Angela would get in touch again. He wasn't miffed that she hadn't come in when he suggested; he got caught up with his own work and was genuinely surprised when she arrived at his Rutledge room on a hard frost day that kept the long grass around the park trees in a punk hairdo until well into the afternoon. The blackbirds and starlings were disconcerted that the ground was too hard for them to forage. He had an appointment in twenty minutes. 'I should have phoned, or sent an email,' she said, 'but I had to come in to see someone.' Her face seemed sharpened by the cold and she wore black stockings. She had gloves on: not the woollen gloves of schoolgirls, but soft leather gloves that wrinkled like flesh.

For the first time he was conscious of finding her sexy as well as companionable, imagined rolling down the dark stockings of winter to reveal her thighs, drawing off the dark leather of winter to display her palms. But all the clothing he took from her was her coat, and he hung it behind his legal door. 'Do you notice something new about my room?' he said, and she picked out the inlaid box from the auction, and told him wherever it was that she had placed the glass inkwell within her house. It seemed they had only begun to talk, when his first afternoon appointment arrived. 'How long are you in town for?' he asked, and she said there were two calls she needed to make. 'Come back at four if you can. If that's okay. If you make it we can have a decent talk. I don't even know what it is you do at the hospital.'

She did make it, and Brian had hustled old Mr McIvor through a settlement in favour of his grandson, so work was over for the day. Angela's coat was again hung behind the door, and she and Brian turned the two client chairs towards the window and the park, took up glasses of Central Otago pinot noir, and talked about their lives. She was a relief anaesthetist at the hospital, driving into the city most days, just as Brian drove out one day a week. She had worked in

Sydney, Vietnam, England, and was pleased to be local again; excited to have a few acres of old orchard and a cottage to transform; relieved that her partner was making a recovery from shingles. And she listened well too, so that Brian had the novelty of talking about his personal life with someone who took more than a perfunctory interest. Since his wife's death that had become increasingly rare, and he found it enjoyable to talk lightly of things for which he wouldn't be held accountable, and to have a listener who wasn't paying for the privilege. They were easy and relaxed together as the early dusk of winter obliterated trees, yet not unaware of the possibilities in a new friendship. That potential was a profitable charge in their talk: the boundaries between them had not yet been agreed on. They didn't part until after six thirty. 'Be very careful driving home,' she said, 'after the wine.' It seemed a long time since anyone had been concerned for him in that way.

She came to his Rutledge room twice afterwards, and on that second Tuesday it snowed, which was unusual even though the town was a good way from the coast. Brian and Angela stood together by the window, in the warmth of the room he had been working in all day, and they looked out on the small carpark and the park beyond it, and watched the snow drifting in from the south although there was no obvious wind. It melted on the tarseal, but built into skeins on the soil of the garden under the park wall. Angela said she remembered snow well from her childhood; it seemed the climate was changing, people said, and getting warmer. Without touching any other part of her body, Brian kissed her cheek when she left. He felt her hair brush on his forehead, and her skin, although white, was warm to his lips. 'You've never seen my Christchurch place,' he said.

So Angela came to his house in Avonside on an evening not long after the shortest day, and it seemed colder than any time they spent in Rutledge, though there was no snow. Brian had a fire in the lounge, but he apologised for the temperature in the other rooms as he went with her through the house. He told her it was built by a successful carrier just after the war, and the two dining room sideboard cupboards were the originals. 'It's a beautiful house,' she said.

'My wife had a good eye for compatibility.'

'And you do to.'

They came to the main bedroom last, and although that wasn't planned, nor the words which followed, Brian found he knew exactly what he wanted to say. 'I'm hoping you and I will spend some time in here tonight.'

'Oh, God,' she said, 'I told myself on the way in that I wouldn't: that friendship's what we've got and best left there.'

'I'd so much like you to. Maybe we just kiss a bit, whatever you're comfortable with.'

'It is nice to be together, isn't it,' she said.

It was very cold in the bedroom, though, too cold to lie down easily, and Brian made two trips to fetch heaters and turned them full on so that their gradual incandescence gave a soft, red glow to the unlit room. Angela stood at the window and looked out at the sloping lawn and the dogwood trees in the fading day. 'Can anyone see in? she said.

'No.'

'Don't turn the lights on,' she said, 'and we can leave the drapes open. Then it's like your Rutledge room when we can always see outside.' Brian brought their glasses in and the bottle of wine.

'It'll soon warm up here,' he said, 'but we can go back to the fire if you like.'

'It's okay,' she said. 'I like the window and the garden. I like that you've chosen this room. Tell me how you and your wife came to buy this place.'

It was a story trivial enough to be told to a stranger, but with its own interest and coincidence for two people fond of each other, and they took off their shoes and top clothes and lay back on the large bed. He knew from her smooth body that she'd never had any children. Her breasts were small, as he'd noticed when he had first met her, but she had full hips, and her thighs were a cool expanse beneath the palm of his hand. 'I haven't had a good fuck for absolutely ages,' he said. 'In fact I haven't had any sort of fuck for absolutely ages.'

'So which do you want then: a good one, or any sort at all?' and that had them smiling.

As the winter light faded in the motionless garden, the red glow of the heaters inside seemed to intensify, reflected in the darkening window. They lay together for a long time before they made love, touching and talking, and the time both relaxed them in each other's company and created a profitable anticipation of pleasure. Brian had always found it an exquisite moment, the mutual, unspoken understanding that a woman has been won, but not yet yielded. When they kissed, the taste of wine was in their mouths, and her nipples had the same taste it seemed to him. The condom sachet was small, tightly sealed; he was clumsy with it in the heaters' indirect light, and Angela took it away from him, opened it and rolled it up his cock. He watched her hands busy with such an intimate task, and being ministered to in that way was immensely gratifying. 'Jesus,' he said shakily, and she looked up and smiled again. For a moment he imagined her fingers in the dark suppleness of the leather gloves.

She left at midnight, going reluctantly from the warm glow of the bedroom into the still chill of winter. They didn't make a specific time to meet again, both unsure whether something had just begun, or ended.

For the first time, Brian was reluctant to ring her at home, but when she didn't come to his Rutledge room the following Tuesday, and left no message, he phoned. It was her cool voice again. Why would he expect otherwise when at first she'd have no way of knowing who was calling, yet he missed familiarity even in her first words. That's how love is. 'Are you coming to see me again?' he asked. 'Here at the room, if you don't want to come to Christchurch. No strings at all.'

'Why don't you come out here. I'd like that.' There was a pause. 'We'd like that,' she continued firmly. There were many ways to interpret that sentence, and Brian, a lawyer most of his lifetime, waited for more indicative information. 'Cath and I want you to come out and see us — have a meal if you've got time,' she said.

'Cath?'

'She's my partner. We own the place together.'

Afterwards, Brian wondered why he was so surprised. It was the twenty-first century and he considered himself liberal in his views. He had gay and lesbian clients; he was friendly with gay colleagues within his profession; he had supported legislative changes that removed legal discrimination against such people. But there was nothing in his close experience which accustomed him to anything other than a heterosexual view of the world.

'We'd really like you to come out on Sunday and have lunch,' Angela said.

Sunday was the archetype for a Canterbury winter. As Brian drove from the city to Rutledge in the late morning, the frost was white lace in the shadow of the farm hedges, and the sun bright in a pale blue, burnished sky. A landscape of absolute, painterly stillness, except that faint smoke rose straight up from the occasional farm-house and feathered in the air. While driving, Brian was in a small world of subdued and efficient mechanical noise, but he knew that outside was a dramatic quietness as well as remarkable stillness. In that cold, bright air the cry of a magpie, or the bark of a border collie, could startle like the rush of an arrow.

The small orchard block was only ten minutes beyond Rutledge; well back from a gravel road, and the entrance was protected from wandering sheep, or cows, by a cattle-stop made of railway tracks. The uneven drive went through the fruit trees, and Brian was surprised at how small they were, unclothed for winter, despite their obvious age. He didn't know what fruit they would bear, but a few in one corner had been bluffed by the good weather into venturing puffs of white blossom that mimicked frost, but promised an opposite.

The old house was weatherboard, newly painted cream, and a verandah on the north side was roofed with bowed corrugated iron. There was a large tank stand with its pipes swathed in sacking so weathered that it had turned grey, and there were new rose plots rimmed with bricks and mulched with pea straw.

Angela and Cath came out to meet him, and Brian took especial care to meet Cath's eye, to listen to her and respond, rather than looking just at Angela as was his inclination. 'Angela mentioned that you've had shingles recently,' he said.

'A hell of a thing,' said Cath. 'Just so difficult to get rid of it. I must have had three or four relapses before coming right.' She was a tall, straw blonde with large features, a quick smile and the slightly weathered skin of the equestrians Brian saw on television. In Cath's case he assumed it more likely to be the effect of fruit picking and gardening rather than riding. 'Come onto the verandah where we can have lunch in the sun,' she said, and as they walked, 'My father was a solicitor.'

Angela talked well; it was one of the things that first attracted him. Cath was even better. Not only did she combine knowledge and humour with a turn of phrase, but she encouraged others in a conversation to rise to her level of interest and involvement. The three of them sat facing the winter sun and chatted as they ate a plain lunch with chardonnay. Mostly they talked about China and South East Asia, where all had spent more than tourist time. Angela and Cath had shared World Health Organisation postings in Cholon just south of Saigon, and Brian had worked in the Hong Kong judiciary for four years. The extremes of the Asian character were a long way from an early Canterbury farmhouse, and Brian, in the midst of his account of a high-level political murder in Hong Kong, had a sudden dislocation, as if it were the experience of someone else and he had fraudulently commandeered it. How remote and implausible it seemed, when they were sitting on a plain, wooden verandah, in the sun, with all motionless before them, the small, bare trees most of all. 'Don't we seem a long way from all that now,' said Angela, as if she guessed the reason for the almost imperceptible faltering in his tone.

Angela and Cath were not excessively demonstrative; Brian wondered if he would have realised they were partners if he'd not been told, but with new awareness he noticed Angela put her hand on Cath's arm when reminding her that the tray would be hot, and that almost every time they looked at each other both would smile.

Their history of affection was a subtle aura, not at all a deliberate exclusion of others, yet he felt wistful just the same.

After lunch the three of them walked down the track to the cattle-stop and back again. Cath said they'd thought of taking out the fruit trees and planting grapes, but that a Lincoln report on the soil hadn't been favourable. 'It's more lifestyle anyway, isn't it?' said Angela. 'If the apples and pears pay for the property's outgoings that's enough for us.'

'We have the privacy of millionaires,' said Cath. They looked over the small orchard, and the flat paddocks around it with occasional shelter belts. Only one other house was visible, reduced by distance and a macrocarpa hedge to a crayon slash of red roof. 'Rather different from Hong Kong, eh, Brian?'

'Absolutely,' he said. And it was a long way too from his bedroom in Christchurch, and Angela and he lying close there with the glow of the heaters reflected in the big window. Angela murmuring yes, yes, and he replying with the same words just as urgently.

The sunlight remained bright at four o'clock, but already the shadows were long and the still air was cold when Brian left. Cath said goodbye in the house, asked him if he'd handle their legal business, said they wanted him to come again. 'God knows we need more intelligent men friends,' she said.

Angela came to the car, and Brian found it surprisingly easy to come right out with the questions that mattered: perhaps they had been forming throughout his visit. 'Will you come and see me again?'

'Oh, sure,' she said. 'And, as Cath said, we'd like you to come here.'

'But Christchurch,' he said. 'Will we make love again? Are we going to be lovers?'

'I don't think that's on.'

'It was on the other night.'

'I was curious, I suppose. Cath and I have been together eleven years, and shingles isn't a very romantic ailment, but we're true partners. I don't want you to think any other way.'

Brian told himself that he should leave it there: he sensed he didn't understand Angela's life with Cath well enough to go on, but he did anyway. There was an apricot tinge behind the scissor sharp outlines of the Southern Alps. 'I thought maybe what we had wouldn't matter to two women.' Her small laugh showed him his understanding was even more deficient than he feared.

'It's different, but it doesn't make any difference, if you understand.'

'I didn't mean to be crass,' he said.

'You're not crass, Brian. You're a nice guy, but I'm in love already, and it needn't be any more complicated than that. It's my fault that wasn't clear.'

He drove down the track with the low sun making tiger stripes through the bare fruit trees. Inside the car he could hear only the soft, efficient workings of the air-conditioning, and he told himself that both women would make excellent friends.

As he crossed the cattle-stop, and turned onto the road, he could see that Cath had come out of the house and both of them gave a wave. Two tall, attractive middle-aged women, one dark and one fair: partners in life. And he knew he'd never come to this place again.